Author Bio

H R Conklin grew up in the rural mountains of Northern
California where her mother gardened and her father played the
bagpipes, as well as spending long hours in the theater where her
parents were a dancer and an actor, which undoubtedly led to her
overactive imagination and love for nature. She currently lives in
San Diego with her husband, two children, three dogs, and one
cat. She is an Educational Advisor to homeschooling parents at a
public Waldorf charter school in which she tells many fairy tales
to their children, and makes up stories in her spare time. Connect
with H R Conklin on her website WildRoseStories.com

May you always!
Believe in yourself.
♡ HR C.

H R CONKLIN

Also written by H R Conklin

The Trinity Knot

Celtic Magic Book 1

The Witch's Knot

Celtic Magic Book 2

Dedicated to my mother,
Sue Ellen
With her eternal optimism,
she taught me to believe in myself.

CONTENTS

Celtic Magic

Be wary the gifts the faeries may give;
We know not how they influence the life we live.

The Witch's Knot

Autumn is a time for change
Covering the earth with blankets of leaves
Underground the dead are bustling
Following the stories a faerie weaves.

KA

Here and There
August 15th, present

Tobias pumped his legs, racing as fast as he could through the tunnels leading into the Faerie Realm, wearing the spirit shape of a black cat. He had felt a new power at the Witch's Gathering, a force stronger than any witch known to their Coven had ever possessed. The power had emanated from the very earth, and the witches had murmured their concerns, heads swathed in black pointy hats intended to call the forces of the Heavens into their incantations.

The evening had started like any other, full of boiling brews and chanted spells as Tobias had watched in his spirit cat form, hiding in the shadows. His actual body was lying motionless in his bedroom on the other side of the world, a prisoner. To be fair, no one held him captive. He was trapped in his own body because every part of him except for his eyes could not move without his mother's help. He often pretended to be ignorant, too, not just immobile. He was as smart as any able-bodied teen, probably smarter, but he found he was allowed to hear more, thus learn more, if people thought he was an imbecile. That was how he had learned to be a powerful witch himself, without anyone knowing. By watching and listening, either at home in his physical body or sneaking about in his spirit form of a black cat.

Lying in his bed, he had actually detected the force radiating from the Other Lands, the Faerie Realm and the Spirit World, long before his mother's coven had, and he'd been curious enough to go in search of the source. Sending out his Spirit Self, his Ka as he'd decided to call it after studying the ancient Celtic-Egyptian connections, he was freed from his almost catatonic physical self. In his favorite shape of a black cat, blending in with the shadows was easy and he was able to slip around undetected and spy on others. He was unable to do anything about his eyes, though, which were a vibrant shade of blue with a tinge of lavender and they glowed in the pitch-black dark of the tunnels.

On silent feline paws he ran through the passageways beneath Scotland, where he had first entered. After a while he felt a shift and he knew he was in the land of the Faeries. Only then did he slow down, peering around corners cautiously, aware that sharp-clawed Pixies or bloodthirsty Red Cap Gnomes could attack at any moment. He turned a corner and that's when he saw it: the source of the energy force. A bubble of light surrounded a tall girl about his own age; her wild red hair floated about her head like static electricity, and her green eyes were wide with fear and determination.

But that wasn't the most remarkable part of her. It was her hands he stared at the most intently, as they shot out bolts of red electricity through the walls of the bubble, hitting an old druid Tobias had not noticed at first. The druid fell to the ground in a scream of rage, instantly wrapped up in a cocoon of energy, turning his scream to a shriek of peril. Tobias wasn't sure if the druid was dead or not, though it was likely. He turned back to the wild girl and watched her focus a green energy on a boy lying inert on the ground, and the boy rose as if healed from some terrible ailment. Then, the three, for there was a younger blonde boy in the group, had hobbled away down the corridor.

Tobias followed them; his interest was piqued by the possibilities of his own body being healed forming in his mind. Curious where they would end up, he watched them for hours, listening in on their few muttered conversations, and discovered that they left the tunnels in his own time and place. Not in Scotland where Tobias had first entered the tunnels, but in California, though not the part of California where he lived. It was much too forested to be Southern California. Still, the coincidence pleased him.

Tired, he left his cat form, dissipating like a puff of smoke, and returned his Ka to his body to rest. He slept for days, feeling the ministrations of his loving and caring mother, as embarrassing as it was, as she bathed and fed his useless husk. When he awoke, he listened to the customary sounds of Kate's house, the house he and his mother had recently moved into, missing the sounds of other people, especially his own age, or even the noise of the witches he'd visited as Ka. Instead, the house was filled only by the whispered tick-tock of a grandfather clock, the musty smell of dirt tunnels replaced with the herbal scent of home. They were in San Diego, having tea. Not that he was having tea, but his mother and Kate were, and the smells were delicious. Whimpering a bit, he managed to get a cup of lukewarm peppermint tea brought to his lips. Ignoring the familiar humiliation he felt at being at someone else's mercy, he gagged in his attempt to swallow the drink.

As he lay savoring the residue of peppermint in his

mouth, he overheard Kate, the Matriarch of the Coven. She was an old woman, with blonde-gray hair cropped short, always dressed in black dresses embroidered with a Mexican flair. He and his mother lived with her, having moved in after his father abandoned them. The memory of the accident was too much for him, which caused all of their money to eventually dry up. Living with the Matriarch had its privileges, like more frequent conversations for him to eavesdrop on. She was now talking about the girl in the tunnels, which didn't surprise him because he had sensed that the witches too had taken notice of her.

"I saw her in our Visioning. My own granddaughter!"

Tobias choked at this revelation and his mother reached over to automatically wipe the dribble with a handkerchief.

"She's not had any training as a witch. Her parents never allowed me to get that close to her. My son insisted his children would not be subject to my odd ways." Kate sniffed and took a drink of her tea. "Huh! No daughters of my own, and my only granddaughter kept at a distance."

"Then, how did she come to be so powerful that you felt her magic?" Sonja, Tobias' mom, quietly asked the older woman.

"Long ago, I tried to scrye about my daughter-in-law's family," Kate answered, tilting her silvery-blonde head to peer into her tea as if the answers might await her there, "just out of curiosity, but there was a blockage." She shook her short bob. "I only got a blank scene. For all I know they are magical, though not witches, or surely I would've heard about them, yet now I'm learning that a great force, a shifting of the natural world, is due to my own flesh and blood— my granddaughter Mairi."

"You must find out more about her. Does she live near us?" At the Matriarch's nod, Sonja went on. "Then get to know her better. What we could do with a witch as powerful as her in our coven . . ." Her voice drifted off.

Tobias rolled his eyes. His mother dreamed of changing

the world, of using the Coven's powers to save the planet. She was an eternal optimist. That's probably why he hadn't been locked up in a hospital. She was certain he wasn't just a vegetable. Tobias attempted to laugh, but it came out as a gurgle, and his mother moved by his side to wipe the spittle from his chin.

"Maybe she'll have the power to heal you," she whispered with longing, pushing his black bangs off his forehead and planting a kiss there.

Tobias blinked in agreement. He wanted to be healed, more than anything else in the world, and maybe this Wild Witchy girl would be able to finally do it. He'd have to find out exactly what it would take to get her to use her powers to give him what he most wanted.

HOPE
San Diego, California
September 15th, present

He's dying, Mairi thought as she stood next to his bed, blood staining his lips, the smell of iron and sickness making her nauseous. The room was permeated with the smells...putrid smells...ghastly smells. Her mom reached for Mairi's dad's hand, beckoning for Mairi and her younger brother, Jamie to also sit beside him.

"We all need to be here for him in these last moments," her mom said, voice quivering. Mairi cringed, then felt crushing guilt that she was cringing at her own dad, whom she adored.

The room was dimly lit; paisley and floral fabric covered the two small windows in her parents' bedroom, mid-morning sunlight filtering through, adding an eerie glow. Shadows in the corners played tricks on her mind. It looked like little people were hiding there, waiting to see what happened with her dad. Mairi closed her eyes and shook her head, and the shadows were just shadows again.

Trying to find comfort, she squeezed onto the same chair where her mom sat, Jamie to the right on a kitchen chair that had been pulled into the room for this purpose. Her Granny Kate stood on the other side of Mairi, caressing her son's head. Other relatives stood in the doorway, friends waited in the living room, and the woman from hospice watched over everyone from a corner.

Is this really happening? Am I losing him for good? An overwhelming fear came creeping in from every corner of the room, threatening to overtake her. *But I haven't said everything I meant to say. I want more time! I thought I would have more time!* Suddenly, Mairi could see he was taking his last breath. "I love you!" she blurted out, eyes wide, shock setting in. *Is this really it?*

On either side of Mairi she heard sobs. Her grandmother wept into her handkerchief, the one she always carried with her initials and a strange symbol embroidered on it, the one that smelled of thyme the same way her mom's clothes always smelled of lavender and Granda always smelled of sandalwood.

Why do older people always smell of herbs? Mairi wondered. A moan beside her brought her out of her thoughts and back to reality. *Dad's dying and there's nothing I can do to stop it.* The thought hit her like a blow to the chest.

She watched her dad's face as he looked up at the ceiling...beyond the ceiling. *He's smiling,* she noticed. Then he released one last shuddering breath from his body, and everything went slack: his jaw, his brow, his skin . . . especially his skin. *He's gone,* she realized. Her whole body felt numb, even her mind, but not her heart, which was racing.

Somehow, she let go of her dad's hand that she'd been holding along with her mom, and stumbled to her feet, out the front door, falling down on the weed-filled grass. She pulled her knees up to her chin, rocking there, and still no tears fell. It was as if she were dried up, an empty shell, and all the sadness that threatened to fill her up and overflow her was held at bay by sheer will. This she could control. Not his cancer, not his death, but she could hold onto him forever if she never let him flow away with her tears.

Then, something miraculous happened: he came to her. Walking across the lawn, dressed as he always was, in swim shorts and a billabong t-shirt, he came right over to her. He reached down with his hand, and Mairi put hers in his, letting him pull her to standing. She reached out her other hand and patted his cheek, sun-kissed and golden from too many days surfing, healthy as he was a year ago.

"Daddy? You're here?"

"I'm always here, my Celtic Princess." He held one of her red curls in his free hand, smiling into her green eyes. "I've always been here. You just have to know where to look. Keep looking for me and you'll find me." He pulled her into a bone-crushing hug with a strength he hadn't possessed for months. She didn't want him to ever let go, but then he did, and she crumpled to the ground, head landing on an unexpectedly soft mound of grass. She felt the familiar sorrow, and newfound wonder covered her like a blanket as she drifted off to sleep.

Mairi lay still, head on her pillow, all the covers except the top sheet pushed to the bottom of her bed. She carefully unfolded her stiff joints, stretching all the way through to her toes, enjoying the cold she discovered at the end of the mattress after feeling overheated. The night had been hot and the sunlight filtering through her blinds warned her the temperature was quickly rising. Watching the dust floating in the stream of golden light, her mind wandered through the myriad of dreams she'd just experienced, the way her Granda's eccentric neighbor, Helena, had taught her to do each morning. She had said it was the beginning of controlling her energy, her magic.

8

Something about homework . . . and her friends hanging out at the mall. Mairi skipped through the dreams as if they were pictures in one of her mom's old photo albums. The last dream she'd had, the one she had just woken up from, was elusive. *A hug . . . I was hugging someone.* Suddenly her heart rate went up, her palms became sweaty. Had she really dreamed her dad was still alive? *What did he tell me? That he's 'always been here. You just have to know where to look. Keep looking for me, and you'll find me.'*

Mairi froze. She barely breathed. *Maybe he is still alive. Now that I've come into my magic powers, he's trying to tell me to come save him. Save him how? How can he still be alive? I saw him die.* Mairi shook her head, unable to shake off the feeling in her gut that he wasn't dead. *There's got to be something I'm missing...*

Mairi hardly dared to take a breath, for fear of losing her train of thought. *I don't know, but I bet there IS an explanation for how he could still be alive. It's not as if I haven't seen strange things happen before.*

Her mind raced through images of ancient castles and angry druids, and most recently her Gran transforming from a white cat back into an elderly woman. Out of habit, Mairi's hand drifted up to the necklace she wore around her neck, a silver pendant in the shape of a Celtic Trinity Knot with three interlocking loops and a circle around all. She still found it hard to believe that the necklace had been the beginning of her magical adventures over the summer.

Her calico cat, Peaches, chose that moment to jump up on her bed and mew plaintively. She'd been the last present Mairi's dad had given to her before he'd died. He'd let her pick out any cat she wanted on the Tijuana Humane Society webpage. Peaches had practically jumped out of the screen at her. They had bonded in an instant and now she was the only one who could get Mairi up early on the weekend.

"All right sweetie, I'm getting up," she said, scratching the cat between her ears.

Slipping out of bed, she knew just what she would do. After feeding her cat, she'd text her cousin Danny at UCLA, asking him to send her everything he knew about Scottish beliefs regarding death. He was bound to know something since he was studying Scottish Folk Lore. She'd do her own Internet search, too. She'd find the answers somewhere. Somehow, she'd figure out how exactly to save her dad, whatever that meant.

As she poured Peaches' cat food into a bowl on the counter, a little part of her mind warned her that she was crazy to think her dad was still alive. Mairi quickly pushed the thought away, shoving it deep into her consciousness. Rather, she chose to enjoy the hope that blossomed in her chest with each passing minute. *Less than a month ago, I thought faeries weren't possible, either, and they are. I went to their Realm, talked to their Queen. So, surely my dad could truly be alive.*

"What better use of my druidic powers could there be?" she asked Peaches, leaning against the counter and pulling out her phone to start researching. Peaches mewed her agreement, happily crunching her fish-shaped food.

ALLIANCE

Isle of Skye, Scotland
September 15th, 1700s

Ewan MacDonald rode his horse across the moorland of Skye, still seething about missing his opportunity to take revenge on the powerful young girl and her two male companions for the death of his father, Ian MacDonald, one month ago. He wasn't entirely sure it was the girl who had killed his da, but he was certain she was involved. Ever since blocking his powers while she and her friends made their escape into the Faerie Realm, Ewan had been working on a plan for how to find them.

Rummaging through his father's belongings found at the entrance to the Faerie Realm after Ian had jumped through and disappeared, Ewan had come across an old drawing of a faerie giving a necklace to a woman, while a Highlander played the bagpipes in the background. This was the first clue that the faeries might be involved more than Ewan had previously realized. Usually, druids and faeries worked separately, though both groups drew their energy from nature, from the Earth herself.

Ewan swept his druid's robes aside as he jumped from the back of his black horse, one of the largest horses owned by his clan because Ewan was one of the most massive of the MacDonald men. He could have easily been a Highland warrior, one of the best if he'd wanted, but his destiny lay in the mystical powers, so he'd chosen his path as druid at the young age of ten. He'd followed in his father's footsteps, succeeding him as Arch Druid when his father aged past his prime.

Ewan enjoyed the power he held as leader; the Clan Chieftain often turned to him for advice in war and governing the clan. Normally, he did not let his father's curious notions infiltrate his business with the chieftain, but ever since his father had died after nearly regaining the Silver Faerie Chanter, Ewan had made it his business to avenge his father's death.

Ewan raised his hand, placing his palms on a huge boulder covering the entrance to a burial mound. This particular burial mound Ewan knew to be his father's favorite thinking spot, and it had dawned on him that perhaps his father had communed with the faeries here. *It is worth looking into*, Ewan thought as he heaved the boulder aside, acknowledging that his aged father would have had to use his druid powers to make such an enormous rock move for him while Ewan only needed his brute strength.

Robes dragging in the dust of a smooth path winding deep into the earth, Ewan made his way carefully into the depths of the burial mound, past the bones of Highlanders who had died over many past generations. A glow in the dark up ahead caught his attention and Ewan paused. Putting a beefy hand on the cold wall to steady his thoughts, while his other hand held firmly onto a torch he hadn't yet lit, he called out, "Who is it that passes in the dark beyond?"

An ethereal female voice responded like the echo of a

bell, "Hello, Ewan. Your father spoke little of his family, but of course I know all about you." A tall willowy woman with black hair, surrounded by a soft lavender glow that arched upwards into the roof of the mound as if it were wings made of pure light, emerged from the shadows. "Aah, you are so like your father was as a young man," she said. "Humans are delightful in how alike each other the old and young are, yet you each believe yourselves to be unique. At least, you have this quality for me to enjoy." The faerie smiled, as a cat might when deciding to play with a mouse for a bit. "You may call me Cali."

Ewan cleared his throat, ungrateful that he was feeling in awe about another being, especially a female. He did not like that this faerie woman might naturally be superior to him. Rising to his full height, which was barely taller than the faerie woman, and puffing out his ox-like chest to emphasize his muscular stature, he felt better. "In fact, Cali, I am here to ask ye about my father. What can ye tell me about the Silver Faerie Chanter he was searching for? And what do ye know about the necklace in this picture?" He held out the parchment drawing.

Cali sighed, "This . . . again? Humans are so persistent." Flicking her long fingers as if to brush away a spider's web, she answered. "Yes, I know about this picture. I told your father all about it; how the necklace and the silver chanter on the bagpipes work together to transport the owner from place to place and from time to time. I do seem to recall there is a curse associated with them, something about worshiping faeries at a shrine dedicated to us." Her laughter tinkled like chimes in a soft breeze. "He seemed so obsessed with these trinkets." Her eyes narrowed as she smiled sideways at him, "Are you?"

Ewan shivered, the air suddenly cold enough to show his breath. *She's got powers beyond my imagining*, he thought before saying, "I do nae really care about these things. I just want yer help catching the lass and two lads I saw with the silver chanter and this necklace. I think they are responsible for my da's death. I do intend to take the silver chanter and necklace in my da's name, then capture the girl to avenge him."

"Hmmm," Cali intoned. "This might be a fun activity to help you with. I really didn't like the interest my Queen took in the girl anyway," she said, more to herself than to Ewan, though she hardly kept Ewan from hearing. "The girl you are talking about is Mairi, and I know just the way to get her attention," she answered. "Return to this same spot on the Autumnal Equinox, midday, and you will realize what needs to be done. In the meantime, I will see to a certain family the girl is related to."

As the lithe faerie retreated into the depths of the tunnel, Ewan noticed a pair of blueish-lavender feline eyes staring at him in the darkness before they turned and disappeared after the faerie, a barely visible black tail swishing in the air.

NORMAL
San Diego, California
September 16ᵗʰ, present

It was over 100 degrees as Mairi walked home from school with the warmth of the afternoon sun beating down on her head. No one had picked her up after school, so she was left to walk the two and a half miles home along the busy suburban streets. She kicked a rock and watched it through a haze of heat as it skidded across the sidewalk, bouncing to a rest in the gutter. *Too bad Jamie and I can't just play the bagpipes and wish us home. Why does our magic power have to be something so loud?* The thought rattled around in her mind for the hundredth time, stuck on repeat. Not that she wasn't grateful for any sort of magic, since it was all she could think about most of the time, it just sucked to have a magic that basically announced itself to the world every time she and Jamie used it.

It was especially hard to be back in school studying, particularly history when she knew she could travel back in time. *Wouldn't that be a better way for me to learn history?*

Not sitting in some stuffy classroom without AC waiting for the bell to ring to release me. She used to be a really good student, last year, before she had spent the summer with her grandparents and discovered she was part faerie, and, if she was being completely honest with herself, before her dad had died.

For a few minutes, she stared at the back of her little brother Jamie who was walking ahead of her, his blonde hair unkempt even in the still air. He had met her on the corner as he walked home from his middle school where he was in the 7th grade. She kind of wished her brother were already in high school with her. Two months ago, she would have never wanted that, but now he was the only person near her age that she could actually talk to about magic. She didn't count her cousin Danny, even though he had been with them in ancient Scotland, because he lived in LA and at 18-years-old, he seemed too busy with college to respond to her calls and texts very often.

Another thing getting her down was that the first Faerie Shrine they had built next to her grandparent's house worried her. They had built a Faerie Shrine like Titania, Queen of the Faeries, and Mairi's great-great-ever-so-great grandmother, had told them to, but it hadn't worked to transform Gran, so they had built another one up on the Oak Knoll. Still, there was something about that first shrine that bothered her. She decided to call her Cousin Danny when she got home to ask him if he had found any research about Faeries being bad. She had called him last week to share her odd feeling. He had taken her seriously and promised to investigate it. She also needed to see if he'd gotten her text yesterday morning about her wondering if there was any possible way her dad had not really died.

Mairi still felt certain her theory about her dad somehow being alive, perhaps in the Faerie Realm, was a valid one. She had spent a good portion of her time yesterday researching Scottish beliefs about death and she'd come across a fae creature called a changeling, a sickly or unruly faerie, usually a child, that was swapped with a human. The faeries would keep the human for their own entertainment while the changeling lived and died with the humans.

Does this mean that my dad was swapped with the faeries as a child? No! Mairi shook her head, not liking the idea that her dad hadn't been human her entire life. *Maybe he was an adult human swapped with a dying adult faerie. That would explain his sudden illness.* She nodded with satisfaction, liking the hope again blossoming in her chest, but decided sharing her theory with her little brother didn't seem like a good idea, so she kept it to herself. *He'd just laugh at me, or ask too many questions.* Mairi sighed, *or get his hopes up. I haven't actually found any stories that show adults were swapped.* She kicked another rock. *I bet Danny will have better luck if I can just get ahold of him.*

However, all chances for calling Danny when they got home disappeared. Her dad's mom, Granny Kate, was at their house waiting for them. Mairi hadn't seen her since her dad's funeral.

"I'm sorry I didn't pick you up at school, but I completely lost track of the time. Most likely it's from the jet lag. I hope walking wasn't too much of an inconvenience." Granny Kate sat at the dining table, having let herself in, wearing a long black Spanish-style skirt paired with a black Spanish style shirt embroidered with flowers in bright colors. Mairi enjoyed the feelings of normalcy she felt in seeing her Granny look like she always did.

It's nice that some people never change, Mairi thought. *She's simply my granny, nothing more.*

Sensitive to her Granny's sincerity, Mairi wiped the sweat from her forehead, pulling at her shirt sticking to her skin as she reached for a glass of water. "No big deal," she said, trying not to sound sarcastic. "Welcome back. What's going on?"

"I want to take you two out for ice cream. We could go to that little place down the street." Picking up her purse, black like the rest of her outfit, Granny Kate stood and walked to the front door.

Mairi narrowed her eyes. She wasn't used to her Granny Kate being interested in her and Jamie. She lived fairly close, near Old Town in a little house on a hill, and was always generous on their birthdays and holidays, but mostly they didn't see her for weeks at a time. Mairi had wondered why they hadn't stayed with her in the summer, when they were instead shipped up to Northern California to stay with her Granda, her mom's dad. At the time, she was told Granny Kate was away on a trip. *I think she said something about having jet lag. Maybe I should ask her about her trip?* Mairi didn't do small talk very well and the idea tasted sour.

"Yum! Let's go!" Jamie said, saving Mairi from her indecision, motivated by his stomach. "Can we get burgers, too? I'm starving!"

Granny Kate smiled at his enthusiasm, but Mairi just shrugged and trudged to the car.

So much for talking to Danny.

Mairi mindlessly swirled her vanilla and chocolate ice cream together, barely noticing as it melted into one muddy color of tan.

"What's going on Mairi?" Her Granny's crisp question interrupted the flow of jumbled thoughts.

"Wha..?" Mairi looked up, not realizing her long fiery copper-colored hair had cascaded off her shoulder and landed in the muddy puddle of ice cream. Her grandmother reached across the bright orange table and caught the wet sticky hair in a paper napkin.

"Earth to Mairi! What is wrong with you?" Jamie demanded.

"Nothing! What's your problem? Mind your own business!" Mairi glared across the table at her brother, annoyed at his sudden immaturity.

She caught the stern look her grandmother was giving them both and ducked her head in shame. She didn't mean to be annoyed, but lately everything just really bothered her. *What was I thinking about, anyway?* She tried to catch the thought, but it swept through her fingers like the evening fog that had rolled in most nights at her Gran and Granda's mountain home over the summer . . . *something to do with surfing in Baja with Dad.* With a start, she realized this had been the first summer in her life she hadn't gone on a summer surf trip with him. She let a huge sigh escape her lips, and looked up into her Granny's eyes.

"I miss him, too, you know," Granny Kate said in a soft voice. "Your dad was a really good son, and an even better dad to you kids."

Mairi nodded, grateful her grandmother wasn't the mushy type, not grabbing her into a big hug, but just quietly letting her affections be known. Mairi sometimes wished she could be more like her, especially when her redheaded temper flared in public.

"I just wish I had more time with him, that's all," Mairi whispered, looking around the ice cream shop, a place her dad used to bring her and Jamie to when their mom was too busy to make dinner, or was gone on a girls' trip. Lately, everywhere she looked, something made her think of her dad. She didn't know if she liked it because sometimes she just wanted to stop feeling, stop thinking.

"Cancer just sucks!" Jamie said. Mairi looked up and saw he was frowning now. *Great! Now I've made everyone sad, even my goofy brother.* Nothing about today seemed good anymore.

"I like your necklace."

Mairi instinctively reached up to cover the silver Trinity Knot pendant around her neck. She knew she shouldn't wear it, shouldn't risk losing it, but something compelled her to wear it all the time. Jamie frowned at her, and she shrugged her shoulders. "It's just something passed down in my mom's family. She gave it to me this summer."

"I see. It is lovely. The Trinity Knot is a symbol of Mind, Body, and Spirit. A perfect symbol to wear when someone we love has passed away."

Mairi liked this new meaning given to her necklace. She'd gotten used to thinking of it as Past, Present, and Future-a means for Time Travel. This new meaning brought new ideas. *Did this necklace only work for Time Travel in connection with the silver faerie chanter attached to bagpipes? Or, could it also have other magic hidden within it?* Feeling her granny scrutinizing her, Mairi looked up into Granny Kate's hazel eyes.

"How was your summer? I'm sorry I couldn't stay home with you, but I'm sure it was nice for your mom's parents to get to know you."

Mairie shrugged, puzzled by the sudden interest being paid to her. "It was okay. More interesting than I expected." She heard Jamie snort across the table, so she kicked him, reminding him to keep their secrets to themselves. Mairi looked down again, away from her granny's mystified look. *Why a sudden interest in our summer? Does it have anything to do with her noticing my necklace? Maybe I'm being paranoid. She's just being our grandmother, making sure we're okay.*

"I have a gift for you, too." Granny's voice interrupted her thoughts, and Mairi looked up from her bowl of soupy brown ice cream. "I brought it back with me from my travels to Scotland last week.

"Hang on, you were in Scotland last week?" Mairi asked, surprised. Exchanging a questioning glance with her brother, she waited for Granny's response.

"Yes, all summer, actually. I try to get to Scotland at least once a year to see my Sisters." Granny rummaged through her purse and pulled out two small sheer black bags. Peeking in the bags, she handed one to each of her grandchildren.

Mairi pulled out a pendant on a long black cord. The pendant was another Celtic Knot, this one being four interlocking loops made from one continuous line, etched into the face of an iridescent stone with blue, green, and gray colors.

"This knot is the Witch's Knot. It's meant for Protection. The stone is labradorite, also for protection. I hope you don't mind wearing two necklaces, Mairi. You wear yours, too, Jamie." It sounded like a command.

Mairi looked at her brother who was holding the same pendant, smiling. Granny continued, "I'd really appreciate it if you'd put it on. It seems to me you two have been getting yourself into all sorts of trouble lately."

Mairi looked at her brother whose eyes mirrored her confusion. *What does she know? Is there more to Granny than we originally thought?* Mairi acknowledged it wouldn't be the first time someone in her family had kept secrets from her.

SICKNESS
Isle of Skye, Scotland
September 19th, 1700s

Anne trudged through the mud drenched ground, attempting the futile task of holding up her long woolen skirts with one hand, while trying not to spill any of the water out of the wooden bucket she held in her other hand. Walking from her home to the village spring up by the edge of the moor was a difficult enough task after the first rains of Autumn, but after her tenth trek back and forth, her mud-covered boots felt like a ton of bricks. Arriving back at the threshold of her house, she did her best to kick the mud off against the big rock her da had placed there for this purpose. Admitting it wasn't working, she reluctantly stepped onto the damp hay covering her family room floor, narrowly missing tripping over a black cat as it came darting out of the doorway.

"Hello, Kitty. Do be careful ye are nae stepped on." Anne addressed the cat as she'd been taught to by her maternal grandmother, with kindness and as an equal, *for I never know when a cat is actually a witch woman in disguise.*

Blinking in the doorway to let her eyes adjust to the dimly lit room, and to let her breathing grow accustomed to the heavy animal stench in the air, she carefully made her way over to the bed on the floor at the opposite end of the room. Her da lay on the straw mat, pale as the full moon and sweating as if it were midsummer, where he'd been since taking ill yesterday morning. Picking up a cloth hanging by the fire as she passed, she dipped it into the bucket of cold spring water and gently mopped his forehead and neck.

Her maw came in at that moment, carrying a plucked chicken by its legs. As she stepped through the doorway and headed for the pot of water boiling over the fire, Anne's older brother Wills came through holding the chubby hand of their little sister, Carrie. Both her siblings were haloed by their reddish-blonde hair, exact opposites of Anne with her hair as black as a moonless night. She favored their Irish grandmother who had the Sight as well as healing powers like Anne, while her brother and sister favored their father's Scottish clan, the MacLeod's.

Anne ran over to her little sister, scooping her up in a big bear hug. She was Anne's pride and joy for she had helped her parents hold fast to her while inside their mother's belly, assuring the baby would not arrive until good and healthy. Unlike several previous pregnancies after Anne was born, and before Anne came into her healing powers, Carrie had been born a squalling pink baby, very much alive. The little girl was entirely adored by their family. Carrie patted Anne's cheek with her dimpled hand, smiling with delight at her big sister.

"Anne?" Her da's voice came out cracked and barely above a whisper. "So thirsty."

She set her sister down and made her way back to the fire where wooden ladles of varying sizes and several large cups hung on the wall. She took a ladle and one of the cups over to her father who writhed on the bed. Filling the cup with the spring water, she reached behind his shoulders and helped him to sit up. He was lighter than a man of his size ought to be and Anne cringed.

Why cannae I heal him? She asked herself yet again. *I've healed all sorts of ailments since first getting my moon cycle. Why does this sickness fight me so?* As she lifted him she concentrated all her energy into the water he gulped down, envisioning it full of life's essence. She watched the water glow pale silver, as if it were a cup full of starlight. She knew from experience earlier in the day that it would not cure him, but at least it would help give him strength to survive a little longer. *But how long will he hold on?*

CHARMS
San Diego, California
September 20th, present

Tobias lay in his wheelchair in a corner of Matriarch Kate's tidy two-story house. She had lived alone, ever since her daughter-in-law and grandson had moved to LA, so Tobias and his mother had been asked to move in. Tobias liked it. He learned much from the conversations the two witches often held over cups of tea, sitting at a small table looking over a well-groomed herb garden. Tobias enjoyed the garden in which his mother often wheeled him about, stopping in the sunlight hopeful that the vitamin D and herbal scents would work a miracle on his helpless body. It never did.

Now Tobias listened intently to the conversation his mother was having with Matriarch Kate. They were talking about the girl again, and he wanted to know more. He hadn't been able to get her out of his mind in the long month since he'd first come across her, and he'd been too busy doing a faerie's bidding to spy on Mairi.

"Have you gone to see her since you came back from Scotland and since we felt your granddaughter's powers?" his mother was asking.

"Yes, I saw her a few days ago. I gave her a Witch's Knot pendant to wear for Protection. She thinks it's a souvenir from my trip to Scotland."

"Did you find out anything else? Is she a witch like you?" Tobias thought his mom sounded too eager, though he knew she had every right to be excited because she was right. The girl was a witch, a powerful witch.

"No, I didn't want to make them suspicious, though I definitely felt something more than I've felt in Mairi in the past. They're going to visit their grandparents in Northern California for the equinox, so I will invite them over to our house for dinner when they return. Meanwhile, we should get ready for our own celebration of Mabon in two days."

Tobias used to enjoy listening to their plans for the festival day, one of two days in the year when day and night shared equal time in the 24-hour span, but their conversation rarely changed, and he didn't feel like hearing it all again. He would much rather return to his Ka form and roam the Faerie Realm.

Tobias closed his eyes, appearing to be sound asleep to the two women at the table, but he was actually in a deep meditation. He envisioned the throne room of the Faerie Queen, and found himself silently running on four soft paws, long tail up in the air like an energy barometer, antennae feeling for any fae creatures who might pass too close beside him, playing their faerie tricks. He especially didn't care for the pixies, the little fae who liked to pull his hair and whiskers, zipping away in fits of giggles before he could bite their wings with his fangs. Or if it was during the Winter Court, he had to beware the Red Cap faeries, little brutish gnomes in red pointy hats who would pretend to pet him but actually dig their razor-sharp claws into his back. It was times like that he would shed the charm that gave his spirit body a physical solidity. As if in response to the memories, Tobias' cat form flickered like a ghost might. He hurried on his way, certain he would find Cali near the Summer Queen's throne at this time of year. He needed a new charm.

It wasn't long before he came through the tunnel he'd been in and entered the Throne Room. It was glorious in its Autumn splendor. Trees with a palette of color splashed all over in the form of leaves, some of which drifted slowly to the ground to join a carpet of fallen brethren. The sun was shining down on them, though it wasn't the sun of Earth, but a distant cousin, smaller yet just as bright. Pixies in varying shades of browns and purples flitted about in the trees and on the backs of squirrels and owls, from a distance appearing more like balls of light than the humanoid figures they often wore. Tall and willowy faeries wandered languidly along the brook that babbled its way through the throne room or they lay on the banks, fingers trailing in the water. Others sat under the trees, nibbling on a midday meal of grapes and berries, most likely harvested from the human world, though many fruits were grown in the Faerie Realm in the Golden Meadow.

Tobias paused and looked around for his mistress. He'd met her when he was still quite young, and she'd befriended him by offering him a single strand of her long black hair, loosely wrapping it around his neck like a chain, giving his spirit form a solidity. As with anything in the fae world, it came with a price. Her price was that he should spy for her on whomever she wished him to. Having been with Cali in the tunnels while she spoke with the druid Ewan, Tobias had been given the task of delivering the faerie spell to a man named James that would make him ill beyond healing, except by a true faerie.

"Ah Tobias. There you are." Her long arm with perfectly tended fingernails beckoned. When she used his true name, he had no choice but to come . . . foolish mistake made by his childish self. When he had given her his name, he hadn't known true names were binding when freely told by one's own voice. "What news have you brought me today?"

Like a junkie needing his fix, Tobias needed his charm to give his Ka substance. It was the only way he could move and feel like a whole creature, unlike his broken human body. Lying around like a sack of potatoes, useless to him for anything other than a set of eyes and ears, he desperately loved his Ka to be a solid physical form, even if it meant the pixies and redcaps could hurt him, so he always returned to Cali for his charm and she used his name to get him to obey completely. It was a dangerous cycle.

"I have none, other than to say the illness has been delivered." Tobias guessed Cali would want to know what he knew about the red-headed girl Mairi, but he would hold onto the info he had about her until directly asked. It was the only way he could avoid giving out information he didn't wish to divulge. He didn't want her to be made a human pet, as Cali was known for collecting interesting people.

"Now now, Tobias, you must bring me something to entertain myself. You know how I enjoy stories of the human world. Hurry and think of something to tell me when I return, for my Queen summons me. I mustn't upset her, or she will wonder about my doings and I can't have that." She petted Tobias' furry head as she got up to leave, "I will also give you your next task in this little game we are playing."

Knowing he had no real choice, Tobias curled up on the lush blanket and cast his mind about to think of some anecdotal story to appease Cali, hoping her next task wouldn't be too cruel. He always needed his charms.

PROMISE
San Diego, California
September 21ˢᵗ, present

"You two please be careful. Don't go anywhere except to your Gran and Granda's." Shaylee gave her children a stern look, arms crossed, as she stood in the doorway of their living room watching them pull their overloaded backpacks onto their shoulders.

Jamie grinned, "Of course, mom. We promise. But should we have to go anywhere else, we have Granny's Protection charm."

Shaylee sighed, not bothering to look at the new necklaces Jamie and Mairi wore. "I'm sure it's just a tourist's bauble she picked up on her trip. It couldn't possibly be magic like our necklace."

Mairi patted the new necklace hanging between her breasts, the grayish-green stone dangling beneath her black t-shirt. There was a distinctive hum vibrating against her fingers. "I'm not so sure, Mom. It feels like magic. Isn't it possible there's more to Granny than we know?"

Shaking her head, Shaylee said, "I've known her for 20 years, Mairi. She's never made any allusion to being part of magic. Your dad certainly never mentioned it."

Flinching at the mention of her dad, Mairi bent over to tie her converse shoes a bit tighter, thinking, *You kept your secrets from all of us my entire life, Mom. I bet Granny has hers, too.* Mairi knew she should voice her thoughts, because not doing so fed her anger, but they'd been through this too many times in the past month. She couldn't let go of her confusion about being raised without knowledge of her mother's magical family. But, Mairi just wanted to get to her Granda's house in Northern California and see how Gran was doing.

As she stood up, Jamie was pressing their mom to come with them.

"Come on Mom, it's perfectly safe. You know it is. And I'm sure you want to see Gran. She's got to be stronger now that she's not a cat anymore and has had a month to heal."

"Thank you, Jamie. Another time. I'm not staying simply because I am not ready to travel by magic. I have a lot of work to do. Please give my mother a hug for me, and my father, too. I'll be going up there for the winter holidays when I have some time off. Now hurry, you two! The sun is only getting higher in the sky. Have fun celebrating Mabon."

Shaylee hugged her son, breathing in the sandalwood-scented shampoo permeating his blonde hair, and simultaneously brushed Mairi's hair back from her face. "I love you kids!" she said fiercely, as though they were going off to war.

"Jeez Mom! It's just for the weekend. We promise we won't go anywhere except Gran's. We won't go see Uncle James and our cousins until the Yule, like you asked, even though we can only go see him on eight days of the year." Mairi rolled her eyes at the injustice of having her magic ability to travel through time being held back by her mom's fearful nature.

"Good! James is a dad. He'll understand when we explain at midwinter." Shaylee stepped back as Jamie raised the bagpipes to his lips, blowing up the bag and starting the first droning sounds quickly followed by the Celtic traveling song.

Mairi reached for her brother's shoulder with her right hand, and held onto the Trinity Knot necklace with her other. "I wish we were at our Granda's," she said out loud, while visualizing her grandparent's house that resembled a miniature castle, carefully nestled on a flat on the side of a steeply sloping mountain in the community of Harris in Northern California.

Mom and the familiar living room full of paisley print curtains and vibrantly colored Mexican blankets disappeared as a cloud of black enveloped Mairi and Jamie. They were pulled and squashed, as though through a small rabbit hole. It had been a full month and Mairi again experienced surprise at how separate she felt from her body, watching as if from above as it was squeezed and stretched like taffy, while also seeing from within her body and wondering why she didn't feel any pain. Then it stopped, and she dropped, unharmed into Gran's garden.

Surrounded by the bright morning light, the lingering summer scent of dry rosemary and lavender bushes washed over their senses, intermingling with the incoming Autumn smells of drying leaves crunching and decomposing under their footsteps. They hastily made their way onto the front porch of their grandparent's ornate wood and stone house, pulling open the huge double doors carved with the same symbol of the Trinity Knot as Mairi wore around her neck.

"Jamie! Mairi! You're here!" Gran's feeble voice called out from across the house. Mairi ran through the kitchen, Jamie was close behind wielding the awkward shape of the bagpipes. In the living room, Gran lay on the couch, propped up on embroidered woolen pillows, tucked under a tartan wool blanket, long white hair braided to one side. She reached out frail arms pale as the white cat she had once been, pulling the children in for a gentle hug.

Mairi gasped out loud. Gran was barely more than bones wrapped in tissue paper skin. Mairi pulled back, afraid of breaking the fragile woman.

"It's okay, Mairi, you won't hurt me." Gran looked at her granddaughter, their identical green eyes connecting. "I'm weak on the outside, but I'm still strong on the inside."

"Why are you...?" Mairi was at a loss for words. She hadn't expected to see her Gran still weak from the curse. They'd broken it, after all, following the Faerie Queen's instructions to the letter, even getting extra input from the Celtic Goddess, Elen of the Ways. "Surely you should be strong by now."

"Aye, she should be." They turned toward their Granda's voice as he was descending the stairs behind the couch, shoulder length white hair swept back in a low ponytail, plaid flannel shirt rolled up to the elbows. "We cannae figure out what ails her. Helena has been to visit, bringing with her many recipes. To no avail."

"Have you talked to Mom?" Jamie asked. Their mom was trained in Ayurvedic Medicine, and she was an herbalist as well. Asking their mom seemed like a good idea to Mairi, but they hadn't, or they would've heard.

"We do not want to worry your mother, but her advice might prove to be necessary. We just do nae seem to possess the magic needed to heal your Gran."

At the mention of magic and healing, Mairi's mind shot back to her journey to ancient Scotland over the summer, and meeting her cousin Anne for the first time.

"Jamie!" She whispered to her brother. "What about Anne? I bet she could help. And I know she'd want to, since Gran is her grandmother, too."

Jamie's face perked up and he nodded emphatically.

"We have to go back and get her, bring her here." Then his face fell. "But we promised Mom we wouldn't go."

"What are you two whispering about? We might be old, but we are still able to hear. What do you think our other granddaughter can do for us?" Granda spoke in his direct way. When she'd first met him, Mairi had thought his directness was his way of being mean, but as she had gotten to know him, she'd come to realize that it was more likely a result of his upbringing. Granda had been born and raised until 18-years-old in Scotland in the 1700s.

Jamie and Mairi took turns reminding Granda of how his granddaughter Anne was a healer in the ancient customs, drawing on her dual lineage of faerie magic.

"Surely she'll be able to help," Granda agreed, a smidge of joy showing through his rock-solid features. "We have to retrieve her and bring her here at once."

"That sounds like a wonderful idea. I'd love to meet Anne. You will have to wait until tomorrow morning, though, for the official start of Mabon. Time travel magic will only work then," Gran gently reminded them, closing her eyes.

Jamie and Mairi exchanged a silent look. They'd only been away from their mom for less than an hour and already they were preparing to break their promise. Looking at Gran on the couch, almost asleep from the little bit of excitement taking too much of her limited energy, Mairi decided going against their word to their mother was the right thing to do.

And, if she was honest with herself, she realized that this also meant she might be able to learn more about changelings and her dad by spending time with her cousin Anne. Going back in time was what she'd wanted all along.

ELEN
Harris, California
September 21ˢᵗ, present

Mairi went upstairs to her mom's old bedroom. It was the room she had used over the summer and it felt familiar, especially as the lavender scent came wafting out of the doorway. She noticed the room was starting to gather a layer of dust again, but not nearly as thick as it had been when she'd visited the first time back in June. *Granda must have someone come dust once in a while, since Gran is obviously too weak to help and Granda must be busy with her.* She shook her head. *Poor Gran and Granda.*

Leaning over the desk, she looked out of the upstairs bedroom window and gasped. *The deer! She's here again . . . or still.* Mairi corrected herself, not knowing which was true. Mairi's heartbeat sped up and her palms started getting clammy. The last time she'd seen this deer, the totem animal that was truly Elen of the Ways, it had been in a dream, but she'd seen her many times over the summer in real life, too.

The doe looked up at her, big brown eyes imploring, rabbit-like ears sticking out, one with a notch in it and velvet antlers stretching up like the branches of a tree, the obvious sign that it was Elen and thus not of this earth, for no female mule deer ever has antlers. The doe turned and walked slowly through the blanket of leaves covering the forest floor next to the house. Several feet back, alongside the garden and still in view, the doe turned and looked up at Mairi's window again. Shaking her antlered head, the doe stamped her hoof.

Mairi understood. She was to follow.

Grabbing her sweatshirt from where she'd left it dropped in a pile with her backpack, she pulled it on as she dashed down the stairs and out the front doors, anticipating the evening air would be cooler up in the mountains of Northern California. The cool breeze that swept over her as she dashed through the garden and out the back gate proved her right.

The gate opened onto a deer trail that paralleled the fence down the side of the house in one direction, and in the other direction it continued up the steep grassy slope, making its way into the woods. Mairi knew this trail well.

Mairi shivered as she entered the woods. Even in her sweatshirt, the cold from the shadows of the trees in the setting sun cooled the air that much quicker. Ahead, a flash of white from the doe's tail marked the direction she had gone and Mairi hurried to catch up with her.

As she crested the hill, she saw the deer down the other side and under an oak tree. The sun shone golden on this side of the mountain, spotlighting the doe as she raised her head, antlers bathed with gold like a majestic crown, ears twitching as if listening.

Mairi frowned and shook her head. *Wait, that's not the deer I saw outside my window. That's not Elen's totem deer.*

This deer had no notch in its ear. This was not Elen. The deer below Mairi was actually a buck. Staring hard at the buck, wondering why Elen had brought her out here, Mairi followed the gaze of the deer and was horrified at what she saw. Hidden in a clump of bushes was a man flattened onto his belly, dressed in camouflage clothes, aiming a rifle directly at the deer.

"No!" Mairi screamed, startling the buck that looked up at her then leaped into the air to make its escape. A resounding BANG! rang through the air, taking down the deer in mid-leap. Mairi's heart plummeted to the bottom of her stomach and she almost threw up her lunch.

Without thinking, she took off running, hopping and jumping over clumps of yellow grass and dips in the hill under her feet. Miraculously, she did not fall.

"Hey! What are you doing?" The man had risen and was shouting at her as he ran to the deer, gun lowered and aimed at the ground. "You're lucky I didn't accidentally shoot you! You're on private property!"

"You . . . you . . . " Mairi pulled up next to the man already crouching beside the buck. She stood there, staring down at the buck lying lifeless on the ground. "Y...you killed him!" she finally managed to sputter.

"Yeah . . . so what? He's on my property and I need to feed my family." The hunter looked up at Mairi with weary eyes set in a dark, weathered face. "I didn't break any laws. It's hunting season. I've got my license."

"But . . . " Mairi looked from the man to the animal on the ground, and quickly back to the man. Blood was beginning to pool at the wound and to drain out of the buck's mouth. Her father's lifeless face flashed into her mind. Shaking her head to rid herself of thinking about her dad, she said, "He didn't do anything to you. Why'd you kill him?"

Pulling out a giant knife, he grabbed onto the front legs of the deer. "Listen, girlie, I gotta feed my family and I'm not a rich man. I don't have sheep or pigs, no time to raise them. What I do got is five measly weeks to kill my quota in deer and turn it into jerky, so my family can eat for the rest of the year. So, just take your drama and head on back from where you came from." He paused, holding the knife to the deer's throat. "Where did you come from anyway? You don't live around here, that I ever seen."

"I . . . I . . . " She had just realized what the hunter was about to do with his knife and she was having trouble remembering his question.

Seeing her discomfort, the hunter let out a long breath and put the knife down. "Look, I gotta drain this guy before all the meat gets flooded with too much blood. Say who you are and be on your way, or the buck's death will be for nothing and my kids will go hungry."

Mairi focused purposefully on the man's shoes, old and worn out, covered in dirt and clumps of dried mud before looking up at his face, staring him squarely in the eyes. "My granda is William MacLeod and he lives just over the hill," she gestured behind her. "I was following the deer and I didn't realize I was on private property." She continued staring at him, feeling her fingers twitch, acutely aware that she hadn't learned to control her magic and she could easily harm this man whether she intended to or not. Balling her hands into fists, she turned on her heel and retreated over the rise.

Mairi burst into her grandparents' home, hot with anger. "How dare he kill that beautiful creature?" she shouted to no one in particular, throwing her sweatshirt over the back of the couch in the living room. "And why did Elen ask me to come out and see that happen? Why?" She shouted the last word as loud as her lungs would carry it, high into the rafters of the ceiling two stories above.

"Oh honey, it'll be okay. Elen never shows anyone something unless it is necessary." Mairi looked up to the balcony above the couch and saw their eccentric neighbor

Helena leaning on the railing, the sleeves of her scarlet red silk blouse billowing over the edge mixing with her long, gray and purple highlighted hair. "Hold on, I'll come down."

"Here, dear. Sit by me." Gran meekly patted the spot next to her on the old floral couch. As Mairi sat down, Helena descended the stairs and sat on the other side of Gran. Jamie came out of their uncle's old bedroom off the kitchen and joined them.

I guess my shouting got everyone's attention, Mairi observed with a twinge of embarrassment.

"What happened, Mairi? What got killed?" Jamie asked.

So Mairi described the scene that had just unfolded, putting in as much detail as she could stomach. As she finished, Helena chuckled slightly.

"I remember the first time I saw an animal killed. It was slaughtering season and my dad was killing off the sheep we didn't need for milk or wool. I cried and cried. I loved those sheep with all my heart, and I still do. But, we all have a place in this world, and sometimes an animal's place is to be eaten."

"He was so alive, though, so beautiful standing in the setting sun. Then he was dead, just lying there in the dirt, gone. The hunter kept saying he was feeding his family, but couldn't he feed them something else?"

"Sure, he could. But if it's the family that lives right next to this property, I know that hunter and he isn't exaggerating when he says he has little money to feed his children anything else. Life has been hard on him. Besides, you eat meat. You eat my sheep I slaughter and send over to Granda in exchange for his help on the ranch," Helena patiently explained.

Mairi's shoulders slumped as she realized the truth. "Maybe I'll become a vegetarian," she muttered in defeat.

"That's your choice, child," Gran said in a soft voice. "We've all got to follow our hearts. But let's consider why

Elen would want you to witness such an act. What do you think, Helena? You've studied her more than anyone I know."

Helena straightened up a little at the deference to her knowledge. "Well now, I think she is showing you a Way. That's what she does . . . she teaches us how to follow our hearts and decide which way to go."

"I don't understand. I don't like that Elen showed me something so horrible." Mairi realized she felt betrayed. *She's supposed to help me understand my magic and to do good, not show me animals dying.*

Helena took Mairi's hands. "Goodness child! Your hands are near burning!" Mairi attempted to pull them away, but the older woman held onto them. "It's okay. I'm familiar with powerful hands, and I've seen your aura. You are a formidable young druid. After we get your gran settled, you and I need to have a talk."

Helena patted her knee. "For now, don't think about it too much. Time always tells." With that she stood up from the couch and climbed back up the stairs, calling down to Gran, "Caroline, I'll have your bed ready in a jiffy, and William will be back any minute to bring you upstairs."

Gran nodded her head, then laid it against the wing of the couch, and drifted off to sleep.

"Helena's right," Mairi whispered to Jamie. "I don't have time to worry about Elen or my magic. We have to take care of Gran or she will be the next to die. Be ready at dawn. We have to get Anne first thing tomorrow!"

FOCUS

California to Skye
September 22nd, Present to 1700s
Dawn of Mabon

Mairi and Jamie tiptoed quietly out of their bedrooms at the crack of dawn. They were dressed in the clothes of ancient Scotland, so they could blend in. Jamie came into the living room wearing a kilt in the dark blue, almost purple tartan of the MacLeod clan and Mairi in a long plaid dress also in the MacLeod tartan. These clothes were faded and looked old, so they would not seem out of place amongst the hard-working crofters of their cousin Anne's village. Bright clothes were reserved for festivals, and the Autumnal Equinox wasn't as festive a holiday as Samhain would be in just a few weeks, or Lughnasadh had been during the summer. They took a few provisions, a bag of crackers and some dried fruit from their granda who had woken up with them, and filled their water bottles. Gulping down the lukewarm oatmeal Granda prepared for them, they were finally ready to travel through time.

Not wanting to wake Gran, they walked outside, following the driveway towards the Oak Knoll where the powers of the earth were stronger under the Old Oak Tree, especially since they had added a faerie shrine to the sacred space. Granda accompanied them only partway, not wanting to leave his wife alone for too long. He headed back to the house when they left the dirt driveway, and began the hike uphill on a well-worn path to the Oak Knoll.

Traveling back in time for the Autumnal Equinox would be in stark contrast to their previous travels on Lughnasadh six weeks earlier. Gran (as Star), Granda, and mom had all joined them and there had been a ritual in which everyone took their place at the four directions, calling upon the corresponding elements. It would only be the two of them today, though. Last night, their granda had sat with them and explained what they would need to do. He had said he knew they didn't have to follow through with such a ritual ceremony, for the magic in the pipes and the necklace could work without it. However, he had learned from experience that when he started with the ritual steps of asking for the guidance of the four directions and the elements of Earth, his travels were smoother.

When they reached the knoll, Mairi took the items from the bag Granda had prepared for them. She walked to the East, where an orange glow was beginning to show behind the silhouette of the mountain rising behind the knoll. She lit a bit of Amber incense to ward off evil intentions, wafting the smoke in a spiral with an orange and brown chicken feather.

Next, she turned to the North, moving Widdershins like Granda had told her to, "because going back in time is like the sun going backwards across the sky." That was the way he had explained it to them. She took out a small ceramic pot and scooped up a handful of soft earthy soil, filling the pot halfway. She pulled out a little bag of thistle seeds, downy tufts soothing against her fingers, and placed them on the soil. "Thistle grows in both Scotland and California, offering a connection between the spaces you will be moving between," Granda had said in his matter-of-fact tone. *How many kids can say their grandparents teach them about time travel,* she wondered, smiling a little to herself.

Refocusing her thoughts, she turned and faced the West "toward the Pacific Ocean" Mairi murmured to herself, feeling the familiar pang of longing to once more be surfing with her dad. Shaking her head to clear her mind, she focused instead on pouring a little vial of water onto the Earth, serving as a sacrifice for asking to be moved safely through time. She noticed as she looked up that the mountains in the distance were indeed varying shades of purple just like the song she remembered singing in fifth grade, "for purple mountains majesty above the fruited plain . . . "

Sighing at her inability to stay focused, she finally faced the South and lit a small candle she held in her hand. Mairi sincerely wished she could ignite it with her powers like Granda had the last time she'd time traveled, but she still needed to be trained. *I'll have to talk Mom into letting me visit my grandparents more often,* Mairi vowed silently, *so they can train me.* Allowing the candle to burn for one full minute as instructed, she then blew it out, since she could not take the lit candle with her nor could she leave it unsupervised.

Standing in the center of their cast circle, Jamie began blowing up the bag on his Highland pipes and played the traveling song. Mairi placed her hand on his shoulder, wrapping her other hand around the now humming Trinity Knot necklace, and wished they were on the Isle of Skye, visualizing the rock in the meadow where they'd first met their Uncle James. Used to the pull of darkness by now, they waited for the glow of the Scottish dawn to welcome them, signaling they had arrived safely.

Mairi and Jamie landed in the wet grass with a harder thud than anticipated. Mairi's knees buckled and she sat down flat on her bottom, feeling thick mud begin to seep through her dress. *I bet it's because I couldn't stay focused!* Mairi blamed herself as she gasped, the wind knocked out of her.

"Ouch! Ouch . . . Ouch . . . Owwwch!" Jamie yelled into the semi darkness. Mairi could scarcely make out his form in the gray morning light. He was on his back clutching his leg.

"What happened?" Mairi crawled on her hands and knees to his side, getting muddier by the second. Reaching out to inspect his leg, she put her hand on his ankle.

"No! Don't touch it! I think I broke it," Jamie moaned in the growing light, his voice loud in the stillness of dawn's awakening.

"Oh crud, Jamie! It's my fault. I'm just not good at staying focused, so the magic didn't run smoothly. I'm so sorry! Can you put any weight on it?"

Jamie rolled over and pushed his body up on to his one good leg, allowing Mairi to grasp him under the armpits and help him balance. Gingerly touching the ground with the foot of his hurt ankle, he collapsed against his sister, "No."

"Okay Jamie, I've got to go get Anne. She can help you."

"How come you don't try? You healed Danny when the druid Ian MacDonald attacked us."

"I can't, Jamie! I just don't know how to call up my powers unless we're being attacked, or something. I'm sorry! But, I'm sure Anne can heal you if I can only get to her. It'll be quicker if I run to her house and bring her back here. We can head back to Gran as soon as Anne heals you." Nodding his agreement with clenched teeth, Jamie worked with Mairi to get him settled against the rock, bagpipes resting across his legs.

"Maybe you should hide the silver chanter. You won't be able to fight anyone off if they try to take it from you." Jamie nodded again, in too much pain to say anything. She unhooked his tartan scarf draped across one shoulder, letting the voluminous fabric fall across his legs and thoroughly cover the bagpipes along with the silver chanter. Leaving his water bottle and snacks within his reach, Mairi turned in what she hoped was the direction of the moor and her uncle's home.

Mairi ran with the sun rising to her left, and the scent of heather wafting off the moor ahead of her, the way she remembered traveling with Uncle James in the summer. Dodging the patches of mud and ribbons of streams interspersed throughout the moor, she wasn't sure why she bothered as she felt all the muddy patches on her clothes. *The sky is so clear right now! When did it rain?* She couldn't help but wonder at the dichotomy of weather.

Mairi slowed her pace a bit, looking around at the wet landscape. *I hope this is the right direction! It wasn't so wet before...it looks so different. She* doubted her memory. She didn't feel as sure of herself as she had when she and Jamie had sat up the night before discussing their plan. Part of her had always expected Uncle James to meet them at the rock like before, especially since he'd waited at the rock every year on every Celtic holiday since he first became trapped back in time. After her brother had yelled out in pain, she'd expected James to jump out from behind the rock. *You'd think he'd anticipate that his family would time travel to see him after our visit this summer.*

"Never mind that we almost didn't come at all," she muttered to herself, not forgetting her broken promise to her mom.

Pushing aside her residual bitterness towards her mom, she went back to thinking about the problem at hand. *It's really odd that he's not here,* Mairi thought, just beginning to let the nagging feeling take hold of her when she noticed someone running towards her over the expanse of wet heather covering the moor. Diving behind a rock outcropping, heart pounding, Mairi peaked out to see that it was her Cousin Anne.

"Mairi, is that you?" Anne asked as she came closer.

"Anne? This is really weird meeting you here." Mairi stood up, attempting to wipe the mud off her dress, and giving up with a shrug. "How did you know to come?"

Anne gave her cousin a quizzical look. "My da insisted he come wait for ye at the Faerie Grove like he always does." Anne explained between gasps for breath. "He was sure ye would come now that yer necklace is working again. I tried to talk him out of it, especially after a black cat came with the dawning sun telling me not to take my da, that bad things are brewing. But my da worked himself into a tizzy. He is so sick I dinnae think he knows what he is saying. Ma is away at a birthing and he needed both Wills and I to help him to travel, so we agreed to assist him, if only to calm him down."

Mairi looked behind Anne then back at the raven-haired girl, puzzled. "Where are Wills and your da, then?"

Anne knit her brows together. "He could nae make it. He near fainted. I bid Wills lay him down a ways back while I ran to see if ye had really arrived." Anne's face brightened up. "And ye are here! I am sure ye will help my da's health improve; he'll be so happy to see ye. Please, we should go!" Anne took Mairi's hand and started to pull her back the way she had come.

"Oh Anne! We have to go help my brother first. He might have broken his ankle when we arrived, and he can't walk at all. I'm hoping you can heal him."

Anne let out a big sigh, shoulders drooping under the weight of so many pressures, understanding that they must first go for Jamie before returning to her da. "I should have asked where Jamie was. I've just been so distraught over my da being sick beyond my healing. I am at a loss! I cannae heal him and I've always been able to heal every malady," Anne explained as they jogged back the way Mairi had just run from, sharing about the illness that had taken over her da the past day.

For the first time it dawned on Mairi that maybe asking Anne to heal first Jamie's ankle then Gran might be too much for her cousin. *What if nothing can heal Gran?* The thought came unbidden to her, making her heart stop for a moment. As they made their way through the slippery mud, Mairi explained why she and her brother had come back in time.

Anne nodded grimly at the news. Mairi was not sure if she was ready for time travel, or if she could even leave her da in his current condition. *We'll just all have to go*, Mairi silently decided.

TAKEN
Isle of Skye, Scotland
September 22nd, 1700s
Midmorning of Mabon

"**W**here is he?" Anne asked of no one in particular. Jamie and Mairi certainly had no answers the first time she asked, or this last time. "Where is my da, and my brother, too? I left Will and Da right here," she gestured at the woods beside the wetlands they had all just finished trekking over after retrieving Jamie.

Mairi tried to pay attention, her mind in a whirlwind about what she had just witnessed with Anne's healing powers. Upon arriving back at the rock, Mairi had assisted Anne by removing Jamie's boot and sock, a stinky business that almost required plugging her nose. Mairi still grimaced in memory. Anne had quickly assessed that Jamie's injury was a sprain, simple to heal, but painful all the same. Hovering her hands just above his black and blue anklebone, she'd closed her eyes and remained still for several minutes, quietly intoning a spell of some sort. Mairi was sure she could see the space between the palms of Anne's hands and Jamie's ankle glowing a soft shade of green. Jamie was soon jumping up and down, laughing in his amazement that he'd been healed so quickly, and by magical means to boot. Never again would she doubt her cousin's ability to heal. In fact, she realized she might be able to learn a thing or two from her about focusing her own magical talents. *How does she call on her powers so easily? I haven't got her control.*

Then, Anne had immediately rushed them back across the moor, only to discover that her da was nowhere to be found.

"Maybe Wills convinced your da to go back home. Let's go there and see," Mairi suggested.

Anne looked up with hope, and a little bit of doubt. Throwing her hands up in despair, she declared, "I guess! I dinnae know what else to do."

Trudging the rest of the way over the moor was a muddy affair, with all three of them covered in the gooey mess from the bottom down. "Now I know why we invented pavement and created sidewalks," Mairi stated to Jamie, a comment that earned Mairi a questioning look from Anne. It required a long explanation, with both Mairi and Jamie offering information about something they had once taken as so commonplace.

"If the ground is covered with this pavement, how does the Mother Earth drink the water? How do the wells get filled? It sounds a little like the roads built by the Romans, but I never thought much of them." Anne did not seem to think the modern road was an improvement on living.

Mairi didn't know how to answer. She had never given any thought to where the water ran to once it hit the gutters along her street. *At least Anne's mind seems to be distracted from worrying about where Uncle James and Wills have ended up,* Mairi thought with some relief. Wrapped in conversation as they were, they soon found they had arrived back at Anne's village, exhausted from their morning sprints.

The minute they reached Anne's home, Anne ran inside expecting to grill Wills on why he'd left instead of waiting for her. Blinking back the blinding darkness in the hut, barely lit by the fire burning low in the center of the room, Mairi bumped into Anne. She had stopped stock still just a few steps inside the room.

"He is nae here . . .Wills! Where is Da?" Anne demanded of her brother.

Wills gave her a puzzled look from the corner where he was folding up a blanket. "He's where I left him. He was shaking with the cold, so I came back to get him a blanket."

Anne's shoulders wilted. "Oh Wills," she said with a sympathetic voice. Mairi remembered that her cousin Wills was a bit slow; he was an amazing shot with the spear, but not very quick-witted. "Ye should nae have left Da in his weakened state, nae matter how much ye believed he needed a blanket." Anne spoke neither with anger nor with condescension, simply weariness, as she might to a very young child.

She's tired, Mairi realized with acute understanding. *She's the one holding her family together.* "Where's your mom?" Mairi asked, looking around now that her eyes had adjusted, wondering why Anne seemed to be doing everything to care for her family. Jamie pushed past her.

"Is that her, Anne?" Jamie asked, pointing at the bed at the end of the room.

Anne looked at the bed, puzzled. "Maw? Are ye okay? Why are ye in bed? Ye are supposed to be seeing to Claire MacKenzie's birthing."

For the first time Mairi realized there was a grown woman sitting slumped in the bed, quietly whimpering.

"I came home. Something tis wrong with yer sister. I cannae figure her out. She will nae stop crying," Anne's mom looked up as she spoke.

Anne darted across the room, instantly at her sister's side. "Let me have her!" Anne insisted, her voice rising with alarm.

Mairi realized it was the little child who was whimpering, not the mother at all. As Anne took the child into her arms, the whimpering escalated to straight out wailing. It grew quickly, getting louder and louder until it was almost unbearable. Mairi covered her ears to shut out the horrendous sound, like nails on a chalkboard magnified tenfold by a microphone, but still the shrieks broke through her fists, tearing at her eardrums.

"Make it stop!" Mairi shouted, but no one did anything, or more likely no one heard her.

Doubling over to block the sounds, Mairi just barely heard Wills shout out, "I think she is a changeling, Anne! She is nae longer our baby sister!"

At that word, Mairi almost forgot the wailing. She dropped her hands to her sides and stood up, stunned. *Did he say a changeling?* Looking closer at her little cousin, she didn't see anything physically different from a human. *Of course, I never saw her before in my life, so does she look like she did before?* Mairi immediately got her answer as Anne held the child from her breast and looked her squarely in the eyes. Mairi saw something so odd she doubted she could ever erase it from her mind. The child grinned a most wicked grin, her eyes gleaming with an unearthly glow, and went back to wailing at the top of her lungs.

Anne gasped. "She is nae my wee baby sister! She is no of this world!"

"Nae!" Anne's mother wailed, grabbing at her child in desperation. "Do no harm her! She cannae be a changeling. We did everything, all the usual charms and protections to keep her safe. She is my own!" Anne's mother hugged the shrieking, wailing child (if child she truly was) to her breast, her face riddled with rivulets of tears, her hair stringy and whisked this way and that. Anne's usually neat bun was slowly releasing from its carefully constructed prison, untwining as the rest of Anne sat rigid on the bed. She was frozen with indecision.

Watching all of this as if in slow motion, half her mind on the current scene while the other half weighed the odds of her own father being a changeling at his death, Mairi saw her cousin Wills stride across the room, closing the space in three steps with his long legs. He wrenched the child from his mother's arms and held her over the water slowly boiling away above the low burning fire. His mother moaned.

"What are you doing?" Anne screamed.

He looked up at everyone watching him and slowly explained his actions, "If . . . she is . . . a changeling . . . the fire will burn . . . the demon out." He frowned, "It says so . . . in all the stories. . . Maw has told us." He looked around with an innocent expression while the creature writhed in his grasp.

"No!"

Mairi turned towards the voice, seeing that it was her own brother who had shouted. The scene was terrible, escalating so quickly that she'd almost forgotten Jamie was in the room, too.

"No!" he shouted again. "Don't burn her. I've heard of a better, less barbaric way to tell. Changelings don't like the sound of bagpipes."

Something clicked in Mairi's memory. Dad never listened to bagpipe music! With this thought came another, more terrible realization. *If my dad was a changeling since childhood, he was never my dad at all . . . or am I part changeling?* Too terrible and bizarre to fathom, Mairi returned her attention to the horrifying scene in front of her.

At the mention of bagpipes, the child who hung precariously close to the hot blackened kettle stopped her caterwauling and glared with a decidedly ancient look. "Nae! No that!" the child said in a creaky voice so unlike the angelic voice of toddlers that any doubt the onlookers might have held onto immediately disappeared.

Looking from her brother, who had stopped in shock with the bagpipe chanter just brushing his lower lip, to Anne and her mother sitting mouths agape staring at their once-beloved child, Mairi almost could not believe what she was witnessing.

"Ah! I see ye have the Silver Faerie Chanter," the wicked child spoke again, her voice barely easier to bear than her earlier shrieking. "There are some who would vera much like tae know ye have brought it here, some who dislike ye so much they have destroyed yer family, taken yer da," he looked at Anne on the bed, "tae pay the seven-year tithing." The changeling wrenched itself free of Wills' grasp and skipped out of the hut, laughing as she went.

They ran to the doorway, only to see the changeling wink out of view in the middle of the road. They stared at each other as the bizarre events slowly sank in, none of it making sense. Then, they turned to face Wills' and Anne's puzzled mother.

"Oh Maw," Anne turned to her mother, gently touching her arm. Her mother had gone catatonic, not blinking or even registering Anne's gentle touch. "I will get her back, I will. I promise ye, even if it means I must enter the Faerie Realm and chase her to the depths of the fiery earth. I will bring our little Carrie home. And Da, too."

Mairi could see a faint glow of lavender light as it radiated from under Anne's hand where she touched her mother's forehead. The room became decidedly calmer in the faint glow of lavender colored magic and the orange light of the fire. Anne's mother closed her eyes, letting out a long sigh, seeming to fall into a deep sleep.

Carefully tucking her mother in, Anne turned to her brother. "Wills, stay with Maw. Make her hot bone broth and feed it to her. Give her plenty of water to drink. Tell her every day that I will return with wee Carrie...and with Da, once I figure out what the Changeling creature meant by 'to pay the seven-year tithe.'"

Opening the door to leave the darkened house, Mairi nearly stepped on a little child, for there lay the wee bairn Carrie in the dirt.

"They've returned her," Jamie said, going on to explain to Mairi how all the tales say if the changeling is found out the human child is returned.

So, I might be able to return my dad to our world if he truly was just a changeling when he died. Mairi's mind whirled with possibilities.

Anne pushed past Mairi and snatched Carrie up, hugging her tight. Carrie stretched and when her eyes focused on her big sister, she clapped her pudgy hands and wrapped her arms around Anne's slender neck. Anne's mother was still out, so Anne kissed the child's sweet-smelling cheek and laid her gently next to their mother's side where she promptly fell back to sleep.

"The Fae must have enchanted her, otherwise I cannae explain why she is nae full of her usual energy. But nae matter, she is here," Anne told them.

That's when Mairi saw it, the fine silver chain dangling from Carrie's ankle. "What is that?"

Anne followed Mairi's pointing finger and saw the shiny delicate chain. "I dinnae ken..." and try as she might, she could not break it off. Even when Wills fetched out his hunting knife and tugged at the chain with the sharp blade, it would not break. "I fear she is still a prisoner of the Fae Folk. I know nae what this means, but it cannae be anything good."

"Maybe Gran will know about the chain. Mairi, we've got to get going," Jamie said, eyeing the sun creeping toward the western horizon.

"We'll have to make one last search for my da where I

last saw him before we can return to yer time," Anne addressed Mairi and Jamie.

"You still want to come with us to help Gran?" Mairi couldn't help sounding incredulous. "After all you have to do here, you are still willing to heal our grandmother?"

"Mairi, I dinnae know what to do just now. It is beyond my knowledge. This is nae something I can heal with my hands." Anne stared down at her delicate hands . . . hands that Mairi had believed could solve any ailment. She watched as Anne balled them into fists and looked up at her and Jamie. "I dinnae ken how to get my da back. I need advice about faeries, and at this point I think Gran might be the best person to help me."

Mairi and Jamie nodded in unison. "You can count on us, too." Mairi said this without hesitation. *There is no way I'm going to let her face the faeries alone. Especially if some of them are as wicked as that changeling.* She also secretly hoped to find out more about her own dad, though now she wasn't so sure she liked the idea of his being a changeling half as much as she used to. Following her brother out into the bright daylight, she realized Jamie might have been more helpful on this subject than she'd previously considered. She vowed to turn to him for help more often from now on.

BARGAINS

Isle of Skye, Scotland
September 22nd, 1700s
Midmorning of Mabon

Ewan struggled slightly under the dead weight of the muscular, extremely ill man he half carried, half dragged down the dirt tunnels, the entrance into the Faerie Realm. The tunnels were getting darker as he walked further from the opening, and he wasn't sure he could keep going between his heavy cargo and his constant stumbling in the waning light, when the tunnel lit up with a purple glow ahead of him. *She's here. Finally!* Ewan sighed a bit and leaned against the tunnel wall, letting the man slide to the floor where he came to a rest on the ground.

"Oh good! You brought him," Cali's tinkling voice broke the oppressing silence. "I have just the thing for him." Ewan watched the willowy faerie bend over and spill a tincture of some sort into the man's mouth.

"Who is he? And how did ye know he would be laying on the mound outside at exactly the time ye told me to look?" Ewan knew he shouldn't be asking questions, he was trying to earn a favor from the faerie lady after all, but he was used to politics discussed by chieftains around a roaring fire, not commands from a winged woman that miraculously played out to the finest detail.

"Aaah, he is the uncle of your Wild Druid that you so eagerly asked me to help you exact revenge upon. He is also the great-great-ever-so-great grandson of my *beloved* Summer Queen." Ewan did not miss that beloved was said with dripping sarcasm. "I'm guessing his clan name is MacLeod, but we can just call him *bait*." Her tinkling laughter was cut-off by the deep moan of the man hunched against the wall. "Mmmm . . . he awakes."

He recovers as if from the dead! "What did ye give him?" Ewan asked, clenching his fists at his side in his frustration at appearing so weak by asking another question.

She looked at him like a wise old owl sizing up a cat to be sparred with, "An herbal concoction infused with a bit of Fae Magic, as you humans call our particular form of healing. His faerie-induced illness was easy to remedy, considering I caused it to be placed in him to begin with." Turning to the man, Cali offered him her hand, "Come love. We have a dance to get to. The Winter Queen is waking up and so we must prepare to greet her."

Ewan barely concealed his awe as the faerie appeared to float back down the tunnel, the MacLeod Highlander trotting along behind her like a large hound puppy following a favorite master.

"Wait!" Ewan called out, and the duo stopped as one.

Cali raised her brows at Ewan. " . . . Yes . . . ?"

"What am I supposed to do?" Ewan felt helpless. He didn't like being at the whim of someone else's plans, and these plans were supposed to be to help him, not the other way around.

"Be patient," she replied and disappeared around the

bend, leaving Ewan in utter darkness, other than a pair of lavender-blue eyes staring up at him. Ewan stepped back in surprise, then they blinked shut and disappeared from his view. Again.

Ewan turned on his heel, determined to make plans of his own from now on.

ABUNDANCE

Harris, Northern California
September 22nd, present
Evening

Wasting no time, they arrived back on their Granda's land, materializing under the towering oak tree on the knoll just as the sun reached its apex. Anne stood up, eyes wide in astonishment, looking about her as she slowly turned. "We are no where we were," she stated simply.

Mairi and Jamie exchanged a look. "She has no idea what she's about to see," Jamie whispered to Mairi.

Mairi nodded, a conspirator's grin on her lips. Taking Anne's hand, Mairi led her cousin down the mountainside to the driveway winding past, leading them to the footpath and over the stone bridge, through the garden and up the steps of the front porch, stopping only to pull off their mud-encased boots. Anne followed suit.

As Jamie pushed open one of the double doors, Anne

caressed the carving of the Trinity Knot etched into the solid oak panels. "Is this the Clan Chief's house? Or perhaps even the King's?" Anne asked.

"No, it belongs to our grandparents," Mairi told her.

Anne gasped.

Making their way past the sitting room on one side and the dining room on the other, through the kitchen, and finally into the living room, Anne's mouth dropped open in awe at the grandeur of her grandparents' home. "How are they able to afford such a house?"

Seeing the house, and maybe even their whole way of life, through her cousin's eyes Mairi realized that next to Anne's tiny one-room crofter's hut this house was indeed grand. "Granda works hard at raising sheep and helping neighbors with their sheep, too." It was a simple explanation, and the truth as far as Mairi knew. "He's probably off doing that work now. But someone, most likely Helena, should be here caring for Gran."

They reached the couch where Gran lay fast asleep and wondered whether to wake her. "Let's get you kids cleaned up first," Helena called from above as she was making her way down the staircase.

"I call first shower!" Jamie hollered, racing to his room. Mairi rolled her eyes at the way her brother could seem so mature one minute and just his age the next.

Helena came to Mairi and crushed her with a sincere hug. "I'm glad you made it home safely! Your mother must have sensed something. She called my house this morning and she's fit to be tied. You should try to text her and let her know you're back."

Turning from Mairi, Helena then gave Anne a gentle hug. "You must be Anne. I've heard you can work miracles with healing, and a miracle is what we are going to need, but I can see you are very tired. Let's get you in a hot shower just as soon as young Jamie is through." Anne was indeed looking the worse for wear and Helena led her to

Granda's big chair in front of the fire. "Rest, my dear."

Anne willingly sat down, feeling the weariness envelop her. It seemed nothing would quiet her aching head, or calm her broken heart. She thought, *How did so much go wrong in such a short amount of time? My da is gone. My Carrie was stolen from us, and though she has been returned I dinnae know if she is yet a prisoner. Even my Gran, who I've not properly met, looks to be on death's doorstep.* With these thoughts whirling through her mind, Anne drifted off to sleep for a few moments, head leaning against the high chair back, only to be awakened by the heavenly scent of herbal tea.

"I hope you like your tea sweet. In our haste to help you, Mairi and I double-dosed your tea with too much honey, but honey is soothing, so drink up this lavender-chamomile tea and we'll get you into the shower after Mairi. I told her to go ahead since you are still getting your bearings." Helena handed her a large clay mug dyed a shade of forest green and stamped with a leaf indentation.

Anne held it tight, enjoying the warmth and taking a sip. "Oh my!" Anne almost dropped the tea.

"Is it too hot?" Helena asked, true concern in her eyes.

Anne shook her head. "Sweet!" she managed to gasp. Anne had never tasted anything so sweet. She knew bees made honey, and she'd seen plenty of honey in a beehive before, but she'd never had access to more than a small drop at a time, usually just to mix with a poultice for a wound. Never would so much be added to one's drink. Anne didn't say any of this to her kind hostess. She was grateful for the attention, and didn't want to show any ingratitude toward her. She quietly sipped the tea, feeling the herbs and the honey soothing her aching body, marveling at the beauty of her grandparent's home.

While she drank her tea, Jamie and then Mairi showed up beside her in odd loose clothing of what appeared to be the softest fabric she'd ever seen. "May I?" she'd asked as she reached out to touch Mairi's shirt. "So soft! What is it?"

Mairi's eyebrows rose. "Cotton." She looked at her cousin inquisitively. "Have you never seen it before?"

Jamie elbowed Mairi as he stood by her side. "Ouch! Why'd you do that?"

"Because don't you know that cotton didn't come to the peasants of Scotland until much later?" Jamie asked in his superior bookish voice.

Mairi grumbled something about not being a know-it-all, but didn't argue. Instead, she asked, "Would you like your shower now? You can borrow some pajamas from me, though they'll probably be too big for you." Mairi stretched a good five inches taller than Anne.

Anne put down her mug of tea. "What is a shower?" She'd never heard of such a thing, but guessed it had something to do with getting cleaner, judging by how pink and shiny her cousins were in their fresh clothing.

Mairi laughed, "Come on! I'll show you! You'll love it."

Grabbing Anne by the hand, tugging her along, Jamie called out behind the girls, "It's like a waterfall, only warm!" Anne liked the sound of that.

CAT SPIRIT
Harris, Northern California
September 22nd, present
Evening

Anne had scrubbed her body like she'd never been scrubbed before, by her own hand of course, once Mairi had set the water falling in a warm gush from the pipes and left her alone in the little room. *Is it called a bathroom? Sounds like the Romans with their Bath Houses.* Anne couldn't quite recall all the things she'd learned just for the simple act of bathing herself, from turning on the faucet to all the different soaps for washing various body parts. Each new bottle she opened smelled like a Summer day in an orchard or a meadow full of blooming flowers. It made Anne's head swim.

The pajamas Mairi had loaned her fit fine once she'd settled on just giving her an oversized t-shirt and leggings. Anne had felt very embarrassed wearing something so revealing of her body until Helena had found her one of

Gran's new bathrobes. The bathrobe felt like the bunny rabbit she'd once held at a festival. Extraordinarily soft.

Heading downstairs, Anne saw that Granda had returned while she was dressing upstairs in Mairi's mom's old room. Anne was too unsure of herself to ask Jamie if she could look into her Da's old room, but hoped it would soon be possible. *Why would ye leave all this luxury?* Anne wanted desperately to ask her da.

Focus first on healing Gran, then she can hopefully tell me how to rescue my da, Anne thought. Fighting back her tears, Anne sat on a stool and focused on her Gran lying asleep on the couch, her grandchildren kneeling on the floor beside her, Granda and Helena standing at the end by Gran's head. None of their noises had wakened her.

They all feared the worst.

Anne ran her hands over Gran's head and shoulders, down each arm, over her heart and stomach in a spiral pattern, and down each leg, coming to rest on her feet.

"She has no injury or illness I am aware of," Anne announced quietly. "I've seen this with herbal women, witches, who can transform into cats at their will. She misses being a cat, and does nae realize that is what ails her. I will need a bit of heather to burn and a feather to call forth her cat spirit, and blessed water to cleanse her of her wanton desires. Maybe with a little training she can call forth her cat form at will and she will be content while in her human form."

Granda just stared at his newly met granddaughter in shock. "She wishes to still be a cat?"

Anne looked up at her Granda, a stranger, and wondered how she would explain to him something she wasn't sure she understood herself. Luckily, Helena chimed in first.

"I suspect, William, that she enjoyed some strength and wisdom as a cat that is different than what she has as a human. Anne has pointed out that Caroline, Gran, is unaware of her own desires. I'm sure she wants to be a healthy human, too."

"I bet if she becomes healthy again, she will like being a human because right now she's stuck on the couch all of the time, so being human isn't much fun," Jamie spoke up.

"And the more she lies on the couch being unhealthy, the stronger her desire to be a cat becomes," Mairi added.

"Yes, I think that is it," Anne agreed. "Now please go get me what I asked for, so I can see about healing her."

At this reminder, everyone jumped up to search for what she needed. Jamie took a feather from the mantle over the river rock fireplace, and Mairi went to the shelves of herbs and found dried heather and a dish for burning it. Coming back to Gran, Mairi saw Granda holding a blue bowl filled with water and Helena stood over it chanting. When it was finished, Mairi asked her, "What were you doing?"

"Blessing the water, of course. I am a Priestess of Avalon, a shaman of sorts."

"Oh, I wondered where we were going to get blessed water," Mairi mumbled.

"Quiet! I am starting," Anne hushed them.

Mairi cringed at being reprimanded, but stared fascinated at her capable cousin. Anne began chanting and wafting the incense smoke. It felt like hours to Mairi, but was merely minutes. The process finally ended with the sprinkling of the blessed water and Anne wilted to the floor. "She was willing to separate from her cat spirit. She did not want to shoo it away completely, the idea of learning to transform at will fascinates her. We need to find a witch to train her, though."

"I didn't hear you talking. How did she say that to you?" Mairi's frown deepened and the knots in her shoulders tightened at not understanding any of the ceremonial healing. She felt like stomping her foot and demanding explanations, but refrained just so she wouldn't disturb her gran.

"Not now, Mairi. Anne needs to sleep. Help her to bed and you can ask more questions in the morning." Helena shooed them all away as she gently covered Gran with a warm wool blanket. "Good night, children. Good night, William. I'll come by in the morning, but I suspect you won't have need for me after that. She is one powerful young lady," Helena made this statement about Anne with obvious admiration in her voice.

Mairi's heart pinched. She hated to admit it, even to herself, but she was jealous of all the praise Anne was receiving.

CONNECTIONS
Harris, Northern California
September 23rd, present

Mairi awoke to the sun fighting its way through a cloud and into the window, its pale glow highlighting a photo on the wall of a young woman in braids and overalls digging in the garden and watching a tiny girl dancing in amongst the flowers and herbs. Mairi saw that Anne lay awake staring at the picture.

"That's our Gran and my mom, Shaylee when she was a little girl," Mairi told Anne.

Anne looked wistfully over at Mairi. "I have never known our Gran before last night, if that even counts."

Mairi nodded. "I know. I've barely known her two months longer than that. Our family got pretty messed up over this magic necklace." Mairi held onto the Trinity Knot around her neck.

"My da told me about that necklace. But what is that other necklace ye are wearing?"

"Oh, this one is from my other grandma, my Granny Kate. She gave it to me as a souvenir from her trip to Scotland last summer. She said it's a Protection Knot and asked me to wear it. Seemed a little weird at the time, but Granny Kate has always been just a bit quirky."

Anne looked at Mairi with a puzzled look on her face. "That is nae just any Protection Knot. It is a Witch's Knot, and when one is carved in the face of a stone like that, it must be quite powerful. May I touch it?"

As soon as Mairi nodded her consent, Anne scooted over to her and held the stone between her dainty fingers. "Oh, do ye nae feel that vibration?"

"I do, actually. It's a lot like the Trinity Knot, so I figure it must have some magical powers. Do you think my Granny Kate felt it, too?" Mairi asked.

"Och! Well, I dinnae know. But, my Grandmother Anne, my namesake, she was a witch of sorts and a stone like this was usually only given away by powerful witches to people they cared vera much about."

Anne let go of the necklace and Mairi picked up both necklaces, one in each hand. If she paid close attention, she could feel that the vibrations were slightly different, and the humming sounded like distinct notes, but in harmony.

Could my Granny Kate be a witch? Mairi wondered.

They lay there in silence for a while longer until Anne said, "What is that delicious aroma?" and Mairi realized she could smell something good coming from downstairs.

"That's odd," Mairi said, getting out of bed and pulling on her robe against the chill. As she headed out the door, she could hear Anne also getting out of bed and pulling on her robe.

"What is odd?"

"Granda never makes anything for breakfast except oatmeal, if he's even around to cook. Otherwise, Jamie and I just have cereal. Someone is making pancakes!"

The two girls walked on soft feet across the carpeted

hall and down the stairs, reaching the wood floor below with an icy reminder that they'd forgotten slippers or socks. That wasn't what stopped Mairi short on the bottom step, though. It was the sight of a very healthy Gran fairly dancing around the kitchen, her long white braid swinging in rhythm as she prepared pancakes, putting a huge stack on the dining table along with a bowl of wild berries and warm syrup. There were place settings for five and Granda sat in one place staring at his wife in awe.

Seeing the girls, Gran beckoned them over to the table. "Please, eat! I don't know about you, but I'm starving," Gran said, sitting down with them.

Jamie heard the commotion and came out of his room, hair ruffled and pajamas askew, joining them and stacking his plate full of several pancakes and a heaping pile of freshly whipped cream covering berries and syrup. "Yum!" was all he said before digging in.

"Gran, it is so good to see ye moving around," Anne stated simply, while Mairi reached over and gave her a huge   hug.

"I've missed you!" was all she could get out, unable to explain her relief. Despite Gran having been a cat the entire time Mairi had spent with her over the summer, Gran's personality had shone through and Mairi could see it was shining bright once again. Then the girls sat down with their own plates, Mairi feeling a little silly for her sudden display of affection.

For several more minutes, all that could be heard was the happy munching of breakfast and the clink of silverware on the plates. Once everyone seemed to get their fill and slow down, Gran turned to Anne and started asking her questions about her da and her siblings and life in general, which inevitably resulted in Anne crying and explaining everything that had happened to her family over the past couple of days.

"I dinnae know what I can do to help my family. I

dinnae know where my da is, nor what has happened to him. What is the seven-year tithe? And my wee sister was returned from the faeries, but she is wearing a silver chain round her ankle like a prisoner. I suspect she is nae so free after all. "

"Oh, my dear," Gran pulled Anne into a hug, stroking her shiny black hair, which hung loosely all the way to her waist. "You've healed me and now you seek my advice? Is that it?" Anne nodded in her gran's arms. "Well, it does seem as if your wee sister is safe for the moment, but your da quite probably is with the faeries. One story does come to mind of a young man who was stolen by faeries as a child and was eventually rescued by a maiden. Perhaps we'll find some inspiration for how to rescue your da. Let's put away breakfast while I remember how the story goes."

After clearing the table and washing the dishes, Gran and her grandchildren settled on the velvet couch in the sitting room with Gran in between the girls and Jamie next to Mairi, still half asleep with his head on the arm of the couch. Granda sat in his chair, a smile on his face.

Gran cleared her throat and began her tale.

TAMLIN
A Fairy Tale
Once Upon A Time

There was once a golden-haired maiden called Janet, who lived near the Wild Woods of Scotland. Her father was a laird and had given her Carterhaugh Hall as a gift, despite rumors it was haunted by a faerie knight named Tamlin. Taking leave of her maiden duties of sitting around weaving and embroidering, her least favorite part of being a Laird's daughter, she wandered to her newly acquired Hall to daydream about being mistress of such a grand place. Though it was old and somewhat desperate for repair, the gardens outside bloomed profusely each year with roses aplenty. As she absent-mindedly smelled the roses, she picked a particularly fragrant bloom to take home to her room in her father's castle.

No sooner had she snapped the thin stem, carefully avoiding being pricked by the sharp thorns, did a man appear. He was as handsome a man as Janet had ever seen, with his blonde curls and blue eyes, and she knew him to be Tamlin.

"How dare you pick my roses!" he called out. "Take your leave now, for it is my duty to guard Carterhaugh Hall, roses and all, for the Faerie Queen."

"Ah, but she does not own Carterhaugh Hall. I do for my father gave it to me and I will do as I please with the roses," Janet said most haughtily, and she tucked the rose into her hair plaited neatly down her back.

Smiling broadly at young Janet's emboldened statements, Tamlin took both her hands in his, causing her to blush. "I see you are not to be run off so easily, so stay awhile with me. I do get lonely out here." So saying, she became bewitched by his charm and they spread Janet's green mantel upon the wild grasses, spending the rest of the day entwined in each other's arms.

The sun began to set, and the shadows darkened in the woods all around. "I must take my leave now, for my father will come looking for me if I do not." So said, Tamlin seemed to fade like mist into the trees and Janet retreated to her father's home.

Time passed, and it soon became clear to all that young Janet was with child. Fearing any of her father's innocent knights should be blamed for her deed, she admitted to her father that the sire of her child was a faerie knight. Unable to face his anger, she ran back to Carterhaugh Hall and looked around in vain for Tamlin.

Alas, she could not find him and fell down upon the grass and cried. Tamlin heard her sorrow and came to her side. Leaning into his arms, she told him all, ending with asking why he was bound to the Wild Woods around Carterhaugh Hall.

"I was taken by the faeries as a young child and I am bound to live in their realm; the entrance is a grassy hill nearby. It is my duty to guard these woods when I am told to. I do love living with the faeries, so beautiful is their world, but I fear that I am to be the Queen's next payment, a tithe to Hell, as seven years has yet again come to pass."

Janet cried out. "How can I save you, my love? What can I do to bring you home to the human world in which our child will live?"

"It will soon be All Hallow's Eve and the Faerie Hunt will come riding through these very woods. Should you wait near the well at the crossroads through darkest hours, you will see black horses ridden by Royal Faeries most dark, then brown horses ridden by the Faerie knights and company. Finally, upon a lone white horse will sit the sacrificial human, myself this time round.

"Should you be so brave, pull me off the horse, though it will seem I do not know you. Hold on fast, for I will be turned into all manner of creatures most hideous, that will snap and claw and attempt to kill you. If you do not let go, I will finally be returned to my own form, naked as a newborn. Quickly throw your mantel upon me and hide me from the Queen of the Faeries for she will be most angry with you, though she will not dispute that you have won, for it is decreed by faerie law."

So it was that Janet returned home to wait the fortnight until Samhain would descend upon the land. Gathering up her green woolen mantle around her shivering shoulders, she ran through the woods until she came to the well beside the crossroads. Hiding herself in amongst the thickets in the woods, she waited for the Faerie Hunt to pass by. Long she waited, or so it felt, and longer still when it began to drizzle then rain, accompanied by lightning and thunder. Shivering, Janet was warmed by the thought of freeing her love and sire to her child.

A flash of lightening lit up the point at which the roads crossed, and there she saw the first of the riders. Shrouded in dark green hoods, dry as if not a drop of rain had touched them, atop horses black as ink only discernible in the bright lightning flashes. Shrinking back, Janet let them *pass, watching closely though her eyes fought to stay open against the torrential downpour. The next flash of golden light showed the brown horses ridden by faerie knights, and as they passed, Janet saw the lone white horse bringing up the end of the parade.*

Janet made ready her body to pounce, and as the white horse passed, she grabbed hold of the rider's ankle, pulling him down by her side. She glimpsed for just an instant her love's face before he was turned into an enraged boar with tusks like spears. She tightened her grip before he was turned into a wild cat with claws that scratched and teeth that tore at her skin, but still she held on tight. Many times, he was turned into the most ferocious of beasts, and though her arms tired, she dared not let go.

At last, Tamlin was returned to his naked human form, and though startled, Janet kept her wits, throwing her mantel over his body, thus hiding him from the Queen's sight.

"I see you have been told by someone our faerie laws," the Queen spat disdainfully at Janet. "Had I realized Tamlin had fallen in love with one of his many human consorts, I would have turned his heart to stone."

Janet did not wait to hear more. She grabbed Tamlin and led him away along the road in a different direction than the Wild Hunt, back to her home in her father's castle.

WARNING

Harris, Northern California
September 23ʳᵈ, present

Mairi sat in the faerie shrine that they'd built next to the house a month ago, the one that had proven to be completely wrong for helping transform Gran from cat to human. She was contemplating all that she'd learned about dark faeries in the last 24 hours. *They are most definitely real. Not all of them are the beautiful butterfly-like creatures I met at first, the ones like Queen Titania, who are full of light and love. Some of them are dark, evil creatures with terrible intentions, I'm sure of it.* An image of Cali came to her, the faerie handmaiden to the Queen, who had led them in and out of the Faerie Realm last summer. It was her cold smile and chilling words about meeting again that stayed with Mairi. *Is she the one behind all these sudden attacks on Anne's family? My family?*

Mairi concentrated on her purpose of finding solitude in this shrine she had helped create. She worked on focusing her attention on meditating as Helena had once suggested to her. This went along with analyzing her dreams.

Trying to remember her dreams from the night before had reminded her to work on her meditating. It had been a convoluted dream about Mairi standing backstage and made to watch Anne onstage being applauded by a faceless audience. She had woken feeling jealous of her cousin, and feeling inadequate. In the morning light Mairi had almost laughed at such a ludicrous dream because she had nothing to do with theater, and Anne had probably never even seen one. It didn't take a genius to understand what the dream meant.

Now Anne was inside the house bonding with their Gran while Jamie joyfully joined in, excited to tell their cousin all about modern life. Mairi had felt herself getting upset that Gran was finally a healthy human for the first time since Mairi knew her, and Anne was getting all the attention. Mairi had slipped away the first chance she'd seen, and quickly made her way back to something she felt in a way belonged to her: the Faerie Shrine she'd helped create.

Mairi sat cross-legged on a mossy tree root growing half in and half out of the rich dark soil. She pulled her sweatshirt closed, fumbling with the laces at the hood trying to block the icy cold North wind that suddenly raced through the grove. Remembering an article about meditation that she'd read online a few weeks earlier, she closed her eyes and took in a deep breath, smelling the sweet scent of decomposing leaves, then she let it out long and slow. She repeated this two more times before the wind blew again, tugging on her hair, pulling her from what she had hoped would be the beginnings of a proper meditator's trance.

She blinked a few times and noticed lights dancing along the low hanging branches overhead. Looking intently at one of the lights, she could barely make out a miniature humanoid figure clothed in spider silk and bearing wings as delicate as a dragonfly's. *It's like when I first used my magic and was trying to run to the Faerie Grove on Skye. I could see the faerie folk who live in the plants.* She sat rigid and still, barely breathing in hopes of hearing the faerie folk, too. She just heard a whispered voice from that miniscule faerie, saying something in a language she couldn't understand.

I bet Anne knows that language.

The thought escaped before she could stop it, bringing her consciousness back to her body. Her insides were a knot of awful feelings of jealousy, doubt, and frustration. All were brewing in her stomach and Mairi felt like throwing up. The faerie disappeared from her sight.

Why is Anne so good at using her magic when I'm not? Mairi formed the thoughts, but knew she was wrong as soon as she thought them. Shaking her head, Mairi answered her own question. *She has always known about her magic. My uncle didn't hide it from her like my mom hid it from me. My dad never would have hid anything like this from me. I just know it.* The anger towards her mom she thought she'd worked through over the summer resurfaced, and an overwhelming feeling of missing her dad washed over her.

Missing our dads is something we both feel, that's for sure.

The tale of *Tamlin* came to mind. *This story isn't exactly about a changeling, but still it proves that faeries steal humans. This could be what happened to Uncle Jamie, but it could also be similar to what happened to my dad. If he was taken, and switched with a changeling, he could be in the Faerie Realm and need my help!*

"Oh Dad! I just need to find you and talk to you!" she moaned aloud to the trees as she leaned against an oak and stared up at the bits of gray sky peeking through the leafy branches.

"We do not always know what we think we know."

Startled by the distinctly feline voice, Mairi looked around half expecting a fluffy white cat to be sitting beside her before she remembered her Gran was human again. She could not find the source of the voice.

"We do not always need what we think we need."

Looking around again, she stared into a pair of vibrant lavender-blue eyes peeking through the shadows at the base of a nearby tree, seemingly without attachment to a body. "Who are you?"

"Who I am is not the point...is it?" The eyes blinked, rising in the air as Mairi realized they were attached to a very black cat, the outline of its body could barely be seen in the shadows. The cat stretched, first arching its back into the air then reaching its front paws out in front of it and bringing its belly to the leaf-strewn carpet of the little grove. "The point is figuring out you. Not so much who you are, but what you are."

Mairi frowned, "I'm a human girl, with a touch of faerie." She realized the voice was distinctly male.

"Yes," the black cat began delicately licking his paws and washing his face. "It seems you might be a witch of sorts, as well."

"Druid, so I've been told, not a witch," Mairi corrected the cat. "Though, I'm not sure of the difference. Either way, I don't know how to control my powers, or what I should be using them for. A . . . " Mairi stopped. *Should I be telling anything to a complete stranger, in particular a possibly dark fae stranger?*

The cat looked at her approvingly, "You are right not to tell me what you think you know. Just rest assured that you *will* figure out what your magic is for as you learn more about your heritage. In the meantime, be wary of rushing off on your own. Trust your family to help you."

With that cryptic message, the cat turned and walked

on silent feet back into the shadows, disappearing without a trace.

"Wait!" Mairi didn't want the cat to leave. She was certain he held a key to the answers she so very much needed.

FRUSTRATIONS
Isle of Skye, Scotland
September 23rd, 1700s

Ewan paced the turret in the MacDonald chief's stone building, the clan holding of Duntulm Castle overlooking the sea. He'd worn his leather sandals precariously thin in his worrying about how to regain control of the situation.

"How dare that faerie wench use me, then shut me out of my own revenge! I dinnae care for her tone towards me," he muttered under his breath.

A whiff of sea air passed under his nose and he stopped his pacing to look over the turret wall, out across the ocean. The day was on the warmer side for the beginning of fall, and the clan fishermen were on the prowl. Ewan took a deep breath of sea air, hoping to clear his head.

"Ahem!" Someone stood behind Ewan, startling him. "Dinnae jump! Who would I go to for advice if ye did?"

Turning, Ewan saw his clan chief: a tall proud man, skin

turned leather over the many seasons of his life. Ewan smiled slightly, though it might have been more of a grimace.

"Just puzzling over a particularly annoying problem, ye ken?" Ewan shrugged.

"Ah, weel, have a bite and walk with me a bit." The chief handed over a strip of venison. The two walked and chewed in silence for a moment before the chief broke in, "Have ye nae heard that the Witch Hunts on the mainland are growing more numerous? It seems that there are more witches in the world than just the one that betrayed the MacDonalds of Glencoe. I am jest grateful we dinnae have any of those women on Skye."

Ewan froze, his mind awhirl. "The Witch Hunts . . . ? On Skye . . . ? Perhaps."

"What is it? Ye appear to have seen a ghost. Are ye disturbed by talk of witches?"

"Nay! On the contrary, I am inspired by it. Ye may have solved my problem. Or at least, I hope so." Ewan slapped his chief on the back. "Thank you! I think I'll go to the kirk now and see what the pastor might have tae say about any possible witches on Skye."

Ewan descended the stairs two at a time, leaving the bewildered chief to wonder what his Archdruid was up to now.

STUCK

Harris, Northern California
September 23rd, present

After dinner, Anne buried her head under the pillows on the bed she shared with Mairi. The bed was unbelievably comfortable, as cushiony as lying on a hundred chicken's feathers. Still, she couldn't get comfortable. Her head was pounding.

"What's wrong?" Mairi asked her as she came into the bedroom. Anne vaguely wondered where she had been.

"I cannae think with all of the sounds! They are nae natural sounds," Anne said, "and my head hurts so."

Mairi nodded with understanding. "Now that you mention it, I do hear the nonstop droning of the fridge keeping food cold and a whining sound from the inverter for the solar panels and batteries is really annoying. I guess I'm kind of used to sounds like that. It's a good thing we aren't at my house in San Diego, or you would really be overwhelmed since we have computers and WiFi and cars driving past."

Anne had no idea what Mairi was talking about, so she groaned and pulled the pillows tighter.

"Can't you use your powers to heal your headache?"

"Och! I cannae think," Anne moaned.

"Hey, let's get out of here," Mairi said, putting a hand on Anne's shoulder. "We can sit somewhere quieter."

Anne followed Mairi downstairs, holding the railing tight so she wouldn't stumble, and then out the front door. They walked through the garden and up the mountainside, following the deer trail. As they moved farther from the house, Anne's head began to calm down. What remained of the pain, Anne could soothe with her magic, now that she could think straight. The girls reached the ridge and lay down in the tall, sunbaked grass, a view of their grandparent's house below them, like a tiny castle complete with rock walls and a single tower sticking up on the far side. It stood at the end of a flat between two streams, looking out over the edge of the valley.

Anne sighed with relief. The only sounds in the meadow were the crickets strumming in the grass and the birds calling from the treetops. The occasional zoom from something odd flying high overhead was as annoying as a fly, but was far enough away not to hurt her head. Anne wondered what it was, but turned to more pressing concerns.

"What am I going tae do?" she asked Mairi. "I need tae get back to my own time, and my family, and before that I need tae get into the Faerie Realm, so I can find my da. But I am stuck here." She rolled over and buried her head in her arms, no longer in pain from strange noises, but filled with the pain of longing for her family torn asunder.

"You need to come to my home in San Diego," Mairi informed Anne, contradicting her earlier statement. "I know it will be noisy, and you'll just have to work some magic to protect yourself while you adjust, but we can't go to the

Faerie Realm without a plan, and so far our best plan is to try to accost Uncle James when the Wild Hunt comes out on Halloween . . . Samhain as you call it."

"Oooh! That is nearly five weeks away! We have tae do something before then," Anne protested.

"I know . . . I agree... we'll keep searching for a better plan. Until then, we should go to San Diego and see if my cousin Danny has any ideas. He's a freshman at UCLA, studying folklore, and he might be able to help us. Maybe he'll come to my house and we can talk in person. Just don't mention it to my mom, because she'll flip out and never let me help you rescue Uncle James in the Faerie Realm. She's way too protective."

In the encroaching darkness, Anne saw that Mairi fiddled with her Protection charm, which seemed to glow faintly orange under Mairi's fingertips. *There is something most powerful about that Witch's Knot,* Anne observed. Shivering in the cool night air, they walked slowly back down to the house, somewhat reassured to finally have a plan.

CONFESSIONS
San Diego, California
September 24th, present

Mairi got up at 10 o'clock the next day, stalling her return to the reality of school and chores. They'd missed two days of school, including today, and Mairi didn't relish the nagging she'd get from her teachers. Jamie's grades were so good he probably wouldn't be affected, but her grades would just land more solidly in the failing category. On top of that, they would have to admit the whole story, or at least the part about going back in time, to explain why Anne was with them. Unable to use her cell phone from her Granda's, which was a virtual desert of no technology, Mairi was grateful for Helena's offer to call on their behalf from her home. She had reported back to them that she told their mom their gran had simply wanted more time with them.

"Hopefully Mom will be so happy at meeting her niece that she won't be too harsh with her punishment," Mairi said to Jamie as the three of them trudged up to the Oak Knoll. They crested the hill and Mairi put one hand on Jamie, who blew up the bag on his bagpipes, and Anne held onto Mairi's other hand. Mairi wore the Trinity Knot pendant around her neck, with the Protection Knot hanging a bit longer on its cord. Mairi pictured her boho style living room in her house and as Jamie played the first few notes of the traveling tune, Mairi said "I wish we were home," and she felt the familiar tug on her body as darkness enveloped them.

"Oof!" The air rushed out from her lungs. *Not the gentlest landing, but hopefully no broken bones.* They all three had landed on the couch that was covered with a brightly colored Mexican print blanket. Shaylee sat in a chair nearby, coffee spilled all over her white poet's blouse, eyes wide open.

"Hey Mom," Jamie said, grinning.

"Hi!" Shaylee set her coffee down and quickly covered the distance to give Mairi and Jamie a big hug. When she stepped back, she stared at Anne, then looked questioningly at her kids.

"This is our cousin Anne. Uncle James is her da," Mairi hoped leading with that would soften the blow once her mom realized this probably meant time travel had been involved. "Anne, meet your Aunt Shaylee."

"Oh wow! You don't have his coloring, but you do have an air about you that reminds me of my little brother. I can't wait to hear about your family!" Shaylee hugged Anne, looking happier than she had in a long time. Mairi noticed her cheeks had a pinch of pink in them. She led the three of them into the kitchen where she put water on for tea. Mairi took a deep breath, enjoying the aroma of drying herbs hanging from the ceiling.

"Let me get this straight," Shaylee set down the new cup of coffee she'd poured, straightened the turquoise, embroidered, Mexican blouse she'd replaced the soiled white one with, and looked ready to explode. Mairi did not like where this was headed. "You went back in time, despite promising me you wouldn't. You ran into a changeling because Anne's little sister was kidnapped by faeries, but returned, though wearing a faerie chain. My brother is missing, possibly kidnapped by faeries, too. And you are all trying to figure out how you can get into the Faerie Realm to rescue him?"

Mairi, Anne, and Jamie looked at each other. *We said way too much.* Mairi had tried to shut her brother up, but he didn't have a deceitful bone in his body. "Mom, you're leaving out the important part about Gran being sick, nearly dead, and we had to go get Anne to save her life, which she did. You're getting all worked up for nothing." *At least we didn't tell her about Jamie's ankle.*

Shaylee sighed and took a drink from her coffee. The silence could be a good thing, or it could mean grounding, Mairi was never sure with her mom's emotional ups and downs since her dad had died. "Okay, that was important. I am glad Gran is feeling better. I still would have liked to have been consulted. I'd like to have a say about whether my children get to play hero. Your Granda did not ask my permission."

Uh oh, Mairi realized her mom's connection to Gran and Granda was tenuous. She had kept them out of Mairi and Jamie's entire childhood until recently. *We need to remember not to throw Granda under the bus anymore,* Mairi made a mental note.

Then Shaylee looked at Anne and changed her tune. "You poor thing. You must be heart-broken. I have also lost your da once, when we got separated through time travel. In fact, I haven't seen him since then. Now he might be taken by the faeries . . . I can only imagine how hard this has been on you. And your little sister's ordeal, too..." Shaylee shook her head in sympathy.

Oh good! Mom might actually let us help Anne if she

feels sorry for her. Mairi was feeling hopeful for the first time since the story started spilling out.

"Why don't you get Anne settled in your room. We have the camping mats in the shed still. Pull one out and I'll get blankets for her from the closet." As Shaylee spoke to Mairi, her eyes narrowed. Reaching across the corner of the table, she scooped up the Witch's Knot pendant that had swung free of Mairi's shirt. "What is this?"

"Um . . . Granny Kate gave it to me. She gave one to Jamie, too. She told us it's a souvenir from Scotland." Mairi sat up, pulling the pendant out of her mom's loose hold, and tucked it back into the neckline of her t-shirt. "Why?"

"It seems... familiar . . . " Shaylee got up and walked into her bedroom. Mairi, Jamie, and Anne stared after her.

"That was weird," Jamie said. Mairi nodded her head, listening to the rummaging sounds coming from her mom's room.

Shaylee returned, clutching something in her hand. "Look, this belonged to your dad. He wore it all of the time when we first met. He said his mom, your Granny Kate, had given it to him when he was a little boy and he'd always worn it. He'd never been sick a day in his life, he told me. He thought it protected him from illness. He stopped wearing it when you were born, Mairi. He said it was just silly superstition, and it was more likely you'd break the old string and choke on it. Granny Kate was really upset about it. She was sure he would regret his decision. Your dad just laughed, telling me his mom was a little nutty, always whispering odd words around the house, talking to her cat, bringing strange friends over to talk Spiritual Science." Shaylee sat down, suddenly quiet, lost in thought.

"What do you think it means?" Jamie asked.

Anne looked at all three of them, one by one, exasperated. "It means yer Granny Kate is a witch! At least, it would in my own time."

Shaylee looked at her sharply, "Do you think so? My husband never said anything about it."

"Maybe Dad didn't know," Jamie pointed out.

"Wouldn't that be ironic?" Mairi asked. "I mean, you kept your family's secret of being druids from me and Jamie and Dad. I bet Granny Kate kept her being a witch from my dad and probably Uncle Adair, too."

"I wonder if she is a vera good one," Anne said. "I mean, she could just be someone interested in witch craft, but nae actually be adept, or she could be a fully trained witch. They can be vera powerful, ye know. As strong as the most powerful druids. In fact, witches were once the Herbal Druids, but when women were forced out of the Druidry they were called witches instead to separate them from druids." She looked at Mairi, "Judging by the energy I feel from yer pendant, I bet she is vera good at witchcraft."

"That would be so cool!" Jamie grinned. "Wouldn't it be awesome if mom's side of our family are druids, and dad's side are witches? We'd be so amazing!" He looked at Mairi, then frowned. "Well, you already are . . . "

Mairi guessed what he was thinking. "Remember what Gran said last summer, you're still young. Your powers will come in soon enough. Besides, I don't feel powerful. I don't have the control Anne has."

"Ye will gain control, Mairi," Anne promised. "Ye have only known about yer powers a few months. I grew up knowing about my powers my whole life, and my gran on my maw's side was a practicing witch who apprenticed me." Anne smiled, "I know . . . I will teach ye."

Mairi nodded, a little jealous of her cousin's control over her powers, and also a little grateful for her offer.

"Well, your Granny Kate has invited us over for dinner in a couple of days. Maybe we'll just ask her," Shaylee pointed out.

As everyone stood up from the table and headed to their rooms, Shaylee called out, "And just so you know, I haven't forgotten that you broke a promise to me. Do not let it happen again."

BONFIRE

San Diego, California
September 25th, present
Dusck

Mairi wiggled her toes in the sand, pushing through the warm granules to the cold underneath. She wrapped her arms tight around her knees, listening to the steady crash of the ocean waves on the shore. Tears threatened to well up and spill over, but she squeezed her eyes closed tight. *Not tonight,* Mairi thought. *I won't cry for him tonight. He might still be alive. His taking the pendant off might have allowed him to become vulnerable and sometime after I was born, my dad was taken by faeries. Maybe before Jamie was born and that's why he isn't powerful in the same way I am.*

Mairi shivered at what she was really implying, that her dad hadn't been her dad at all and Jamie was possibly the son of some odd faerie creature. *Weirder things have happened in my family, though. So, if this is true, my dad is alive and well in the Faerie Realm and I need to rescue him.* She knew this was a bizarre thought, and exactly what Anne must be thinking about her own dad. Only Anne was right and Mairi was just wishing it were true.

She tried to control her focus by returning her attention to the waves, counting the intervals between sets. The longing to be immersed in the cold salt water, once again riding those waves, was rising in her. She sighed. *It just isn't the same without Dad.*

"Hey! I thought you came to hang out with me, not curl up in a ball and ignore us." It was her cousin Danny. He'd finally gotten back to her about her text regarding changelings and he'd suggested meeting on the beach to share stories. "Come over by the fire. We've finally got it going."

Mairi felt her body start to shiver. The days were still scorching hot inland at her house, but on the coast, it was cooler with fog-filled days and cold nights. An offshore wind had managed to blow all the fog away and they were sitting under the clear night sky. The stronger stars usually would be reaching through the light pollution of downtown San Diego to the south and Pacific Beach to the north, but the nearly full moon was outshining them tonight. Ocean Beach was lit up by the moonlight, and the beach was spattered with bonfires from one end to the other. The occasional bark of someone's dog at nearby Dog Beach could be heard. Aside from the longing in her chest, she felt at home in this place.

Mairi walked over to the bonfire and sat in her beach chair. They'd brought them from her house when Danny had picked her and Anne up in Granny Kate's car. He always stayed with her, riding the train down from LA now that he'd sold his piece of junk car.

"Thanks," Mairi said to Danny. "I was spacing out about surfing with my dad."

Everyone nodded.

"Anyway," Mairi said to break the awkward silence. "I don't want to be a bummer for us. You said you had run across a few changeling stories in your studies?"

Danny stood up and grabbed a soda from the cooler. "First, tell me what you guys have been up to. Bring me up to speed. How did your cousin Anne get here from the past?" He looked at her and smiled. "Don't get me wrong, it's nice to see you, but just a bit of a shock is all."

Mairi suspected Danny had a wee bit of a crush on her other cousin. *Weird! But, they aren't actually related, so maybe it's no big deal.* "Too bad Jamie couldn't be here." Their mom wouldn't let him go out with them because she said he was too young. Jamie was trying to get caught up on his homework, so he hadn't been too upset. Mairi guessed her mom had only let her out because Anne seemed so trustworthy. "He's the better story teller, but I'll do my best."

Anne and Mairi tried to tell Danny what they'd been through, including healing Gran.

"That's so great you could heal her!" Danny smiled at Anne, and Mairi sighed, her feelings of inadequacy rising in her chest. "Okay, your sister definitely seems to have been switched with a changeling. You have very strong evidence for that, and she's been returned, so that's good. Now, your da might have been taken by faeries, though your evidence isn't the strongest in his case. I doubt there was anywhere else he would have gone, though."

"We forgot to tell ye the changeling said my da was being taken for the tithe," Anne pointed out.

Danny nodded his head. "Right. That is good evidence, then."

"What about that story you promised me?" Mairi interrupted. "The one about a grown changeling. Maybe that will show evidence . . . about Uncle James," though she really meant evidence in regard to her own father and not her uncle.

"Oh yeah, I'll tell you now," Danny said, and focused on the glowing flames of the fire within their circle of chairs.

CHANGELING

A Folk Tale
Long, long ago

Once there was a pastor whose wife was as beautiful as she was healthy. They had a son between them who was as helpful as he was joyous. They lived together in a little village and cared for their neighbors like they were family and all who knew them loved them.

One sunny day in late winter, all the wives and young children went out into the meadows to gather flowers for the upcoming festival to celebrate the season changing from the cold, dark of winter to the warmth and light of spring. There would be dancing and singing around a pole covered in ribbons and everyone would wear flower crowns upon their heads.

The wife of the pastor was seen to wander off farther from the group and so disappeared from the view of her friends. No one worried for soon she came wandering back and no one thought anything of it. Except, she was *different. Her cheeks were not nearly as rosy as they once had been, and her eyes no longer turned up at the corners as if she were eternally smiling. A shadow had passed over her once vibrant blue eyes, so that they were more of a gray, and her golden blonde hair was limp as though it had not been washed for weeks.*

She made her way back to the village with just a small handful of crunched up flowers and lay down in her bed though the hour was far from evening time. Her darling young son asked his ma what ailed her, and she turned away from him as though she did not know him. He offered her warm tea made from herbs, but this did not interest her until he said he had found some honey and would she like that.

She sat up in a bed, a wicked sort of grin passing over her features, causing the boy to cower at the sight of his own mother. Still, he was a good and dutiful child, so he made the tea and sweetened it with honey so that his mother drank it with loud slurping noises, demanding he bring her more. This went on for the next hour, cup after cup of tea until the honey was left to just what stuck to the edges of the pot. When no more honey could be produced, the boy's mother lay down again upon her bed and refused to look at him or speak. The boy left her alone, waiting for his father to arrive to solve the problem.

Soon his father returned from his work at the church and upon hearing about the strange behaviors of his wife, he sat upon her bed and asked what ailed her. She shrugged her shoulders and grunted most unbecomingly, scooting to the very edge of her bed as far from her husband as she could. As he leaned over her to get a better view of his wife and decide what illness had taken over, she swatted at him causing him to drop the Bible he held in one hand. He raised his brow in surprise, and ignored the niggling thought of what it might mean that his once pious wife should attack the Bible.

Returning his attention to his son, the pastor sent him out to fetch some milk for their supper. Upon hearing the mention of milk, his wife suddenly turned toward him and demanded a glass. Hoping that it was only hunger from an illness, he gave her a glass of the sweet cream milk as soon as his son had it ready. She again gulped down her drink without any show of manners and demanded more.

This went on for some days, and father and son did their best to feed her insatiable appetite. Soon they were out of all stores of honey and their milk supply could not keep up. As there was barely enough for all three, their portions became more and more meager. It wasn't long before his wife showed signs of further wasting away. Just one short month later, at the height of summer, father and son buried the empty husk of the once good and beautiful woman.

Many years passed, and the son grew into a kind and handsome young man. When he was one day visiting friends in a village several miles away, he made the acquaintance of an elderly gentleman and his young wife. Upon seeing the wife come into the cottage with her husband, the young man jumped at her similarity to the memory of his mother. Being caught staring at her, he sputtered out that she was the exact likeness of his own dearly deceased mother. He was pressed further, as the woman wondered if his deceased mother had had any sisters for she had been found wandering in the meadows two years back near his village, without memory of her own name or where she had come from. The young man told them truthfully that his mother hadn't had any siblings, then told of the mysterious change that had come over his mother when picking flowers in that very same meadow.

One of the guests at the gathering was an herbal woman who said she might know how to coax a memory from the woman, suspecting the cause of her memory loss and of the young man's mother's mysterious ailment.

Fetching dried sage and dried rosemary, she burned them in a little seashell and blew the smoke into the woman's face.

Coughing a bit, a spark shown in the woman's eyes and her hand flew to her mouth to stifle a gasp, for she suddenly remembered all in a flash of the day she had been picking flowers and had wandered too close to the fairy mound, beguiled by enchanting music that made her wish to dance. The story tumbled out of her as she remembered dancing down a long tunnel in the very ground leading to a magical chamber alight with stars and a babbling brook, and fairy people in all manner of flowerlike dresses and tunics. Then, as though only minutes had passed, yet it must have been years because her clothing had become rags, the music had stopped, and she'd found herself in the meadow without memory of the fairies nor her own past.

"Then who was it that came into my home when I was a child and demanded honey and sweet cream milk until the day she died?" The young man asked, without truly needing an answer, for he had often wondered if the woman he'd called "Ma' in her final days had actually been a changeling. He had proof now, and needed no more. As his own dear da had died of old age and hard life the previous winter, the young man moved villages to live near his dearly returned ma and her new husband who treated her kindly. Accepting that while this was indeed a strange twist in his time with his mother, it was better than no time at all, and it fit all the stories he'd ever heard of the fae folk.

WITCHES
San Diego, California
September 25th, present

"Do you think this is similar to my da?" Anne asked. "My da did become seriously ill all of a sudden, the type of illness that I could nae heal, which is really odd." She shook her head, not waiting for the others to answer. "But he also stayed loving and kind. He was himself. I dinnae think he was a changeling, but certainly was enchanted with an illness. His fate is more like that of Tamlin. We must still wait for the Wild Hunt to come out at Samhain."

Mairi nodded her head in agreement. "Yeah, Uncle James' fate sounds more like Tamlin's. But at least Danny's story shows us that sometimes adults are switched with changelings, too. I really need to get into the Faerie Realm!"

Danny looked at her closely. "Why do you need to get into the Faerie Realm? Who do you think might be a changeling? It can't be Anne's da because he is clearly being held for the tithe at Samhain."

Mairi looked at Danny, weighing her options, holding her breath. Finally, she came to a decision and sighed, letting out her breath. "I've wondered for a while now if my dad was a changeling. You know, before he died he was so healthy then became sick out of nowhere and suddenly died." Seeing Danny might be about to object, she hurried on. "Listen, he was perfectly healthy, just like that woman in your story, and then . . . he just wasn't . . . and . . . he died." She looked helplessly into Danny's eyes, willing him to agree with her.

Anne walked over to Mairi and placed her hands on her shoulders. "I never realized about your dad. It must have hurt so much to lose him, Mairi."

Mairi glared into Danny's pitying gaze and shrugged off Anne's hands. *I don't want their pity! I want them to agree with me!*

"Don't! Just . . . don't." *I'm not going to cry. Not when I have so much hope. If he was a changeling, I can find him.* "I know there's something in there," and she looked off into the vast darkness of the ocean, seeing the Faerie Realm as it was when they'd visited just last month. "I know there are answers in the Faerie Realm."

"What if we do get in there?" Anne asked. "What then? What will ye have us do? Go looking for your da I assume, but where do they keep the humans they changed out with their faeries?" Looking to Danny, she asked him, "Do ye know?"

Danny shook his head, then shrugged. "I don't know. I haven't found any tales that say, though I'm certain there are more places I can look. I did see a painting once that showed human children captured by faeries wearing delicate chains around their ankles. Like what you said your sister was wearing when she returned after the changeling ran off."

Mairi sat down in her beach chair again. *Are they just humoring me? Or do they agree and want to help?* Suddenly remembering a piece of evidence she'd forgotten to share with Danny, she told him about the Witch's Knot pendant her mother had said her dad used to always wear before she and Jamie were born.

"It's exactly like this one," she showed him the pendant around her neck. "It was from Granny Kate, too. She made him always wear it, but he took it off after I was born. Do you think Granny Kate is possibly a witch?"

Danny sat up straight in his chair, staring at Mairi and frowning. He was silent for a long time, the rhythmic crash of waves keeping the time for them.

"Well?" Mairi finally broke the silence.

"Yeah . . . I just . . . " Danny let out a long breath. "I was just realizing that so many of my memories from when my mom and I were living with Granny Kate point directly at her being a witch. The stories she'd tell me, the herbal concoctions we'd make from the garden, the poems I'd memorize. I thought she was just humoring my love of history and *Harry Potter*, of course. But now I think she was leaving her legacy with me. If what you say is true, that your dad knew nothing about witchcraft, so that would negate you and Jamie as possibilities. I know my dad laughed at her 'battiness' as he called it, but he left us when I was little, so he couldn't stop her teaching me stuff. Maybe she felt a need to leave her knowledge with me since I lived in her home."

Mairi nodded. "That makes sense. But maybe you didn't show any potential as a witch." Sensing she might have hurt his feelings, she hurried on, "I mean, you seem more like a druid whose purpose is more to memorize stories than to do magic. But then, what is the difference between witches and druids, and where do faeries fit in?"

When no one answered right away, Mairi's attention drifted back to the ocean waves, her mind a whirlwind of questions. Out of nowhere, she thought she felt a furry body rub up against her bare leg, and she nearly jumped out of her chair. Assuming it was a dog escaped from Dog Beach, she peered down at it in the glow of the firelight. Lavender-blue eyes blinked up at her, while the body they were attached to seemed to shimmer as though it weren't completely solid. *A trick of the firelight, maybe...*

Then it spoke.

"Hello," It was the black cat who had visited her at her Gran's. "I can tell you all about witches and druids, also faeries and changelings, too. You're right in your need to return to the Faerie Realm. It's the only way to find all the answers you seek, and time is running out. The moon will be completely full in two nights, and that's when I will take you through to the Faerie Realm. Meet me here and I may just help you find what, or who, you seek." And he disappeared.

GRANNY KATE
San Diego, California
September 26th, present

The next evening Mairi, Jamie, Anne and Shaylee arrived at Granny Kate's little two-story house in the older part of San Diego, near Old Town. Danny had headed back to LA for his classes, so he couldn't be there. Before leaving he'd promised to keep researching fairy tales about changelings, and Mairi promised to find out as much as she could about their Granny Kate.

Mairi knocked on the solid oak door and a woman she didn't know answered. Mairi jumped in surprise. She had been expecting the dinner party to only be the five of them, including Granny Kate. *Who is this lady?*

"Uh, Hi. I don't know you." Mairi knew she was coming across as rude, but she was unprepared for anyone, but Granny Kate.

"I'm Kate's friend. My son and I are renting a couple of

rooms from her and she invited me to join you for dinner. I hope you don't mind. I get terribly lonely with just my son, and Kate is so good at cheering me up. My name is Sonja. Please come in." Her upbeat manner was in opposition to her declarations of being in need of cheering up

The frail woman backed out of their way. She was easy to slip past in the narrow hallway as she was barely skin and bones, dressed in a black dress two sizes too big for her; she had stringy black hair half pulled up and caught in a silver clip shaped like a salmon. She melted into the shadows on the stairwell just inside the door and almost became invisible to the entering party. Shaylee, with her fuller figure clothed in a black floral sundress, which Anne had insisted she wear when asked for an opinion, was the last to sweep past Sonja. Sonja closed the door and the strong scent of thyme mixed with rosemary and sage swirled around the tight space.

The hallway was heavily carpeted with an oriental rug and opened onto a small living room with thick area rugs and plump furniture covered in doilies; French doors opened onto a small, but lush, backyard garden. *It feels like a grandmother's home is supposed to,* Mairi mused. *Most grandmothers' homes in picture books and on TV are decorated with doilies.*

Then her mind flashed to a picture book she'd been given by a school friend for her eighth birthday. It was a collection of popular fairy tales, and it included *Hansel and Gretel*, with the witch's cottage that was made of candy and gingerbread, so little children would be enticed to nibble on it and then the witch would capture them. *That witch's house looked just like this,* Mairi realized, *surely Granny Kate doesn't capture little children.* The idea was absurd and Mairi dismissed it, but she was starting to see her Granny's house in a different light.

As Mairi sat down on the light-pink, velvet couch, her freshly washed dark blue jeans felt just a little too tight; she noticed that hanging on the walls were black and white photographs of women from different eras. She'd never paid much attention before, but now she wondered if they were her relatives. They were dressed in different sorts of clothes, from a woman in a Victorian dress with black lace and a tightly-cinched corset to another woman in the loose drop waist Flapper style of the 1920s. All the women seemed to resemble each other, and Mairi decided they must be her great-grandmothers several generations back. A sense of pride at possibly being related to a long line of witches began to well up in her, though she looked nothing like any of them. None of them had her curly red hair.

Noticing the bookshelf, she wandered over to it as she politely accepted the cup of tea Sonja offered her. Taking a cautious sip, she realized it was peppermint, a good tea for keeping them awake and chatting, plus stimulating their appetite for dinner. Stepping in for a closer look at the tightly packed shelves, she saw that there were volumes on astrology, astronomy, herbal lore, gardening, fairy tales from several countries, travel and history books about Scotland, a Gaelic dictionary, books with crochet patterns, and even a few children's books Mairi vaguely remembered reading when she would spend the night with Granny as a little girl. None of them were all that different than what were on her mom's shelves at home, but that could mean a lot or a little, considering Mairi's mom was a druid of lesser powers focusing on Ayurvedic medicine.

"Do these books mean yer Granny is a witch?" Anne quietly asked Mairi. "I cannae barely read them. The English is a little different than what I learned at home."

"I'm not sure," Mairi whispered, then told Anne about how she could see it either way. Granny could be an eccentric old woman who liked gardening and studying the stars, or she was a witch who needed to know about herbs and stars for her spells.

"I think all of these books mean she's a witch," Jamie

said, standing directly behind them and speaking a little too loud. Both girls shushed him. Turning his volume down, Jamie continued in a whisper, "because I found this in her bedroom upstairs."

Mairi guessed that Jamie must have dashed upstairs while the rest of them had sat down in the living room. He was holding out a large ancient tome with a leather cover and uneven pages. On the front, carefully written in old script, was a single word: *Spells*.

"That has to be her grimoire," Anne pointed out. "I have my gran's which was once her gran's and so on. They are vera special. Every time a witch learns a new use for an herb or sees a pattern in the affect celestial bodies have on humans, she writes it in her grimoire. Ye best put that back, Jamie. That book is invaluable."

"Ahem."

All three whipped their heads around to see Granny Kate watching them from one of her plump chairs. "Yes, please put it back with great care." She was sitting with her usual poise, , clothed in a dark purple dress embroidered with green and gold Mexican floral designs; her hands clasped in her lap. "Once Sonja gathers her son to the dining room, we will all sit down and have a nice talk. Please take care to be polite when you meet Tobias. He will appear to not hear you, but I suspect he is a very good listener, and a great deal smarter than he lets on."

Arranged around the formal dining room just off the kitchen and living room, Mairi sat between her cousin Anne and the quadriplegic boy in a wheel chair she'd just met, Tobias. He looked a lot like his mother, though his black hair was shiny while hers was dull. *Obviously, she takes better care of her son than she does of herself,* Mairi caught herself thinking. Tobias was unable to move any part of himself except for his eyes that kept staring at Mairi in a most unpleasant way. Adding to the sour feeling was the sneaking suspicion she had seen eyes just like his somewhere else, but she couldn't recall where. They were such a distinct shade of blue, almost lavender, that Mairi was mentally beating her brain trying to remember.

After their meal of black beans and tortillas had been passed around, complete with homemade salsa fresh from the abundant backyard garden, Granny Kate cut to the chase. "You are all wondering something about me that I should have told you a long time ago, but I've kept it a secret from my family for so long that I have become comfortable in my dual roles. One role is as matriarch of my family. My husband, your grandfather," she said, looking at Jamie and Mairi, "died when my boys were very young, and I've always kept my focus on keeping my family safe and healthy.

"It is my second role that you are interested in, I am sure. As I have seen you suspect, and seem receptive to knowing about me, I am also the Matriarch of my Coven of Witches. We are based here in Southern California, and once a year meet up with other witches from around the world in Scotland."

Jamie grinned, Anne smiled and nodded her head knowingly though she'd only just met Kate, Sonja looked admiringly up at her, and Mairi sat back relieved. It was only Shaylee that looked truly surprised. *Ha! The tables are turned on my mother now.*

"It would seem, though, that I am not the only one who holds onto secrets in this family." Kate looked first at Shaylee and then her gaze settled on Mairi. "It would seem," she continued "that I am not the only one wielding power."

Mairi's eyes rounded in surprise and her breath caught in her throat. *What does my Granny know? How could she know?*

Granny Kate patted Mairi's hand from across the table,

reaching past the tall candlesticks in gold bases alongside the bouquet of baby's breath interspersed with dark red roses in a crystal vase.

"It's okay dear. We witches must watch over each other. I sensed your powers this summer and now we will talk, sharing our knowledge, but not tonight. We've had enough surprises for now. Let's enjoy being here together, a room full of enlightened people. Tonight, we celebrate." Holding up her glass of red wine in a crystal goblet, needing only the pointed black hat to be the classic image of a witch, she said to all in the room, "to us and keeping the Old Ways alive."

Dutifully, and with varying levels of cheer, everyone except Shaylee, who looked to have the wind knocked out of her, held up their crystal goblets filled with wine or iced hibiscus tea; the clinking of the glasses sounded like the chiming of faerie bells.

CAT'S EYE
San Diego, California
September 26th, present

Tobias had meant to leave for the Faerie Realm sooner, but he couldn't pull his attention away from Mairi. She was even more beautiful when he was looking at her through his own eyes rather than his enchanted spirit eyes. He had expected it to be the opposite way, that she would be dull without the influence of the fae realm surrounding her. More than ever in his life since discovering his Ka spirit form he wanted to be a strong human being, not the immobile husk he was. He envisioned asking her to prom or something other kids got to do without a second thought.

In that moment he wished he could punch a pillow to rid himself of his helpless rage. Instead he gurgled, and his mother stumbled out of her bedroom across the hallway from his room. She never turned off the baby monitor though she tried to give him "teenage privacy" as she often told him. *Privacy for what*, he always wondered, since she bathed him and dressed him every day. He appreciated her sentiment, though. She wanted the same thing for him that he did: a "normal" life.

So he wouldn't be conscious for his mother's fussing, Tobias sent his Ka spirit out, and with some relief found he was wandering along the stream in the Throne Room of the Faerie Realm, stars twinkling overhead. He came upon Cali reclining on her favorite purple velvet blanket, a tall Highland Warrior with long wavy blonde hair dressed in ragged plaid clothing was sitting beside her.

"I see that you have James still." Tobias sat down on the velvet bedspread next to the faerie and the highlander, noting the blanket was set for a midnight snack. Bowls of grapes and cherries, strawberries and blackberries, all manner of fruits were set before them. James sat feeding himself grapes and drinking a glass of faerie ambrosia from a golden goblet; a big happy grin spread across his face and he had a blank look in his eyes.

Glancing fondly at James, Cali patted his free hand. "Hush Tobias. We mustn't have the Summer Queen finding out I've enchanted her many times great-grandson. Of all the humans we may snatch from the human world, relatives of the Queens and Kings are off limits. Maybe I should disguise him, now that I think of it."

She tugged a strand of her long black hair from her head, whispered a few words into her palm, and the hair became a delicate silver chain she carefully wrapped around James' neck before sealing the ends together. Before Tobias' eyes James' hair turned nut brown, his eyes a deep chocolate brown, and his clothes changed into a silken tunic in shades of copper and gold just like the fae men wore. Not the most convincing disguise, in Tobias' opinion, but perhaps enough to deter questions. James grinned happily and gobbled down more fruit, purple grape juice dripping off his chin. Cali took up a silken handkerchief and carefully wiped the drip from his face like a mother would her own child.

"I've done your bidding, Cali." Tobias wanted to finish his business with this particular faerie and get back to Mairi first thing at dusk. He needed her to be at her most powerful if his plan would work. "I'm here for my own charm, as promised."

Cali's eyes narrowed. "True, you have done as I bid, yet I sense you have knowledge of something . . . no, someone I would be most happy to know about. What is it, little kitty? Why are you keeping secret from me? Don't make me use your true name."

Tobias glanced furtively at James, trying to think of a way out of this dilemma. He didn't want to tell Cali about Mairi being descended from not only a faerie and a druid family, but also a family of witches. Mostly, he just didn't want to let Mairi go. He was too curious to give her completely over to Cali. Still, he would be forced to tell her if she used his true name. The fact that she hadn't used it yet told him she didn't know that his information was really good. *On the other hand, what can I tell her that will be interesting enough to be convincing?*

Looking back at Cali he said, "I know that his daughter," and he indicated James with a nod of his head, "is a witch with healing powers. She wasn't able to heal her father because your spell specifically forbade it, but she was able to completely heal her Gran, James' mom, from the effects of the curse of the Trinity Knot necklace." Tobias felt relieved he'd remembered that piece of information from the summer spying on both Cali and Mairi. He hoped it was close enough to the truth to appease Cali, but not interesting enough for Cali to become excited. He might need both Anne and Mairi for his own plans.

"Curious," Cali mused. "His daughter is a powerful witch? A healer?" She fingered a strand of James' brown hair. "I wonder if his family would mind if we played a little bit with this human anomaly. So few humans are able to tap into their magic, though when they have a kinship to faeries they seem to have an easier time. Hmmm . . . yes, I think I'd like to stir up the hornet's nest just a little bit more."

Cali turned to Tobias and pulled a strand of hair from her head a second time that night, this one remaining black as she draped it around Tobias' black fur, murmuring a few words to cast her faerie magic. Tobias sighed with relief as he felt the solidity returning to his Ka form.

"There you are, Tobias. I'm glad you chose to share with me as you like me to share with you. Now run along. I must make my plans." She lay down on the velvet blanket, resting her head in James' lap, as Tobias ran towards the tunnels, visualizing the beach in San Diego where he would meet up with Mairi.

THRESHOLDS

San Diego, California
September 27th, present
Full Moon

Mairi tip-toed into the kitchen, pulling out granola bars and bags of almonds from the pantry, knowing she needed to bring food, so she wouldn't be tempted to eat what they found in the Faerie Realm, having read that doing so could enslave her to the Realm's magic. It was nearing midnight and she could feel that the threshold of when magic would be at its strongest was almost upon her. Stuffing the food into her leather satchel amongst her tartan scarf and new druid robes, which she hoped would serve as a disguise should she need one, she took out her water bottle.

Treading softly to the jug of purified water on the counter, she flinched when her shoe squeaked on the tiles. Freezing on the spot, she waited two seconds before continuing filling up her water bottle.

"Mairi."

Startled by the sound of her name coming from behind her, Mairi almost dropped the water bottle.

Turning slowly, she put on a smile for her mom. "Oh, hi. Did I wake you? I'm just grabbing a few snacks for sitting in the canyon and watching the full moon. Jamie and Anne are in the fort waiting for me. I have to hurry." She attempted to pass her mom to exit the kitchen and go out the back door into the canyon.

"Mairi, what are you up to?"

"Nothing . . . why do you ask?" Mairi willed her heart to calm down, feeling her palms getting sweaty. *Mom knows. I'm sure she does.* She willed her eyes to appear innocent.

Shaylee frowned, lips pressed tight. Sighing, she said, "It's getting late, don't stay out much longer. I'm sure you have homework to do tomorrow."

Mairi's shoulders relaxed. "I'll finish my homework tomorrow." Shrugging off the pang of guilt she felt for lying to her mom, since it was doubtful she'd be back by tomorrow, she opened the back door and headed into the canyon to meet up with her brother and cousin. *It doesn't matter,* she justified to herself, *I need to find my dad. Mom will forgive me then.*

Climbing the ladder into the old fort their dad had built them, Mairi ducked her head to enter. In the bright moonlight she could see Anne and Jamie bundled up in hooded sweatshirts, canvas backpacks filled with their own disguises as well as food and water.

"You're late," Jamie pointed out.

"Sorry," Mairi hissed. "Mom woke up and asked a lot of questions. We have to sit here for a little bit and pretend to be watching the full moon. I'm sure she's keeping an eye on us from the living room. Did you bring the bagpipes? We have to get to the beach to meet the cat." Mairi had told them all about the black cat and since she was determined to go, Anne and Jamie had insisted on going, too.

Jamie patted the bagpipes he held under his right arm. "Okay, we have to sneak out the back and go through the neighbor's orchard. We should be able to get far enough away that our mom won't notice the bagpipes."

Jamie shook his head. "She'll know, but there's nothing we can do about that. Let's just go and come back before she has a heart attack."

They climbed down the rope ladder that hung off the back of the fort. Mairi trusted that the old wooden rungs would hold their weight, though she wasn't sure that was wise. As she slipped through the run-down fence dividing their lot from the neighbor's, she froze at the whoosh of wings from an owl swooping past overhead. Shaking off her nerves, she stepped softly past the chestnut and kumquat trees. *Why am I so nervous? I need to get ahold of myself!*

Trudging past the barrel cactus and yucca plants, careful not to get stabbed by the barbs, they arrived at the bottom of the canyon next to the trickling stream, which was filled year-round by the runoff from all the houses on the canyon rim watering their lawns.

"Okay, this has to be far enough. We need to get to the beach."

Standing in the shadow of a tree, Jamie filled up the bagpipes and blew a few tentative notes. The sound was like a blast in the near silence of the night. Almost immediately the deck light went on at their house several hundred yards above them, as well as a few of the neighbors'.

"Quick!" Mairi hissed.

"Is that your maw?" Anne pointed up at the deck railing. Sure enough, there was Shaylee in her white pajamas, leaning over the railing staring into the canyon. Mairi could almost see the wild look that was most likely in her mother's eye. A breeze blew into the canyon carrying the scent of lavender as if Shaylee were sending them a reminder of home, imploring them to stay.

"Hurry Jamie! She's going to guess what we're up to. There's nothing we can do about it now." Mairi grabbed Anne's hand. "Hold onto me. I don't want to lose you guys." Mairi put her other hand on Jamie's shoulder. Jamie started playing the traveling song and Mairi saw her mother's head whip around to look in their direction. As Mairi began visualizing the beach where they'd had their bonfire the other night, her last image of her mother was of her rushing down the wooden stairs leading into the canyon, white pajamas glowing in the moonlight, as she called their names in anguish.

They arrived at the same beach where they'd had the bonfire. The light from the full moon rising over the hills behind them shed an eerie glow on the small waves rolling onto the beach. Their landing was rough. They sat on their backsides, hands buried in the sand, except for Jamie who had deftly held the bagpipes aloft, breathing hard in the salt air. Danny was waiting for them as they'd planned earlier.

"I'm sorry," Mairi muttered, her mind a jumble of emotions. *I need to focus better . . . but how? Everything happened so fast. I hope Mom will be okay . . . we shouldn't be gone too long, I hope.* They were heading into the Faerie Realm, though, so she really didn't know how time would pass while they were there. A day in the Faerie Realm for a human could be one day or one year or even a hundred years in the human world. She didn't know how it worked, and there didn't seem to be any scientific answers, or even rhyme or reason as to how time flowed differently between the two realms. *Or are they different dimensions, or different worlds?*

"Ah, you made it," a voice purred above and behind them, "and with several minutes to spare before midnight.

We need to get to the entrance into the Faerie Realm now. Follow me." The black cat got up from where he'd been sitting on the sea wall waiting for them.

"Wait," Danny called. "I'm supposed to take the bagpipes, aren't I?" he asked Jamie.

Yeah! I can't use them in the Faerie Realm and I know you'll take really good care of them. I look forward to whatever you learn about the markings carved on the Silver Faerie Chanter."

"Now we go!" Ka called out. Flicking his long black tail in the air like a flagpole, he walked along the wall heading under the pier. Mairi, Jamie, and Anne scrambled to their feet, ran to the sea wall, and jumped up onto it to follow behind the cat.

After passing under the pylons of the pier, they jumped off the sea wall and passed the tide pools where children played during the day if the tide was low, catching hermit crabs. It was low now as Mairi leaped over small pools of salt water, following the cat around the bend. To their right, the ocean spread out in all its vast emptiness, and to their left the cliffs grew steadily higher as they picked their way along the crumbling sandstone path.

"What's your name?" Jamie called out. "I don't know what to call you."

The black cat stopped for a moment, tilting his head to the side as if to think about it. "That is a big question in the Faerie Realm, but I can see it is also a necessary one. Maybe you already know this, but do not ever tell your real name to a faerie. If you do, they will own a bit of your soul, and you will have to do their bidding if they use your name against you. So, forgive me if I do not tell you my real name. You may call me Ka, for that is what I am, a spirit form of my true self, a form called Ka by the Egyptians." He turned and continued walking, gracefully leaping over holes in the path as he went.

"Hold on. You're not a real cat?" Mairi asked. "How

many pretend cats am I going to run into this year?" she muttered more to herself, but Anne heard and nodded her agreement.

"No, I am not a real cat. Real cats don't talk," Ka smirked. Looking over his shoulder towards the round moon quickly reaching the apex in the sky, he continued, "Though, we don't have time to discuss it now. This particular entrance to the Faerie Realm is fickle, not easily entered except under specific circumstances. Please hurry!"

At that moment, the moon reached high in the sky, Jamie's watch chimed midnight, and Mairi heard a haunting song coming from the ocean. Looking out to where the moonlight lit up a bit of the water like a spotlight, she could see what appeared to be large fish jumping in the air and diving into the water, only their torsos and heads were human, with long hair trailing behind. The singing came from their direction.

"Mermaids...?" she asked.

"Yes," Ka answered, "their singing provides the magic we need to get into the Faerie Realm at this exact spot, and during the full moon is the only time of the month that they sing. Since several full moons a year bring high tides at midnight, it is only at the low tide during a full moon that we can access this particular entryway. Follow me. We're nearly there."

They rounded the corner and opening before them was a gaping cavern leading deep into the earth. Ka didn't hesitate. He leaped down to the wet sandstone, carefully avoiding the pools of water, and headed into the darkness beyond.

Mairi watched Anne and Jamie scramble down, glancing one last time at the mermaids who were now sitting on a rock rising up from the waves, running fingers through their hair and flicking their long fish fins that gleamed in all the colors of the rainbow. Their song clung to her thoughts as she slid down the ledge on her bottom and followed everyone into the yawning entrance to the Faerie Realm.

STEALTH

The Faerie Realm
Outside of Time

"**H**ow is it that there is an entrance to the Faerie Realm here in San Diego? I thought the faeries abandoned all the areas outside of the United Kingdom as people stopped believing in them." Jamie was trudging along the tunnel behind Ka. The wet entrance of the cavern had led them into the familiar dry tunnels formed of rich soil and giant tree roots.

"There's no way we are under San Diego anymore. We must have passed into the same tunnels that we entered on the Isle of Skye," Mairi pointed out.

"I see that, Mairi, but the actual entrance was in San Diego. How is that possible?"

Ka stopped and looked at Mairi and Jamie. "The entrances have always been possible. It only takes one person believing and then timing it right to create the entrance. You made your entrance on your Granda's land just this summer. The entrance in San Diego is ancient, older than the white settlers, perhaps older than the Kumaai Indian Tribes, but I'm not sure. The mermaids are immortal, so maybe they created this entrance before the tribes were here. Anyway, you never knew this entrance existed because you are only just learning about these things. You can't know something until you know to look for it."

Ka started walking again and they continued to follow, but Anne grabbed Mairi's sleeve and held her back. "Walk with me for a moment," Anne said in her gentle manner, using as quiet a voice as she could. "I have been thinking, Mairi. Who is this cat really? We are following him without knowing who he truly is. We see only his spirit form, which he chooses to possess only in cat shape, but he is really a human somewhere. We dinnae even know when he is from, let alone where. I think he must be the cat that gave me a warning just before my da became ill. Why, I cannae guess. I dinnae feel safe following him into the Faerie Realm. How do we know he means us no harm?"

Mairi nodded understanding, then frowned and pulled away from her cousin. "He hasn't done anything to show us we shouldn't trust him. I need to get into the Faerie Realm to find my dad. Your dad we will most likely find when the Wild Hunt passes through on All Hallow's Eve, but we don't know where. We have a date and a time, and we will figure out the place to intercept the Wild Hunt and rescue Uncle James, but I only know that my dad is somewhere in the Faerie Realm, so I have to search. Ka says he can help me, and I believe him."

Anne shook her head at Mairi. "No one does anything without wanting something in return. What does Ka want? Besides, you dinnae even know if yer da was switched with a changeling. Ye are nae thinking this through. I feel great concern over following Ka."

"Then don't follow him. Go back, or go somewhere else.

I don't care." Mairi stomped ahead of Anne, rushing past Jamie who had stopped and was staring at the girls, a look of shock in his eyes.

"Wha . . . what's wrong?" he asked.

Mairi shrugged. "Ask her," pointing at Anne.

Anne shook her head and said nothing, continuing to follow her cousins and Ka.

Ka squinted his eyes at the girls, realizing he needed to keep the peace long enough to get them to do his bidding.

They arrived at the tunnel entrance behind the waterfall in the Faerie Queen's Throne Room, silver starlight twinkling overhead. There was a hush in the cavernous glen, the only sound was the occasional call from an owl, *whoo-whoo*, as if asking who dared to enter the Faerie Realm.

Mairi wondered where all the faerie folk went at night. *Do they even sleep?* As if in answer to her question, Mairi saw that Titania, Summer Queen of the Seelie Court, sat on her throne beneath the ancient apple tree, murmuring to several faeries dressed in clothing much sturdier than the usual gossamer finery. There was a sinister feeling in the air, and Mairi felt the hairs rise on her neck.

As they snuck past the Faerie Queen and her advisors, Mairi noticed the apple tree was just beginning to show signs of the changing seasons: scarlet and yellow leaves were falling from its branches as a cold winter wind blew through the great hall. When they were far enough from the Queen, Mairi asked, "Where are you taking us?" She hadn't thought beyond getting into the Faerie Realm. Now that they were there, she had no idea what they would do next.

"We must head to Avalon, sometimes referred to as the Isle of the Dead. Others refer to it as the Land of Youth where the Gods and Goddesses of the Tuatha de Dannan dwell. There is a lot of speculation by humans as to who or what that particular realm holds."

Mairi stopped, her body rigid. "Why are we going there? My dad isn't dead."

Ka stopped, along with Anne and Jamie. "Mairi, it's okay. On the way to Avalon there is a field and an orchard of ever-ripe fruit trees and streams of clear water. It's where changelings are kept when they aren't needed to do the tasks of their faerie owners. If your dad was switched with a changeling, he'll be there. Now come on! We have to hurry before the Unseelie Court senses we are entering their territory."

The three humans had to race to keep up with the black spirit cat as he bounded ahead, uncertain of what dangers they were facing.

WITCH HUNT
Isle of Skye, Scotland
September 27th, 1700s

"Tell me about this Anne MacLeod ye say healed yer son when he was sick."

Ewan sat in the cramped crofter's home on the edge of the MacLeod territory. By being on the MacLeod side of the arbitrary dividing line, he was risking the tenuous truce the two clans had set up after their last skirmish, but he needed answers. "She gave your son an herbal drink and suddenly he was better . . . from a disease that had killed your other child?"

The mother sat in front of him in dirty ragged clothes that barely covered her misshapen body pulled and stretched by the numerous children running in and out of her home.

Ewan shuddered, *I dinnae know that I could stand to have so many children. I am just not that interested in their mess and noise.*

Drawing his attention back to the woman, he listened intently as she told him about the petite young woman with black hair and green eyes who had attended her children during an epidemic that spread through her village several months past.

"She came in with her da, she did, and he a great tall blonde MacLeod Highlander. Then she sets about gevin a tincture tae every person who had the bloody cough and pustules all over their body. By morning, all had slept peacefully and woke up with renewed energy and ravenous appetites, like starved animals. I dinnae know what Anne gave them, but it helped, and all of us in the village are grateful for it."

Ewan nodded his understanding. He could see how a village might be grateful even to a devil who saved their families, no matter the price. *But what is the price, I wonder. If Anne and her father are indeed related to the faeries, as Cali claimed, then I bet there was more in those herbal drinks than herbs. There was probably magic, which the kirk would not like to hear about. The Devil's work, they would call it. It should be so easy to convince the Crofters that the healing was the work of a witch. A woman with such powers should not be so hard to turn the people against. Women are not equal to men and I'll not let these Wild Witches wreak havoc in the Highlands.*

"Perhaps Anne gave your son a potion filled with spells to bind your son to her. Has he done anything odd since he was healed?"

The woman visibly shivered and took a breath, but hesitated, not answering. Twisting her skirts in her wash-hardened hands, calloused from scrubbing family clothes in lye, she crossed herself and muttered a prayer. A small child, filthy from playing outside with the chickens, crawled into her lap and she pulled him to her like a shield. "Weel, aye, he 'as, actually. Ye see, he 'as taken tae singing. All the ones who was sick sing a lot now. They are happier now than they was before the sickness. I dinnae know why, but I suspect it was somethin' in the herbs."

She squeezed the child to her breast and went on. "We talk about it, ye know, by the well when we gather water. We ask each other what new odd thing our family who was almost dead, but are nae because of the work of Anne. We whisper, because if the priest who comes on Sunday was tae ask us about it, he would be angry. He does nae want us tae ask the herbal woman, that tis what we call Anne, we are nae s'posed tae ask her for help. He says we are inviting the devil into our homes, into our loved ones." She slumped further into the space between her hard, wooden stool and the mud walls of her small dark home, exhausted from her life. "But we are glad they are alive, so we dinnae tell the priest about the singing."

Ewan nodded, and rose, bidding the woman good-bye. As he stepped out of the gloom and smoke of the little house, he took in a deep breath of the fresh air outside. *Such filth, such stench. I could nae live like that. Why does anyone live like that?* He got on his horse and made his way back to his clan at the southern end of the Isle, telling stories in every alehouse along the way, stories of a young herbal woman who appeared to practice magic. 'Is she a witch in the devil's employ?' he wondered out loud in the company of husbands who returned to their wives, spreading fear like a wildfire, inciting the embers of speculation and finger pointing.

Whispers of *Witch! Witch!* Became the drumbeat of a battle cry, growing with intensity, "Witch! Witch!" Until all the weak-minded crofters were pulling out pitchforks and torches, and sisters were outing sisters for using herbs and blessings to exact cures for loved ones. "WITCH! WITCH!" was shouted and the pounding of feet echoed all over the Isle of Skye, leaping the ocean to Scotland and rushing to join the rest of Europe, as the witch hunts surged again, rounding up women of all ages to be tried and punished for dancing with the devil himself.

All this happened, and Ewan smiled smugly as he entered his chieftain's halls, to be regaled with the latest news of the mainland. The Witches were being hunted more vehemently than ever and wouldn't the world be better off for it? All those women pretending to be druids when everyone knows they were only colluding with the devil. Women needed to be reminded of their place, in their homes and tending their babes, not pretending they had powers equal to men. Ewan raised his mug to his chieftain, cheering the wisdom of men as the ruling gender, and to druids who should only be men.

Now I need only track down this Anne MacLeod and her Wild Witchy friend and make sure they, too, are brought to justice in this new time of putting women in their place. His mind turned to Cali, to the faerie woman who so liked to plot and plan. *She should nae have dismissed me so readily. I am just as able as she is to plan and rule the fates of others.* He downed his draft in triumph, banging his cup down on the thick wooden table triumphantly.

WINTER COURT
The Faerie Realm
Outside of Time

The path they followed away from the Summer Queen's court paralleled the stream that meandered through her throne room, which soon became a rushing river as more and more tributaries flowed into it. The night hours passed swiftly into dawn and on the opposite shore of the river, Mairi could see the mountains rising high in the distance, snow-covered caps reaching into the blue sky. Looking down into the clear waters of the river, she first thought it was only filled with fish flashing golden and silver and salmon pink, but she soon realized that there were more than fish living there. A rainbow fishtail flashed in the sunlight, disappeared under the turbulent surface, to be followed by a beautiful brown-skinned maiden, small as a child yet with the bosom of a young woman covered by a water lily bralette top; she had damp velvet-brown curls cascading down her back. The mermaid leaped from the water and perched on a rock outcrop, quickly followed by more mermaids of all colors, each strikingly beautiful. They sang out in melodic voices a song of want and desire.

"Don't listen!" Ka spat out. "Their words are poison. They wish to pull you into the watery depths of the river and drag you to their ocean kingdoms far away. Most often men are drawn in by their voices, but sometimes women are, too."

Mairi grabbed Jamie's hand and didn't let go as they ran behind Ka, Anne a few steps behind, getting further from the river bank and closer to the edge of a dense forest, the distance muting the pull of the mermaids' songs. They sat down in the grass and breathed in deep the scent of the forest.

"Should we be doing this?" Anne asked. "Seems too risky to be passing through the Unseelie court's domain."

"We have to. It's the only way to reach the meadow near Avalon," Ka explained.

"I'm trying to remember what the Unseelie Court, the Seelie Court are, and who the Summer Queen, and the Winter Queen are. Can you remind me, Ka?" Jamie asked.

"Sure, but we'd better keep walking or we'll be dragged into the woods by any number of dark creatures." Ka stood and stretched his legs and beckoned them on with a twitch of his tail. The three cousins rose and once again followed.

"The Summer Queen, your distant relative, is Queen of the Seelie Court who are faeries that are kinder, gentler than their counterparts, the Unseelie Court. The Winter Queen, a cold faerie who blatantly does not like humans, rules the Unseelie Court. In fact, she resents humans and occasionally declares she will someday make war on them to regain the Earthly realm. She might be all talk, but every year she seems more determined to make it soon come true. They are the faeries who steal humans for sport, either switching them with one of their own kind who is sick and will die soon anyway, glamouring them to look like the human they are stealing. Or, they outright snatch the humans and torture them, sometimes eating them."

Anne's hand flew to her mouth to suppress her horror at what her da might be facing.

Ka glanced at Anne, "More often than not, they just treat them like pets or slaves."

Just then the quiet was shattered by an unearthly scream echoing from the woods, followed by what might have been the chi-chi-chi of a chipmunk, or the evil laugh of a Dark Fae. Mairi peeked into the almost black shadows of the woods and was certain she saw numerous eyes lit up golden or red, blinking back at them. Mairi shivered. Jamie walked a little closer to the girls. They could hear a loud thumping sound in the distance, steadily drawing closer. They picked up their pace in response.

"Why do they hate us humans so? We live in a different world. We could remain separate for all time if the faeries wanted it," Mairi asked.

"Yes, well, humans are supposed to have taken the earth from the faeries eons ago," Jamie answered, and Ka nodded his head in agreement.

Mairi frowned at Jamie. *How does he always know things I don't know? It's got to be all those hours he spends reading.* "How is that possible? If faeries are so much more powerful than humans are, how could humans have stolen a whole planet from them?"

Ka jumped over a small boulder as he answered, "the fae folk are dependent on humans in a roundabout way. In their connection to nature there is a weakness. Humans aren't directly affected by the health of the planet, though more so than humans realize, but faeries are very much affected. If the earth is sick in any place, than the faeries cannot occupy that part of the planet . . . cannot physically stand on a diseased land . . .and so they retreat into the shadow world, the Faerie Realm."

"What is this world, anyway?" Mairi hadn't actually

thought about it until now.

"It's another dimension of Earth. It's still the earth, like a 3-D shadow, but it's becoming more solid and separate as time goes on. It might be its own planet now. The stars are different from our stars, there is no moon, and the sun is a brighter white light." Ka leaped over a fallen tree branch as he spoke.

"They are afraid of what will become of them if the earth is completely lost to them," Anne stated. "I sense that fear in the air."

"Yes, and so some faeries, mostly the Unseelie, want to return to the earth while they can and fight for what they believe rightfully belongs to them, and that the humans are selfishly destroying. Other faeries, mostly the Seelie, believe that humans are also a part of the earth and fate has worked out how it was meant to, so they choose to play with the humans like little children, but to more or less leave them be. The Seelie faeries might attempt to influence humans to care for the nature of earth better, create a more symbiotic relationship, but Seelie fae rarely inflict harm to humans on purpose." Ka looked at them from a rock outcropping and they all stopped to let this latest news soak in. Now they were stopped, they could feel the thumping they had heard earlier. The ground was bumping up and down, vibrating through their bones.

"Basically, train us to be better stewards of the land or kill us all. Is that it? Those are the options the fae believe in for humans?" Mairi asked, too interested in the conversation to pay attention to the strange sounds and activity around her.

"Yes," Ka agreed. Then his eyes grew round at something he saw behind them and he shouted "Run!!" Turning and running across the meadow, the three cousins racing behind him, unsure what they ran from or why.

Mairi looked over her shoulder and screamed.

She wasn't a screamer normally, but she wasn't normally

chased by something as hideous and blood thirsty as what was following them. Crashing through the trees behind them was a humanoid creature the size of a small downtown high-rise building, ragged clothes hanging from its tree-sized limbs, and smelling of rotting flesh. His humongous feet pounded the earth with each footfall; its gargantuan height and bulk caused mini-earthquakes the closer he came to Mairi's group.

GLAISTIG
Isle of Skye, Scotland
Time Unknown

Anne ran as fast as she her legs could carry her, sure this was it, this was when they would die. The hideous creature following them was fast on its giant legs, and probably hungry. *I knew we should nae have come. It is a bad idea to follow spirit cats around just so we can prove or disprove that Mairi's dad is a changeling.*

"Ka!" Jamie called. "Is there any way out of here?"

"Almost there!" Ka called over his shoulder. "There's a one-way door here somewhere."

Leaping behind a rock, Ka disappeared in a crack in the slate gray surface. Mairi squeezed in behind him, then Jamie and Anne were finally there, too. Anne felt the beast's gruesome breath on her back as she squeezed in, and fell down, down . . . down . . . down into a cavern both dark and empty. She fell for long enough, and slow enough, to consider her falling. *This must be why it's one-way. Falling up wouldn't work out so well. But where will we land?*

Then she did land, with a bump, and found herself looking at a large rock. Beside her Mairi, Jamie, and Ka had also arrived. They looked around in bewilderment, until Jamie said, "It's the Bodach an Stòrr!"

Mairi looked at him in confusion until Jamie explained, "The Old Man on Storr." Mairi still looked confused.

"We are on the Isle of Skye," Anne explained. "I think I finally understand why there is a story told about this rock being the thumb of a giant buried under ground."

Jamie eagerly nodded his head. "Yeah! That was a giant chasing us, wasn't it?"

Ka stretched his front legs long in front of him and sharpened his claws on the moss-covered slate littering the ground. "Yes, I have never seen giants in that forest, though. I didn't expect we would be chased by something that might catch us so easily."

"That was crazy! I had no idea giants existed. I mean, I know now that faeries do, but I've only ever seen the winged type and mermaids . . . not a gruesome giant." Jamie exclaimed, more excited than scared.

Mairi fumbled with her knotted curls, pulling strands of loose hair off her head in her nervousness. "I'm sorry I didn't use my magic to protect us . . . to fight . . . I didn't even think of it..." her voice trailed off.

"Mairi," Anne reached out to touch her cousin, sympathy filling her heart, but Mairi pulled away.

"Don't! I don't need your sympathy. I just need to be better at using magic." Mairi stood up and kicked a rock, then walked over to the edge and looked out over the water in the distance.

"What's the story of the giant?" Jamie asked, looking at Anne. "And why do you think there was one in that forest when you've never seen one before?" Jamie directed the second question to Ka.

Ka answered first, "I think that the fae are growing

stronger, building their forces. At least, the Unseelie Faeries. As winter approaches and their rulers become stronger, so do all the Unseelie Folk. Giants are the biggest problem, literally, but there will be Red Cap Gnomes out in force, and other fae coming out of the Shadows, fae that hunt humans for sport. Something is changing, something that will affect humanity, and most humans don't even know it.

Anne waited patiently for Ka to finish then she told Jamie about the legend of Storr. "There are a lot of stories, one of which is that of an old man and his wife, who were longing to be together forever and were offered the chance by fae folk. When the Old Man admitted that his dearest wish was to have his wife always by his side, they maliciously turned them both to stone. Their wish was fulfilled, but not in a way that they expected.

"However, the other legend is that a giant died here and so was buried, with only his thumb left out of the earth. Giants are thought to turn to stone when they die, so that story also fits. And certainly, we were chased by a giant, so I see a connection with that particular legend."

"How come we seem to always end up in Skye or California when we leave the Faerie Realm? Seems like we should be ending up anywhere in the world." Mairi wondered out loud, not really expecting an answer.

"I think," Ka said, "that there is an energy connection between Skye and California that was formed by your Granda and Gran when they first accidentally time traveled. Your family is connected to these places and times. Maybe other families would end up other places, other times."

Mairi frowned, wondering how Ka knew so much about her family. *I never told him, so how does he know?* For the first time, she began to suspect Anne was right to be questioning following Ka around. *But I need him,* so she dismissed her concerns.

"The real question," Mairi said, returning to their side,

"is how do we get out of here? And, by here, we don't even know what time in history this is."

Jamie looked out over the landscape and answered, "Well, I'm pretty sure we're not in the 21st century. There aren't any roads or airplanes passing overhead. We're definitely in the past."

"But how far back? Do you have any ideas, Ka?" Mairi asked the black cat, who was beginning to shimmer in the sunlight, reminding all of them that he was actually a spirit cat. A cold breeze blew through and she shivered.

"No, I don't know. I suppose we'll have to make our way into a village or town and see. Now I wish I'd kept the bagpipes. We could wish ourselves to the Faerie Grove and return into the Faerie Realm so easily. I figured they were cumbersome and unnecessary in the Faerie Realm. I guess we'll just have to walk." He kicked a rock, sending it whistling through the air, and it disappeared over the edge, falling far, far below. "Another question is which way do we go?"

Anne looked around, getting her bearings, and was surprised by the torso and head of a woman popping up over the ridge.

"Excuse me, I don't mean to startle you," the woman said, her long gray hair blowing in the cold wind that was picking up over the Storr, whipping her hair away from the little pointed goat horns sticking up from her forehead. Clothed in a flowing green dress, it took Anne a moment to notice the goat hooves as the woman climbed over the edge and stood beside them. She was a surprisingly tall woman reaching up a foot taller than Mairi, and obviously a fae creature as well. "I overheard your predicament and I'd be happy to point you in the right direction."

Anne recovered first, soothed by Ka's purring, no doubt meant to calm everyone's nerves. She nodded her head at the Glaistig, for Anne recognized what the Fae Woman was. "Yes, that would be most helpful."

Pointing down the way she had just come, the Glaistig said, "Walk in that direction, around the bay of water and back on course. Soon you will come to a well-worn track and that will lead you to the first town in the MacLeod lands."

"Thank you, fine lady," Ka inclined his head. Turning to the others, he said, "we need to pay her for her kindness. Does anyone have something to give her? A stone or a bell or anything? Milk would be preferable, but probably asking too much."

Anne spread her hands out, showing that she had nothing to offer. Mairi rifled through her backpack and, pulling her druid's robes out of the way, she located a small jade stone in the pouch of stones she'd brought with her, Jamie having warned her something like this might occur. "Here, it's the color of your dress. I hope you like it."

"Perfect," the goat lady smiled, and everyone shuffled past her, making their way down the extremely steep incline to see what awaited them next.

CAPTURED

Isle of Skye, Scotland
Time Unknown

Mairi tugged at the heavy druid's robes she'd pulled on over her blue jeans and t-shirt, grateful for the disguise though damp after walking for hours in the drizzling rain. What had started out as an almost clear morning when she'd stood at the Storr looking out over the water for signs of what year it was, had steadily become a gray wet day. At least, they had found a rutted road to follow and there was hope still blooming in her that they would find an inn of some sort in the town the Glaistig had mentioned. A hot tea or soup or something would be wonderful, if only the Inn Keeper would be willing to trade for one of the gold trinkets or pretty stones she'd brought with her.

They trudged through the rain as it came down stronger and stronger. The mud coating Mairi's shoes was getting heavier as more and more of it clung to them. *At least my modern-day shoes are disguised by all of the mud covering them now,* she thought. Watching Ka, she felt envious that his spirit form seemed less hindered by the drizzle, though he still seemed to be getting a little wet. *Curious. Is he spirit or solid? So strange.* Getting ready to beg that they stop and find shelter in the stand of trees off to the right, away from the water, Mairi stopped herself when she saw lights up ahead.

"Do you think that could be an inn or pub or something?" she called to the others.

Jamie looked up, pulling his hood back from where it had fallen and nearly covered his whole face. "Yeah, maybe. There should be a few of them along this isle."

Renewed with hope, Mairi picked up her steps just as Anne reached out to squeeze her cousin's hand. "Oh good!" Anne said. "I do hope we will be warm soon." Mairi nodded, pulling her hand from Anne's. She wasn't quite ready to forgive Anne for not supporting her search for her dad in the Faerie Realm. She winced at a pang of guilt as Anne slowed her steps and walked behind her once again.

What felt like hours later, but could have been much less, they arrived at the inn. There were horses and sheep, small cows and chickens holed up in a corral off to the side, their plaintive lowing and shuffling, kicking and cackling at the cramped quarters reached through the rainfall. There was an oil lamp hanging over the heavy oak door, the only clear indicator of where to enter the gray building; the front step was covered with the mud wiped off of the many boots passing over the threshold. As soon as they opened the door the smell of mutton stew and stale ale wafted out. Mairi's stomach grumbled, and she imagined she heard Jamie and Anne's stomachs, too. Ka was nowhere to be seen.

Oh crud! I didn't expect him to disappear, but of course he has to. Even as a cat he probably can't come in, but as a spirit cat, looking all ghostly, he can't be seen. We should have talked about this... She glanced over her shoulder to see if he was anywhere nearby and she heard a "mew" off towards the animal shed. *Okay, I hope that's him. We'll get back out here as soon as we know what year it is and have managed to warm up our fingers and dried off a bit.*

She turned and followed her brother into the dark smoky room, her cousin right behind her. As they pulled back their hoods and Anne unwrapped her tartan from her head all sounds stopped, and several pairs of eyes bore into them, glaring. The place was barely occupied with people, most were probably home in their own cozy crofts, but the few travelers unfortunate enough to be caught in the downpour had obviously found shelter at this inn. A low muttering started up and more than one burly highlander definitely muttered, "Witch!" From their body language, Mairi was certain they didn't mean it as a compliment.

"This looks bad, Jamie," Mairi whispered in her brother's ear. "Let's just go sit by the fire for a minute and warm up, then we can see if we need to leave." The orange glow of the fireplace beckoned to her drenched body, as the cold had already settled into her bones.

Jamie hesitated, then nodded. "Okay . . . but I think there's something bad going on here."

They sat huddled next to the roaring fire with one other weary traveler who must have also just arrived. Steam rose from his greased leather cloak and Anne envied him his being prepared for the Scottish weather. *If I was home in my own lil' croft, I would be warm and dry, or prepared like him, at the very least.*

Shaken by Mairi's earlier rejection of her attempt at mending the rift between them, Anne worried over what she should do. *I do nae know what I can do to heal our friendship. She is a prickly one, like the red blooming thistles.* Lost in thought, she didn't feel the anger rising around her. An idea occurred to her, and she tugged on the Highlander's hot sleeve. Speaking in Gaelic, she said, "Excuse me, sir, but I wonder if ye can tell me the date today? I've been traveling a long while with my companions and I've lost track of the days."

"Och! Of course! I've been on the road awhile meself. It is . . . "

Mairi leaned in to hear what Anne was talking about with the Highlander, but missed most of what was said when the fire popped and crackled behind her. Anne nodded her thanks to him and repeated the information in English to Mairi and Jamie, joining them to sit on the bench nearest the fire. Their suspicions were confirmed. They were in Anne's own time, and they had lost three weeks in the Faerie Realm.

A barmaid, just coming to offer them a draught of ale if they could pay, stopped short and narrowed her eyes at Anne. "Ye would nae be Anne MacLeod, would ye now? And this yer companion here," she indicated Mairi, "would she be the Witch Mairi?"

Jamie and Mairi caught their breath next to her and before Anne could answer, all the greasy Highlanders and Crofters, and even the Inn Keeper, had stood as they listened for Anne's answer.

Jamie jumped to his feet, "Run! Run now!!"

Without hesitation, Anne and Mairi stood as one and they all pushed past the bar maid, gripping their bags and racing for the entryway. Mairi and Jamie, both taller than Anne, reached the door first. Anne was almost out of the door when she was yanked backwards. She felt herself falling and she landed on the hard-packed dirt floor with a loud THUD.

"Oh no ye don't, ye MacLeod lass. A witch like ye cannae be allowed to escape." A Highlander in MacDonald tartan stood over her, a greasy leg of mutton in one hand, and the end of her tartan scarf in the other. He wiped some of the grease off his face with the corner of her scarf, pulling it tighter around her throat so that Anne coughed and choked. Her nails raked at her throat, helplessly attempting to pull the wool scarf loose from her neck. "Go on! Use yer witchy magic, lass." He laughed a rough raucous laugh and dragged her over to his table, so he could finish his meal.

DESPERATE

Isle of Skye, Scotland
October 16th, 1700s

"I should have realized," Jamie gasped between gulps of breath.

Jamie and Mairi were hiding in a cave they had stumbled into after running for their life. Ka had seen them and followed.

When he could breathe at a normal rate again, Jamie went on, "I think we've arrived when the Witch Hunts are still happening in these smaller villages on the outskirts of Europe. They were incredibly rare in the Highlands and outer islands, but someone told these clansmen to be on the watch for us." He looked up at Mairi and Ka, "Well, Anne and Mairi, at least. I wonder if this could possibly be related to the attacks on Anne's family . . . Uncle James' kidnapping and her little sister's changeling exchange."

Mairi dropped her head into her hands, wet curls sticking to her arms. "They have Anne." She looked up into

Jamie's eyes, then Ka's. "First Uncle James is taken by faeries and now the Highlanders have Anne, and it's my fault. Just because I insisted on going to find the changelings . . . to find my dad . . . we were chased by a giant, and caught in this rain storm in some part of Skye we have no idea how we can get out of here, in MacDonald land, and now Anne is in their grips . . . " her voice trailed off as she dropped her head into her hands again. "I can't even get my magic to be useful right now," she whispered.

Ka purred, using his cat tricks to soothe everyone, before saying, "We'll figure out something. Jamie, do you recall where they would take an accused witch?"

"I suppose they would take her to the MacDonald chief's home before having her stand trial, or a dungeon nearby. We need to figure out where that is. I wish we had a map!"

"I have an idea," Ka said. *I don't want to give them false hope, but I'll go see if I can find a map and memorize where to go.* "I need to go away for a bit, but I'll return soon and hopefully I'll have the answers we seek. In the meantime, Mairi you should work on focusing on fire magic. You might be able to draw enough energy to warm you and your brother. Have faith in yourself. You are a powerful witch . . . druid . . . whatever you want to call yourself . . you are barely trained, that is all. Anne needs you, that is true, but right now your brother and you need to get warm or you won't be of any use to Anne." *Or to me,* he silently added.

As if to prove his point, their chattering teeth could be heard in the silence. Ka faded away and disappeared.

Jamie and Mairi huddled in the cave staring at the spot Ka had stood moments before.

"Want to give it a try?" Jamie asked. When Mairi barely moved, Jamie shrugged, "It would be nice to dry off and get warm. How about you work on your magic, and I'll work on mine." He pulled off his druid's robes, so he could take off his backpack. Rummaging through it, he pulled out a plastic bag with matches and a scoop of pellets. "A scout is always prepared," he grinned at his sister's surprised look.

At least someone is focused and calm, Mairi thought before sinking back into her misery.

Once Jamie got the fire going, a tiny spark just enough to warm their fingers and toes, Mairi huddled beside her brother, as close to it as they could get without getting burned.

"You know," Jamie began, "There's a story about a MacDonald Witch that may explain why these Highlanders were so ready to persecute you and Anne."

Mairi looked up at him, her green eyes dull with self-loathing. "Well, what is it?" *Might as well listen to a fairy tale as sit here doing nothing to help Anne.*

Jamie smiled, despite the situation. "It had to do with the Jacobite uprising and the 'pretender king.'

MACDONALD WITCH

A Historic Tale
1692, Glencoe

Not so long ago, the MacDonald Clansmen slept *peacefully in their beds, their homes nestled in the beautiful valley of Glencoe. With mountains rising on either side of a valley with rolling green meadows and long winding rivers, it was an ideal spot to live and the clan felt blessed. Now the MacDonalds were an unruly clan known for their rebellious nature; they were Highland warriors through and through. They had fought bravely alongside the Jacobites, hoping to overthrow the pretender king and return James to his throne. But it was not to be, and the MacDonald chief was slow in showing allegiance to the current king sitting upon the throne.*

Now in the Highland bens, the tallest mountains surrounding the glen, lived an old woman. The old woman had lived all her life in those mountains and suffice it to say, she was as much a part of the mountains as any creatures who made it their home. She knew every herb that grew there, every rocky alcove to hide from the north winds, every pool and waterfall. More spirit than human, she was often called hag or witch, and she did not mind for she knew things, amazing things. She knew how to staunch the flow of blood from a wound by mashing up the proper herbs, or how to catch a rabbit with the snares she shaped from sticks and bits that nature provided. But she also knew the future, and this sometimes got her into trouble.

One winter night she dreamed the river that ran through the glen flowed blood red with the slaughter of the MacDonald clansmen. She woke immediately and hiked in the moonless dark night along the treacherous trails to the valley below, arriving at dawn. The men were all at their work in the fields, so she warned the women as best she could. Speech was not her best asset, for she rarely spoke to humans, so what came through was not as clear as what she saw. Still, she tried, calling out in her raspy unpracticed voice.

"Terrible tidings do I bring,
Horrible happenings come to bear,
Do not stay idle in your beds,
Run! Run away from where
Your names, Death is sure to sing."

She returned to her mountain escape, to watch what the future had planned, and weep at the slowness of the women in acting upon her warning.

When English soldiers passed through, led by the Glen Lyon, and asked for a bed for the night to keep them from the cold snows, the ever-hospitable clan invited them in. Surely there was nothing to worry about, regardless of the ramblings of women about the mutterings of a lonely witch? Guests and hosts hold an oath in Scotland: none shall raise arms against the other, so long as the roof is shared. But English are not Scottish, and oaths are often broken.

After a fortnight of camaraderie, the soldiers rose in the night and slaughtered their hosts in their beds, while women and children ran for their lives having gone to bed in their clothes and shoes every night for worry of the old woman's warning. Houses were burned, so the women and children had no place to warm their bodies, and thus another forty were dead before the day had passed up in the snowy passes.

And the old woman wept for those she had not saved.

The few who survived spread stories of what had happened, and the old woman's name was whispered from home to home, "witch, witch, the witch knew . . . the witch cursed . . . the witch is to blame."

Her sympathy for her kinfolk was her undoing. She crept from her mountain haven, where no Highlander or English soldier would ever have found her, to search the ruins for signs of the living, for signs of how she might help to rebuild her clan. Before the moon grew full and bright, she was rounded up and brought to the dungeons of Edinburgh, where she was tried and burned as the witch she was, though traitor she was not.

TRUTH
San Diego, California
October 16th, present

When Ka had disappeared from Jamie and Mairi, he had reappeared in his bedroom, arriving in the shadows in case someone was there, and as expected, someone was. His mother sat over his bed, weeping into her hands. "Where are you, Tobias? You've been still for so long. No indication of waking up in there. Do I give up hope? Are you still alive?"

Giving his sleeping husk only a cursory glance in the bed, Ka felt the urgency of getting his plan back on track, so he could return with a fully empowered Mairi and Anne, hopefully ready to heal his body. He did, however, take in that his mother had put him on life support, always necessary when he'd left his body for too long. He felt bad about the cost, but hopefully it wouldn't be necessary ever again if his plan finally worked.

His mother got up then, tucked Tobias into his

blankets, and walked out of the room. Looking out the window, Ka saw that it was nighttime, the same as when he'd left Jamie and Mairi in the past.

To work! Looking at the wall of books, he thought, *this would be so much easier if I had a human form right now. Still, my paws can manipulate my mother's computer.* Her computer sat on a desk along the wall opposite the bed with his vegetative form, bright rainbow colors whirling across the screen. *Good, it's on.*

Ka pushed the mouse and the screen snapped to attention. His mother had left it open to a page about the latest technology for healing a quadriplegic. This was a typical Internet search for her. He pushed the mouse to get the arrow to move so he could minimize the page, then he brought up a new page and tapped away at the keyboard, hoping to find a map of the Isle of Skye depicting the clan boundaries in the 1700s.

Ka sighed. *This would go faster if I didn't have to erase every other letter because my paws hit the wrong keys.* When he finally succeeded, there were hundreds of images and it would take a while to sift through to find one that was actually helpful.

"Hey! Who are you? What are you doing?" Ka whipped around to see Danny standing in the doorway. He realized that here was the help he needed.

"You're that cat spirit that Mairi and everyone followed into the Faerie Realm. Where are they? What did you do with them? How did you get here?" Danny was starting to sound defensive.

Ka put his front paws on the desk and stretched, "It's okay. Everyone's okay . . . sort of." He proceeded to tell Danny about the giant and jumping through a one-way passage out of the Faerie Realm and ending up on Skye in the past, and then about Anne getting captured by a witch hunt. "I'm here to try to find a map of the MacDonald's holding on Skye to hopefully figure out where they would have taken Anne, so we can rescue her and get back to the Faerie Realm before it's too late."

Danny looked stunned. "Uh . . . okay. I can help with that." He sat down at the computer. After several minutes he found a map that would help them. While Ka studied it, Danny stared at him. "So, how come you came here? To this house?"

Ka froze. He reflexively looked back at the sleeping form of Tobias. Danny looked at Tobias, too, then back at Ka. His eyes narrowed. "Oh . . . oh! Wow! YOU are Tobias?"

Ka stared at Danny. "Please don't tell anyone. It's . . . embarrassing . . . I guess. I don't know . . . "

Danny nodded, "I won't tell anyone right away, but you have to and soon. Your mom is a mess about you not waking up for nearly three weeks. If she knew you were roaming about in your spirit form, she'd probably feel better."

"You're right," Ka nodded, thinking about his mother weeping when he'd first arrived in this room. "I have to hurry back to Jamie and Mairi. I will tell her about . . . this," he waved a paw back and forth between the two of them, "but later. I'll explain everything when we return because I have a plan for healing myself. That will make all of this better."

"Yeah, but is it true? Do you really have a plan for healing your body?"

Ka gave Danny a feline smile, "but of course!" then disappeared.

PROTECTED

Isle of Skye, Scotland
October 17th, present

Mairi sat up, stiff and cold next to the blackened pit where the fire had gone out. She glanced over at Jamie who stretched and rubbed his eyes. She sighed, "I don't want to be a witch. Druid is a much safer title. Why did you tell me such a sad tale?"

"You fell asleep before I could tell you the most important part. Even sadder still, in this time where the massacre only happened a few decades ago, the Highlanders are extremely wary of witches and ready to banish, through an unfair trial of drowning or burning, any who are called witch for fear of another massacre. But, in our time when hundreds of years have passed after this tragic event, it has been proven that the old woman meant her clan no harm and in fact tried her best to protect them. For, you see, part of the tale that only some knew was that the old woman went into the burnt ruins of their homes and sought out their chieftain's *claidheamh-mór,* his great sword, what we call a Claymore in English. She carried it to the nearby loch and tossed it in, proclaiming that as long as his sword lay undisturbed at the bottom of the lake, no MacDonald warriors would die in battle."

"Did it work?" Mairi asked.

"It did!" Jamie's face lit up in the orange glow of dawn. "Archaeologists researched it and found that not a single MacDonald was listed as having died at subsequent battles, yet as soon as the sword was dredged from the loch in 1916, so the MacDonald's clansmen of Glencoe fell in the following battles. She had been protecting them for centuries beyond the Glencoe Massacre."

Mairi smiled at that, though bitterness sat in her heart. "How unjust to blame a massacre on a woman for being a witch, as if witch were a bad thing. It seems a witch is as good as a druid, better perhaps because witches heal while druids rile up their people in big political battles." Shaking her fists at the cold fire pit, a spark spit from Mairi's hands, her red hair brightening beneath her changing aura. She leapt to her feet.

"I didn't ask to be called druid! I didn't ask to be called witch! I didn't ask for any of this! I know my magic helped our Gran, but magic is also what cursed our Gran in the first place. Because of magic, Anne was taken as prisoner by druids and Highlanders, Uncle James has been kidnapped by faeries, and I think our dad is held prisoner as a changeling. None of this is good." With each accusation against magic, Mairi's hands glowed brighter orange, sparks of electricity leaping from her hands and hitting the cavern walls. Her still-wet druid robes began to steam as her heated body dried the cloth from within.

Ka stepped into view, lavender-blue eyes glowing, speaking in a soothing voice sounding almost like a purr. "Mairi, share your heat with your brother. Put your magic to good use. He is cold. Help him."

Mairi blinked her eyes, taking a moment to comprehend someone else was in the cave with her. Finally letting Ka's words sink in, she looked at her brother who was indeed shivering uncontrollably. Closing her eyes in concentration and swallowing her anger, she focused on visualizing a bubble of energy, picturing a sun-like ball of warmth, and as she felt it surround herself, she imagined it expanding to encompass her brother as well.

Peeking under her eyelids, she saw that Jamie was inside her bubble and that steam was rising from his discarded robes on the ground beside him, as well as rising off his clothes and backpack. His cheeks took on a healthy rose color and within minutes they were both dry. Mairi dropped her hands to her sides and sank to her knees, thoroughly drained.

"Very good!" Ka exclaimed. "Now you help her," he instructed Jamie, "dig out some of your survival food, protein preferably, and feed her. She's wiped out."

After rummaging through his backpack, Jamie brought a piece of beef jerky to Mairi's lips. With a shaky hand, she took the jerky and bit into it, chewing slowly.

"We'll rest here a little longer, then make our way North to Castle Duntulm, the MacDonald's current home where they should be holding Anne for trial."

Mairi nodded her head, sitting up and habitually running her hand over her necklace, wishing the Trinity Knot was powerful on its own, without the Silver Faerie Chanter so she could whisk them away. Feeling the second necklace she wore, the stone with the Witch's Knot for Protection, Mairi wondered at the irony.

Did my Witch's Knot protect me from being taken as a witch with Anne? Did it protect me from the Witch Hunts? If only I'd believed in its power, I would have insisted Anne was given one, too. But maybe I can at least attempt to rescue her, Mairi thought, gazing down at her inexplicably powerful hands, *if I can simply manage to get angry at just the right moment,* shaking her head at the frustration she felt.

GHOSTS
Isle of Skye, Scotland
October 17th, 1700s

Anne was pulled down off the back of the horse without any decency or decorum. No longer used to supporting her weight after riding hard all night, her legs buckled. She fell into the horse manure-seasoned mud puddle on her hands and knees, only to be yanked back up by the crook of her elbow and barked at in Gaelic.

"I can walk on my own, dinnae ye ken? Let me be!" Anne wrested her arm from the Highlander's surprised grip, only to be grabbed at the nape of her neck.

"We'll nae be letting ye go, witch! Our ArchDruid will nae take kindly tae our losing his bait." The Highlander cackled in glee at his joke.

"Take her below, tae the dungeons. Ewan will be tae see her shortly," a second Highlander shouted across the muddy courtyard of the MacDonald castle.

Made to walk like a cornhusk doll maneuvered by a

toddler, Anne put one foot in front of the other and soon found herself in a dark tunnel smelling of human feces and urine. Tears sprang to her eyes from the odorous gases. A barred door slid open with a loud clang, echoing through the stone passageway, and Anne was shoved into the tiny dark room. Locking the door with a clank and a click, her Highlander escort disappeared back the way they had come.

Only then did Anne sink to a seated position and allow herself to crumble, the tears flowing readily down her filthy face. When she'd sat like that for what felt like hours, though there was no way for her to truly know as there weren't any windows to let in the movement of the sun and the moon, Anne straightened her spine and wiped her face with a corner of her tartan scarf.

I have to stay strong. Mairi and Jamie, maybe even Ka, will do their best to help me. I know they will, even if . . . even if Mairi is unhappy with me. Tears threatened to spill again at the fear that her cousins might just turn their back on her. *Nae! We are family and they will no abandon me.*

With this resolve she set to checking her pockets and pouches tied to her waist and around her neck. She always carried them packed with every dried herb she could find. Certain there would be pennyroyal or lavender or something sweet smelling to counter the pungent odors surrounding her, she finally found a sprig of pennyroyal to rub on her upper lip. *Ah . . . at least I can breathe a little better now.*

More tired than she could ever remember feeling, even when she'd been up all night encouraging a baby to enter the world for the first time, she laid down on the edge of her tartan and fell into a deep slumber, only to have a haunting sound drift into her sleep deprived mind, pressuring her to wake once again.

"Woooaaaah . . . woooaaah . . . "

CLANG CLANG CLANG

Anne sat up with a start. The moaning and wailing, the banging and clanging, were so loud she pressed her hands to her ears.

"What is this?" she asked the darkness of the dungeon. "Are the ghosts protesting their fates . . . ?" Then she remembered all the stories she'd heard on her treks to the village spring and the occasional market visit. Even the women whom she attended in childbirth would tell her stories. *Castle Duntulm* is *haunted! The hungry Hugh MacDonald who died of starvation in the dungeon...*

"Woooaaaah . . . woooaaah . . . woooaaah"

Anne stopped thinking. Stopped breathing. She whipped her head around, wide-eyed, though there was little she could see in the dark of the room. Frozen in place, she dared not move, feared taking even a shallow breath.

Is this the dungeon room where he died? She did not risk answering her own question, afraid to consider the possibility of it being true. She began singing under her breath a lullaby her mother often sang to her as a wee lass . . .

"Baloo Baleeri
Baloo Baleeri
Baloo Baleeri
Baloo Balee."

"Waaah! . . . Waaah! . . . Waaah!"

The faint cries of a baby wailing were followed by a woman's hysterical weeping, filtering in from outside.

A soft glow seeped through the wall beyond the dungeon bars and the sounds grew louder and louder, coming closer and closer.

Anne whimpered and pulled her tartan over her head. *This must be the ghost of the chieftain's babe who was dropped from a castle window, and his nursemaid who was punished by being set adrift at sea. True . . . the stories are all true . . .* Anne stuffed the wool scarf into her ears, pressing her palms harder still against the cloth, and curled into a tight ball, rocking on the floor, continuing her lullaby about keeping nasty fae spirits away.

> "Gang awa' peerie faeries,
> Gang awa' peerie faeries,
> Gang awa' peerie faeries,
> Frae oor ben noo."

She sang to herself until she fell into a fitful sleep, dreaming of her mother's weeping and her sister's wailing for the return of her da.

CONFINED
Isle of Skye, Scotland
October 17th, 1700s

Recovered from the incident in the cave, Mairi and Jamie made their way back towards the Inn, the only direction they knew to go without getting lost. On the way, Ka described the map he had memorized. To reach Duntulm Castle, they could bypass the peak where the Old Man of Storr stood, but they would still need to pass through the Quiraing, a series of steep crags and deep glens with barely a trail to follow. As Anne had been carried off on horseback, the chances of catching up with her and her captors after their overnight delay in the cave were nil. Mairi suggested stopping by the Inn and "borrowing" a horse for their trip.

"But can you ride?" Jamie asked. "Because I know I can't."

Mairi smacked his shoulder. "Don't you remember I

took those lessons when I was 12?" Jamie looked at her blankly, rubbing his shoulder. Mairi sighed, "All my friends were riding horses, so I just had to have lessons for my Christmas present?" At his shoulder shrug, she threw up her hands in exasperation. "Well, I did! So, I'll take the reins and you just hold on behind me. Ka can sit on the horse with us, I suppose."

"No, I can't," Ka responded. "I have to return to my body. It weakens the longer I'm away, and the jump out of the Faerie Realm cost me more time than I expected. Usually I can count on not being detained in the Faerie Realm for too long. *Cali's charm usually prevents that. It must be losing its magic from constant use.* I'll be leaving soon, and you'll have to just head due North to reach Duntulm Castle. I'll check back in a day and see where you are."

Mairi was stunned at this revelation, but took a deep breath and nodded her head. "What's our plan, beyond finding a horse to borrow for the day, what then?"

"We have to see if Anne is being held at Duntulm, and if she is, we have to break her free," Jamie pointed out.

"Okay, IF she is there, how will we rescue her?" Mairi fiddled with her necklace. "If only we had the bagpipes, we could whisk Anne away and return to the Fairy Grove and escape back into the Faerie Realm."

"Yeah . . . " Jamie agreed. "I think we don't even need the bagpipes in our hands. As long as someone is playing the traveling tune while we are wishing to be somewhere using the necklace, we can travel. Isn't that what happened the very first time we used it, that time on the bus?"

Mairi nodded her head, "Hey! Yeah! That's true! Granda was in the field near his house playing the bagpipes and we were on the bus and we wished to be at Granda's already. But . . . this is through time . . . does that matter? And how would we tell Danny to play?"

"I can go to Danny and ask him to play at the exact

moment you're wishing to be at the Faerie Grove," Ka volunteered.

"Okay . . . but is it really the best time to test this theory when we're surrounded by druids hungry to kill a witch?" Mairi shook out her fiery red hair and ran her fingers through it, getting tangled in the multitude of knots.

"I'll go right now and ask him to play the tune. You could try wishing to be at Duntulm Castle." Ka paced back and forth, getting more anxious as time ticked by.

"I don't know what Duntulm Castle looks like . . . " Mairi sighed.

"I don't think we have to know what a place looks like, but it increases our chances of arriving at the right place if we can visualize it." Jamie smiled. "And I studied it when I was studying Skye, so I can hold the necklace and make the wish."

Reluctantly, Mairi took off the Trinity Knot necklace and let Jamie hold it. Then she held his other hand. "Okay, no point wasting time and no point borrowing a horse if we can just magically wish ourselves past the Quiraing. How long do we stand here wishing? How long for you to find Danny?"

Ka stretched, "If he is where I think he is, seconds. I can't return right away to let you know if anything went wrong in finding Danny, I need to return to my body. So, I guess if it doesn't work right away, then keep walking to the Inn."

They all agreed, and Ka disappeared. Jamie and Mairi stood in the glen and waited, holding hands with Jamie focusing on the image of Duntulm Castle he had seen in a book and waited.

Ka returned to his room, which was as silent as a tomb except for the mechanical sounds of the feeding tube and breathing apparatus. He'd been gone too long. He took a quick gander through the house and determined that only his mother was home, asleep in the arm chair in the sitting room by the kitchen, a big medical book open in her lap. *I can't wait any longer. When Danny returns, maybe I can muster up the strength to talk to him and return to Mairi and Jamie to help.*

Then he silently returned to his room, jumping on Tobias' chest, allowing his spirit to melt back into his prison confinement of flesh and bones.

CAGED

Isle of Skye, Scotland
October 17th, 1700s

Anne woke again, this time to the dungeon doors being pulled open and the light of a torch blinding her.

"Awake, witch! The Archdruid is ready tae see ye." She could almost make out the burly form of a Highlander behind the blinding light. Slowly maneuvering to her knees and then to her feet, she stretched the kinks out of her sore body as quick as she could, but not quick enough. The man's big hand wrapped around her upper arm and yanked her in the directions of the dungeon hall. They climbed the stairs back up to the castle courtyard where a little stone house was nestled right in the center. Blinking in the brightness of the morning sun, Anne stumbled as she was shuffled across the cobblestone walkway leading to the entry of the little house.

She eyed a great big cage that was being unloaded from the back of a wagon by a blacksmith dressed in his customary leather apron, and a shiver ran down her spine. As it was dropped to the ground, Ewan MacDonald stepped out of the doorway of the little house, the MacDonald Chieftain following close behind.

"So, this is the MacLeod lass ye are in a bunch about? She's a wee little lassie. Witch, ye say?" The chieftain looked mildly interested.

"Aye, she is a witch, I daresay, for she is known far and wide for her healing talents, though any person of God knows only physicians should be doing the healing. We have the good men of MacLean to do our clan's healing. A witch's healing is a dangerous gamble, fer what she does in goodness such as bringing a wee bairn into the world must be paid tenfold to the devil with feeble cattle or other wickedness. Aye, it is best we do away with all the witches before they ruin our fair isle." Ewan looked over at Anne with a malicious glare as he made this speech, a triumphant grin plastered across his face.

"Aye, it is true, for a witch it was that caused the MacDonalds of Glencoe's chief to be unable to sign the treaty in time, and so it was that the Campbells were set against my clan kinsmen. Do whatever it is ye must with her," the chieftain waved his beefy hand in Anne's direction, "but I must be off to check that my crofters aren't cheating me. Let's away, men." Several Highlanders got into their saddles along with their chief and galloped across the soggy wet moor.

Ewan pointed at the cage on the ground in front of him. "In there she goes. We'll leave her until her Wild Witchy friend arrives to try to save her, then I'll have the both of 'em."

Anne was shoved into the cage, just big enough that she could almost stand, though she had a crook in her back. Grabbing the bars, Anne let out a moan. "Let me go. I have nae done anything bad! Witch is a lie. A druid heals with herbs. How is what I do so different?"

"Careful, you'll take to admitting you are a witch," Ewan wagged his sausage-sized finger at her. "Rest well. We'll be gathering soon as we fetch ourselves another witch, a red-headed one this time." He slammed his palm down on the cage, rattling Anne's bones, his laughter booming out of the courtyard and across the ocean below.

HORSE RAID

Isle of Skye, Scotland
October 17th, 1700s

After Mairi and Jamie had waited several minutes, they sighed and silently agreed that relying on Danny to play the bagpipes sometime in the future wasn't working and their plan to steal a horse was the best hope they had. Checking that no one was around, they were about to run across the Inn's yard when Mairi stopped Jamie.

"Wait! I have one more idea. Just give me a minute." She found a rock to sit on and stilled her mind. She vaguely registered her brother sitting down beside her, dribbling a handful of little jagged stones through his fingers. Mairi thought about the rain the night before, the lingering drops of water on the tips of the grass glistening in the morning sun. She sought out the smell of the ocean in the distance, and she imagined great billowing folds of mariner's fog rolling in like a thick gray blanket covering her on a winter's night. A chill ran up her spine, starting at the base where it touched the rock and it ran out her legs and arms until her toes and fingers tingled. She could feel the fog building to the east, the water-laden ground calling its salty cousin.

Mairi snapped her eyes open. "Hurry! We have about an hour."

Jumping up, Jamie followed suit, and they ran across the rocky terrain back towards the Inn, slowing down only when the tracks of other people drew closer and they could hear the shouts of people nearby.

"Careful Mairi, we don't need to get caught now." Jamie grabbed his sister's hand and pulled her back. "We should go around back of the stall and see about taking a horse that way."

Picking their way through the mud and manure, their druid's robes more brown than white at this point, they came to the back of the stall. From this point of view, they could see the boy who was supposed to be mucking out the stalls, only he was just lying on a stack of hay asleep; his tartan scarf had been discarded by his side.

"Good," Mairi whispered to Jamie. "I'll get his horse, you get his scarf, we need different clothes now, so we aren't recognized if we are seen."

The horses in the back must belong to the Innkeeper because they don't have any harnesses on, and the ones in the front of the stall are still harnessed as if the owners will leave soon. If I take a horse from the front, I'll be seen. If I take a horse from the back, I have to tack it and that might wake up the boy. Deciding the boy would be easier to deal with than the men in the Inn, she carefully pulled a harness off the wall and found what she hoped was the nicest mare, leading her out into the sunlight momentarily breaking through the heavy mist.

Jamie followed behind. "No saddle?" he whispered.

"No! We need to hurry." Slipping the bit into the horse's mouth, she pulled the strap over her ears and buckled it under her jaw. "Okay, we'll use this . . . "

"Hey!"

Mairi and Jamie looked over their shoulders to see the boy standing in the stall door staring at them.

"Oh crud! Use the fence to get on the horse!" she whispered harshly at her brother, not wanting to alert the attendants in the Inn. Jamie scrambled onto the horse's back and Mairi followed to do the same. The boy lunged at her, grabbing at her foot. She kicked him in the head with her other foot, knocking him to the ground.

Scrambling onto the horse's back, Mairi nudged the horse in the ribs and pulled her head to the left around the stall and towards the rocky terrain of the Quiraing Mountains. As they galloped into the crevices and crags, the fog grew thicker, enveloping them in a cloak of invisibility while the boy's shouts faded behind them.

The route proved harder than they had imagined. The fog had lifted hours ago, and they were able to keep an eye on the sun and know what direction they were headed, but the journey was long and windy as they made their way around one rocky outcrop after another. The steep climb was easy for the horse, but every time the terrain dropped into a glen, the horse slowed her steps and Mairi was certain they could travel faster on foot. They were grateful to be on horseback and not on foot, but the number of times their horse slipped on loose rocks made them nervous. They considered returning to the muddy roadways they were attempting to parallel, which was nearly impossible to do with the towering rock formations causing them to wind this way and that, but they didn't dare return to the road for fear that if they did a traveler would pass by and see them, so they stuck to the precarious pathway.

Finally, as the sun crept past noon, they saw the sparkle of sunlight gleaming on ocean waves and the towering walls of Duntulm Castle stood proud in the distance. "Please let our cousin be held there. And please let us be able to escape with her at our side."

As they neared the much-used track stretching between the castle and the inn they had left behind, Mairi and Jamie slid off of the horse and let her go, hoping she would return to her home, so that they hadn't actually added horse thievery to their growing list of wrong-doings. Finding a gully to hide in, they lay down to wait for Ka's promised return, as the sun was beginning to set.

ALONE

Isle of Skye, Scotland
October 18th, 1700s

Mairi lay in the gully a ways off from where she could see Duntulm Castle standing guard over the cliff above the Atlantic Ocean. She was waiting for Jamie to come back from sneaking around trying to find where Anne was being held. He had decided they needed to have some information before Ka showed up, in case Danny was going to be able to play the bagpipes after all. They still hoped the bagpipes would work and that Ka simply hadn't found Danny the previous day. They were also trying to come up with a plan B.

Mairi wasn't sure she liked her little brother being on his own this way, but the people in the Inn had been looking for Mairi and Anne, not Jamie, so he stood a better chance of being safe, though he had most likely been added to the Most Wanted list after being seen at the Inn. Mairi clenched her fists, frustrated that her little brother was being put in danger.

Nevertheless, wrapped in his druid robes and draped with the stolen MacDonald tartan from the stable boy, Jamie appeared to be a young druid apprentice, which was how he planned to identify himself. Though, if he spoke, he'd have to also claim to have been sent from an American family and the whole plan just sounded insane to Mairi. "Just stay hidden," she had implored her little brother. She could tell Jamie was enjoying playing a bigger role in rescuing their cousin, and she knew he still waited with great hopes for his own powers to kick in. At almost thirteen-years-old, his fifteenth birthday felt like a long way off for him.

Anne squatted in a corner of the cage, watching the people of Duntulm Castle trek back and forth across the inner courtyard, young boys running errands from one end of the castle to the other, young men sparring with swords as they bragged about how many English soldiers and Cameron Highlanders they would have killed if allowed to fight for the honor of their Glencoe kin, scullery maids hauling buckets of fresh water to what Anne imagined was the kitchen. Every drop that sloshed out of the buckets reminded Anne how very thirsty she was with the unusually hot Autumn day warming her head. She draped her scarf over her forehead and shoulders, preferring the warmth of the wool to the glare of the sun.

Every so often a handful of wild highland children, boys and girls alike, would run to her cage and rattle the bars or throw pebbles at her, taunting her with sing-song chants of "Witch! Witch!" She simply smiled sadly at them, knowing they were just wee bairns imitating the fears of their elders who had conveniently forgotten how many times women like her had saved their loved ones from death by illness or infection.

She stared down at the ground now, tired of seeing the

good and the bad in the people surrounding her. Her own dear baby sister's face came to her and she wiped back a tear that escaped from her longing to hold Carrie's chubby body in her arms again. *Please let Wills be taking good care of her and our Maw. He is a simpleton, but he knows how to hunt and cook a rabbit. Surely, they are nae hungry, and Samhain is only a couple of weeks away. We will be a family again, soon.*

She wondered, again, what was happening to her Da in the faerie realm, a captive of the Unseelie Court. *I pray to the goddesses that he is in bliss and nae knowing the worries I have for our family, and for myself. I know Mairi has it in her to free me, I will hold my faith in her, in family. And we will be at the ready when the Wild Hunt winds its way out of the Wild Wood, where ever that might be. We will rescue my da and . . .* she paused, *. . . and myself.* She tried to forget she had to be rescued first, but every time a pebble hit her, or her cage bars clanged, she was jolted back to her reality.

"Och! Enough! Be off with you!" She lost her cool and stared up into the pale blue eyes of a little girl in filthy clothes and bare feet. The girl laughed a harsh laugh, showing her gap-toothed grin belying her age. "Aye, ye are jus' a wee bairn, nae much more than six. Dinnae choose unkindness child." The child laughed again and grabbed the bars to shake the cage, though her small strength didn't budge it at all. Anne stared at the child, and then she saw someone new behind her, in the shadows of one of the outer walls of the castle.

Squinting in the bright sunlight, she thought . . . hoped with all her heart . . . could it be? But yes, it had to be Jamie. *Oh, be careful little cousin,* Anne worried. He held up a hand in a half wave, and she nodded her head to indicate she had seen him. Then he slipped away, and she was alone again in a sea of strangers.

Jamie returned to his sister with his report. "She's in a cage in the courtyard. The place is bustling with so much happening that I slipped in and out without a single question. I think I can do it again and hold her hand and wish to be away if Ka comes with me and disappears to tell Danny at the exact moment."

"Won't I be doing anything?" Mairi asked, feeling jealousy seep into her bones, . . . jealousy and uselessness.

"Mairi," Jamie looked at her in exasperation. "Of course, you will do something. You will keep a look out and as soon as we are at your side with Anne, we will have to disappear again. You'll do your magic stuff to make us disappear. Will it be fog again? Or a bubble of energy?"

Mairi nodded, chagrined. "You're smarter than I give you credit for. I . . . I'm sorry I keep getting pissy when it comes to Anne."

Jamie patted her shoulder, "You're too insecure for your own good. I wish you could see yourself the way others see you."

Mairi wanted to ask how it was others saw her; her imagination could take it in so many directions, but Ka arrived at that moment just as he'd promised, and her question would have to wait.

"Danny's ready, we have to hurry. What's the plan?" Ka asked. Jamie quickly explained what he'd relayed to Mairi and before Mairi was ready, they had left to enter the castle. She stilled her body and meditated on what magic she would conjure up to do her part in rescuing Anne.

RESCUE

Isle of Skye, Scotland
October 18ᵗʰ, 1700s

Ewan paced in the chieftain's little house in the courtyard, watching the witch in her cage through a window, waiting for the news that would tell him the red-haired witch who was responsible for killing his father had arrived. He was sure she would attempt a rescue. *It's only been a little more than a day. Surely, she'll come. The messenger who came earlier brought reports of a stolen horse at the Inn where this witch was captured, and the rider was a boy with blonde hair and a young woman with long red hair. They must be on their way.*

He stared outside, watching as little children threw rocks and poked sticks through the cage, as grown women mocked the witch with the water they carried, as warriors stopped to curse at her, and the witch did nothing, said so little. *How dare she sit there so confident? She ought to be crying out for help, begging for mercy. Instead she sits calmly, as if she is waiting for something to happen.*

Ewan stared at her small build, black hair, matted and dirty, wide eyes that glanced around shining green in the sunlight, and her MacLeod tartan scarf draped over her forehead and shoulders. *Of course, the MacLeods would harbor a witch!* He spat a gooey glob of phlegm in the witch's direction as he thought this.

As he watched his spittle land in a mud puddle, a cold wind blew in from the ocean and danced through the courtyard, pulling at scarves and kilts alike, twirling in the mud of the busy courtyard and sending bits of straw and grass flying into the air.

Ewan's loose hair fell into his eyes, and as he stared, the air began to shimmer and then there was a young druid where none had stood seconds before, and a black cat shining ghostly in the sunlight. Ewan hesitated for a moment, barely registering that the very thing he'd been waiting for was actually happening.

"Guards! To the witch!" he commanded as he threw open the door and ran towards the cage.

Anne whipped her head up and lunged to her feet as Jamie materialized before her eyes.

"Grab my hand," he yelled, and Anne did so without hesitation.

As the small tornado blew around them, Jamie whispered under his breath and they were gone from the cage, landing in the grass beside Mairi who was sitting still as a stone, looking in the direction of the castle. Jamie reached over and grabbed Mairi's hand and he yelled, "We wish to go to the Faerie Grove!"

As they dematerialized for the second time in less than a minute, Anne heard a guttural growl rise up from behind the castle walls. Ewan knew she had escaped, and he was very angry indeed.

Anne landed rougher than the first time, her mind

overwhelmed by the squeezing in and out of space, and lay sprawled out on her back, the first full body stretch she'd had since being moved to the cage earlier that day.

Jamie nudged her with his hand from where he sat beside her. "You okay?"

"Aye," she answered, and grinned at him. "Ye did it! With Mairi and Ka, ye did it! Thanks be to Lugh and Brigid!" She looked around for Mairi and saw she was also lying down. Mairi gave her a half-hearted smile as Jamie threw her a granola bar.

"You're safe," Mairi whispered. "I'm so sorry you don't have one of these to protect you." She held up the Witch's Knot pendant. "We really have to get you one."

"It's fine, Mairi, I have got cousins instead." Frowning then, Anne looked around. "But where is Ka? I saw him with you, Jamie, when ye first arrived beside my cage. Did he nae travel with us?"

Jamie jumped to his feet and looked all around him, then ran around every tree and bush nearby.

Mairi struggled to sit up, staring into every shadow. "Ka?" she asked. Mairi turned frightened eyes to Anne. "We can't get back to my time without Ka. If we enter the Faerie Realm without him, we could end up stuck there for hundreds of years, or a single day, there's no way to know, and who knows what place we would end up at. Ka is the only one who seems to know how to control such things. Has he just left us?"

Jamie, who hadn't stopped looking, stepped out from behind the nearest Oak Tree, the one that guarded the faerie door in the mound. "He's here, but he seems . . . he's . . . something isn't right."

Anne and Mairi did their best to hurry to Jamie's side. When they looked behind the Oak, they saw Ka lying on the ground, opaque and immaterial as a ghost.

"What's wrong with him?" Mairi asked.

"He has nae enough energy to sustain his astral form,

and he is too far removed from his body to return," Anne pointed out. "He is dying."

JUMPSTART
Isle of Skye, Scotland
October 18th, 1700s

"We have to do something!" Mairi cried out, feeling guilty that she'd jumped to the conclusion that Ka had abandoned them. "Do you know what to do for him?" She looked at Anne, tears welling in her eyes. Brushing them away with the back of her hand, she swallowed her sorrow and fear. *I am not going to start being a crier now, not after all I've been through.*

"Mairi," Jamie looked at her sadly. "First, remember what Ka told you the other night in the cave. You need to eat that granola bar. You must be so tired from using so much energy making that tornado at Duntulm Castle."

"I can't eat at a time like this!" She growled at her brother, then grudgingly took a bite because she knew he was right.

Anne stared at Mairi, her wide eyes narrowing to little slits.

"What!?" Mairi sputtered through peanut butter and oats, automatically reaching for her backpack and water bottle to wash down the sticky goo in her mouth.

Anne looked down at Ka and back at Mairi. "Ka needs energy," she said. "Ye have energy, an excess of it. That is one of the reasons for yer magic, because ye practically overflow with energy, even if ye are depleted after using it. But I suspect that is only because ye have nae the control yet."

"I don't understand what you mean," Mairi said.

"I understand," Jamie said. "Like a baby rattle snake who has the same amount of venom as a grown rattle snake, but because it's a baby and lacks control, it pumps all of its venom into its victim rather than just a little bit like the grown snakes can do."

Mairi gulped down the cold water, swishing some in her mouth before speaking. "Okay, I can see that I use energy, and might have more than someone without magic, but I must have the same amount of energy as you, right?" Noticing Anne was eyeing her water bottle, Mairi handed it to her, watching as she glugged down several gulps.

"Oh jeez! I bet you're starving, too. I feel so stupid!" Jamie pulled out another granola bar and handed it to his cousin, who ripped the wrapper off. Pausing, she looked at Ka and sat down beside him.

"Sit by me. I will explain before I eat this." Anne patted the wet moss and roots on the ground next to her.
Mairi and Jamie sat down, finishing their granola bars and drinking water. Mairi was starting to feel stronger.

"Mairi, when I look at ye, yer like one of those torches ye have attached next to the front door of yer house. I think ye call it a light bulb. When it was dark out and ye touched that button thing, the light was so bright my eyes were blinded. But, when it was daytime, I noticed the light was nae so bright, barely noticeable. So, it is like that with ye, ye kin?" Anne paused and ate a bite of her granola bar.

"No, I don't know what you mean, and I think we have to hurry. Ka is getting fainter." Mairi desperately wanted to pet the black cat, but in spirit form he was like a phantom.

Swallowing her water, Anne continued, "Aye, ye will help him in a minute. Ye have to be back to full energy to do it."

"But how can you tell if she's at full energy?" Jamie asked, impatience filling his normally calm tone. Mairi could tell he really liked Ka.

"Because, she usually shines like that light at night, so bright it nearly blinds me. Even non-magical humans can sense her brightness, I see them awkwardly look away. It mostly shows in the copper gleam of yer hair and the shine in yer eyes. I have some of the Sight, the ability to see faeries just a tiny bit in our world, from time to time, so I can see yer energy, and it is getting brighter since I first met ye. It dims once ye have used it, but brightens pretty quickly. Like now, so ye are ready. We have to heal Ka."

Anne took Mairi's hands and told her to hover them over Ka. Anne did the same thing and Mairi imitated her form. "Jamie, you put your hands here, too."

"But I don't have any magic," Jamie calmly stated, though Mairi thought she noticed a hint of disappointment.

"Ye do! How else do ye think ye were able to use the Trinity Knot necklace? And I can see yer light beginning to shine very faintly around yer body." Anne grabbed Jamie's hands and pulled him over to Ka.

"Of course!" Mairi nearly shouted, "I can't believe we didn't realize that, too. But he's only 12 . . . ?"

"I was 13 when I came into my powers." Anne's statement was so simple, but left so many questions for Mairi, questions that had to wait; Ka needed their attention now.

"We cannae physically touch him, like we would if his physical body were next to us, but this will do. Energy hovers around a body anyway. Now, quiet yer mind and concentrate on seeing energy pass from yer hands to Ka. I will do the same and we will give him some of our energy."

Mairi nodded and Jamie said, "It's like jumpstarting the battery on a car. The cables connect the battery in one car to the battery in the other car and energy . . . electricity passes through."

"Shush!!" Anne's stern look caused Jamie to clamp his mouth shut, and Mairi quieted her mind. She visualized the sunlight reaching through the trees and flowing into her head and shoulders, into her spine, and passing down through her arms into her hands. She imagined little lightning bolts flashing from each of her fingertips and passing into Ka's astral form. Just as she saw this with her mind's eye, she heard a loud 'ZAP!' and a jolt ran through her body.

Her eyes flew open and she saw Ka blink his eyes, every spirit hair on his astral form standing up like he was one of those cartoon cats. Mairi pressed her hands over her ears as he let out an ear-splitting yowl.

"What happened to me?" Ka screeched.

"You almost died, buddy," Jamie said in the same voice he used on Peaches when she was afraid of the neighbor's dog. "We zapped you back to life, like the doctors do in the ER."

"Well, thank you . . . I guess . . . " Ka sat down and groomed his fur, bursts of electricity occasionally zipping off his body. Jamie, Anne, and Mairi sat down to eat and drink while everyone tried to regain their calm, though Jamie had a Cheshire cat grin plastered to his face.

PATHS DIVIDED

The Faerie Realm
Outside of Time

After several minutes, Mairi pointed out they really had to get out of the Faerie Grove because Ewan was most definitely going to be searching for them there, and soon. That kicked everyone into high gear and they grabbed their backpacks. Jamie handed Anne hers since she had become separated from it when she was captured. They ran to the Faerie Door and Mairi was about to fix up the altar they'd set there back in August, the last time they had visited, when Ka walked right into the hillside. Blinking Mairi pushed her hand to where she remembered the door being, and it went right through the soil. Pulling her hand back out, she saw that it wasn't dirty at all.

"How...?" she sputtered.

Ka stuck his head back through. "Come on. If you've been into the Faerie Realm before and the current Queen, in this case the Seelie Queen, Titania as you call her, wants you to enter, then all you have to do is walk through. Though," he added, "it can't hurt to refill the water in the alter and clean it up a little."

Mairi nodded and did just that, as fast as she could. Jamie spied his Sgian Dubh, that he'd left outside the faerie entrance the last time they'd passed through. Sticking his dagger into the ground near the faerie entrance was supposed to ensure that they didn't come under the spell of the Faeries, but it hadn't mattered because they were part faerie, so their magic worked differently on them than on regular humans. Wiping off the mud, he put it into a pocket of his backpack.

"Okay, that's good. Let's go!" called Ka's head, the only part of him sticking out of the faerie door in the mound. "We've got to hurry now."

Mairi stood up and stepped through the door, moving out of the way, so Anne and Jamie could follow. Anne held both Jamie's and Mairi's hands, so that seemed to earn her a pass. It should have been dark in the tunnel, as there weren't any windows or lights, and technically the tunnels were underground in the Earth, not quite in the Faerie Realm and not quite on Planet Earth anymore, an in-between place. And just as before, Mairi and Jamie glowed in the dark. Anne did too, because they were all descended from the Seelie Faeire Queen, but this time Mairi lit up like a full faerie herself, minus the wings and Jamie was a little brighter than before, though not as bright as Anne.

"It is as I said: your powers are increasing," Anne smiled at her cousin.

They turned and began the walk to the Seelie throne room, which wasn't a room at all, but more of an outdoor patio throne room. Realizing that they would probably be coming through the most obvious entryway, the one in plain view of the entire faerie court, Mairi asked, "How will we sneak past the court this time?"

"I dinnae want to sneak through," Anne said. "I want to

meet the Queen this time. She is my distant grandmother, too, and I would like to talk to her like ye once did, ye ken?"

"I ken," Jamie grinned.

Mairi looked away from her happy brother. *I do not want to stop and talk to Titania. I want to get on with finding my dad.*

"Ahem . . . " Ka sat down in the dirt ahead of them. "I will not be continuing on. I must return to my body for a day or two. You know to follow the stream through the Unseelie Court's territory where it will come out at the sea. There is a meadow along the shore where changeling humans live when not needed by their faerie family anymore. If your dad isn't there, Mairi, they will know where he is, IF he is a changeling."

Mairi raised her eyebrows at Ka, and threw her hands up in disgust. "Great! Now you're abandoning me, too. And just how am I supposed to get past the mermaids and the giants and whatever else is lurking in those woods?"

"Mairi, it will be okay, better even if you're alone. You can hide more easily, and I promise I'll catch up with you just as soon as I can." Ka even purred in an attempt to sound more soothing.

Mairi looked at Jamie and he shrugged his shoulders. "I just want to talk to Titania for a minute. You could wait for me and then I'll go with you."

"If she sees us she won't let us go off exploring the Faerie Realm. But, whatever! I'm just going to go alone," and before anyone could say anything more, Mairi marched past them and down the winding path leading into the faerie realm.

I know I'm being grumpy for no reason, she thought, *but I can't help it. I'm just so tired of solving other problems when all I want to do is solve the one involving my dad. Jamie should want that, too. What's so important that he has to stop and chat with Titania? Geez! Let him stay with*

Anne, for all I care.

The fading glow that was Mairi disappeared within minutes as the path dipped lower and lower towards the Seelie Faerie Queen's throne room. Ka stretched his cat body and disappeared from view, too. Anne sighed and looked at Jamie.

"Ye dinnae have to stay with me. I will be okay. I think Mairi really needs you," she pointed out.

"I know, but I just wanted her to wait a minute. I want to talk with Titania for a bit. Maybe Mairi is right, though. Maybe the Queen *will* stop me from catching up with her." Jamie kicked at the ground, the tip of his shoe emitting a faint light that arced through the dark following the path of his foot.

Anne gazed in wonder at the light then looked at her own glowing body. "It is beautiful, ye ken?" she whispered to Jamie.

"It is," he agreed. "The light reminds me of this article I read once about how plants give off a soft glow of phosphorescent lights. Most humans can't see the light with their naked eye. It takes an ultraviolet light to make the phosphorescence show up. The pictures were beautiful. Now I wonder if we would glow like that under a UV lamp. I think I'll try when I get home again."

Anne just stared at him, this time completely perplexed. "I dinnae understand the words ye are using, but if plants glow and so do we, that really is something. Perhaps faeries are more closely related to plants than humans, and since we are descended from faeries, we are also related to plants. Now I have even more questions for Titania." Hiking up her skirts, she started down the path, the same direction as Mairi, and Jamie followed closely behind.

As they made their way into the Throne Room, the cavern walls faded away so that there was nothing solid about them, but the nearly invisible path beneath their feet.

It was nighttime in the Faerie Realm and Anne saw the stars blinking above her and the soft glow of faeries below her, their chime-like singing rising to their partly fae ears. The familiar stream bed could be heard chuckling as it made its merry way beyond the vast space, and glimmering fish illuminated the waters.

I suspect those are the mermaids we saw before, Anne speculated. The sweet scent of flowers wafted through the air and Anne felt she might be ready for a good long rest.

REVENGE
Isle of Skye, Scotland
October 19th, 1700s

Ewan kicked at the door into the burial mound. *How did they get away from me so easily? I dinnae see or hear the bagpipes they usually carry and use to escape. I dinnae see the red-headed witch. One second the black-haired witch was in the cage and a young druid approached her . . . the next second, they vanished, a tornado of wind in their place.*

Flattening the palms of his hands against the door of the mound, he used his oxen-like strength to push it open and he stepped into the damp murky darkness.

"Cali!" he shouted, not knowing how these rendezvous worked, just knowing that when he'd called in the past, the faerie had shown herself.

"Cali! Show yerself and explain how this plan of yers is working."

He continued calling as he made his way deeper and

deeper into the darkened tunnel, wondering at the faint glow becoming more obvious the deeper into the tunnel he went.

The eerie glow that always preceded the elegant faerie began to grow around the corner of the tunnel beyond the buried clansmen. Ewan straightened his plaid and ran his fingers through his long red hair, more to pull himself together than out of any concern for what the faerie might think if he appeared too rumpled.

"You called?" Cali stood before Ewan, a smirk of amusement, eyebrows raised, arms crossed, a hint of the malice she bore all humans dancing across her face.

"I want to be caught up on how *our* plans," and he emphasized *our* to make his point, "are going in regards to avenging my father's death. Ye have the man who is the uncle to the red-headed witch who killed my da. I demand to know what has become of him and how that has helped with my seeking vengeance."

Cali's amused smirk disappeared. "You *demand?* YOU demand?" Her voice lost its customary tinkling sound, now replaced with the harsher tones of glass breaking. "Careful puny human, no matter your distant relation to the fae, choose your words wisely. I do not take demands from anyone, least of all humans. Try again. Diplomacy is an art you must have not learned, though your da had led me to believe druids were better at it."

So chastised, Ewan's white skin flushed blood red to the roots of his hair sprouting from his forehead, his mind a whirl so that he barely caught her insinuation that he was descended from faeries. *A preposterous idea!* "I mean, I would like to know how our plans are going. I'd like to be of assistance in the avenging," he stated, through clenched teeth.

Cali smiled, her voice returning to the melodic sounds of wind chimes in a gentle breeze. "That is more like it. So much easier to work together if we are civil, now isn't it?"

She paused, waiting for something, so Ewan nodded his agreement. "Good, well then! Let's give you a position in the grand game we are playing."

She paused again, scrutinizing Ewan with her violet eyes, tapping her long nails together. Then, she stood up straighter, clapping her hands and startling Ewan.

"I've got it! You shall be a witness at the tithing. When James is brought forth on horseback along with the Wild Hunt on Samhain, you will be there to witness it. James' death will be in equal payment for your da's death. An eye for an eye, as humans have said, or someday will . . . " She frowned at Ewan, "You humans with your Time moving in only one direction . . . " She sighed, "so troublesome. Time is so much easier when you let it flow around you like water and you simply jump out of the current whenever and wherever you like."

Shaking her head and laughing with a sound like bells jingling, Cali smiled at Ewan. "Be here the day before Samhain and I'll lead you to follow our Wild Hunt and bear witness."

Then she was gone, and Ewan was plunged into darkness again, save for the tiny glow of light clinging to his skin like sweat. He took a swipe at it, but it was a part of him. He grunted his annoyance, turned and made his way towards the tunnel entrance where a shaft of sunlight could be seen, towards reality where Time was predictable, and games were among men, not dependent on the flight of a faerie's fancy.

"I cannae wait for this to be ended. I'll take the battles of the clans and the trickery of young boys before I tangle with the Fae again," he muttered to himself. *Two more weeks and this will be all in the past. I'll have done right by my da and I hope the Witches will be vanquished.* He climbed onto his horse and rode back to his Clan's castle, to bury himself in his work as the Arch Druid of the MacDonalds, until it was time to return for one final meeting with the Fae, and more specifically, with Mairi.

QUESTIONS
The Faerie Realm
Outside of Time

Anne and Jamie stepped off the path that had led them into the Throne Room and bowed to Titania, who sat upon her moss-cushioned, crystal throne beneath the apple tree. The Queen smiled at them, her wings outlining her in their shimmering essence. "Ah, another grandchild. Welcome back young Jamie. Who is this you have brought to me?" Anne and Jamie rose from their kneeling position.

"This is my cousin, my Queen," Jamie indicated.

Anne curtsied again and smiled at Titania. "I am so overjoyed to meet ye! Please do forgive my filthy appearance."

"The pleasure is all mine. I sense you have recently had a very rough time. Come, tell me child, what bothers you?" Titania took Anne's hand and drew her to sit upon a moss-covered stone bench beside her, gesturing to Jamie to join them. All around on the ground were leaves in golds and reds, browns and fiery oranges, like a thick carpet under their feet.

Anne told her everything, starting with her dad being unusually sick, so that she was unable to heal him, then his disappearance and their suspicion he'd been taken for the faerie tithing on Samhain. She explained how she had helped heal Gran so that her spirit reconnected with her body, and that they had made a spirit animal friend who was helping them see if Jamie and Mairi's dad was possibly a changeling, and then she had been captured by angry Highlanders proclaiming she was a witch and the abuse she had suffered in the cage.

Anne broke down and cried, soothed by Titania's ancient presence, made to relax and let it all out. She felt so safe wrapped near Titania as if wrapped in a silken blanket made of butterfly wings, a soft scent of roses washing over her. Jamie patted her knee.

"I see. That is a lot for you to have gone through. Called 'witch' as if it were a bad thing. So often healers are revered, the gratitude of those you heal raises you up on a pedestal not of your making, and then that proclaimed awe is quickly turned to fear as someone points out how powerful the healer is, how easily a healer might harm. Though the healer rarely harms. It isn't in your nature, is it?"

Anne shook her head. *To hurt another person or creature is unfathomable. I cannae!*

"But I see that it is your father's disappearance that has you the most distressed. What is this about his being sacrificed as a tithe? Do you mean by the Wild Hunt?" At Anne's nod, Titania's clear green eyes turned amber brown for a moment and her brow wrinkled. "What is my Sister of Darkness up to now? It's bad enough she takes humans, but taking humans related to the faeries? That has never been done before."

Titania stood and walked across the leaf carpet, eddies

of bright colors swirling about her feet as she walked; she rested her hand on the gnarled trunk of the eons-old apple tree. For one brief moment, Titania appeared as an elderly woman, her shoulders bowed, her forehead resting against the tree. They could hear her murmuring to herself, as though she'd forgotten they were even there.

"Does she want to start a war between our Courts? It has been many years since we battled. The separation from earth, from nature, is taking its toll on us. Perhaps she is finally holding to what she so long ago threatened to do: incite war against the humans and reclaim what was once ours. And what is it I am supposed to do? Fight her? Fight the humans? Let them sort it out?"

She took a deep breath and sighed, a sigh so deep and long that the very winds were stirred to action and the carpet beneath their feet swirled into a whirlwind before settling back to the earth.

Titania squared her shoulders, straightened her spine, and turned to face her many times removed great-grandchildren. "I must speak with my advisors. Thank you for bringing this to my attention. Long I have enjoyed the peace that is my way, but I should not have lost touch with my Sister, the Queen of the Unseelie Court. Her Court is strongest in the Earthen Winter, from Samhain to Litha, and my power weakens. I must call her to a meeting, after I speak with my advisors."

She turned then, away from Anne and Jamie, and called forward several tall, lithe faeries that had been so blended with the trees and nature around them, as to be almost invisible. They stepped forward in their green and brown tunics, spines rigid, jaws set. The air around them chilled as they all snapped to attention, soldiers heeding the call of their Queen.

Jamie took Anne's hand and pulled her away towards the stream. "Let's get out of here and find Mairi. Something is seriously about to happen, and I think she might be in danger if she's alone in the Unseelie Lands."

"Did ye not have your own questions for Titania?" Anne asked Jamie.

"Yes, but nothing important enough to interrupt her concerns with her sister. I'll ask her another time, if I get another chance."

Stopping for a moment along the edge of the stream, Anne washed as much of the mud from her arms and face, and even leaned her head into the water and washed her hair. She didn't dare swim in the water, remembering the mermaids from earlier, though she did not see them in this part of the Faerie Realm. The sun was shining bright upon her back and the water dried quickly from her skin and hair.

As they walked along the bank, following its meandering path out of the Seelie Court and into the lands beyond, Anne spotted a deer. There were plenty of woodland creatures in the Faerie Realm, bunnies and squirrels frolicking in the grass alongside tiny points of lights which, when they stood still Anne could see to be Pixies, so seeing a deer wasn't that unusual. But this deer, a tall reddish-brown deer, decidedly female but crowned with long branching antlers, stood in the grass grazing, every so often glancing at them as if she was waiting for them.

Anne nudged Jamie, "Do ye see?"

Jamie nodded, "Let's follow her. Elen is a goddess that takes deer form that my sister told me sometimes guides her. I think she's guiding us now, hopefully to find Mairi and return home."

"Mairi will not want to just return home. She is determined to find your da and prove that he dinnae die, that only a changeling died in his place." Anne picked her way through the dew-covered grass, the noonday sun beating down on her head.

She frowned, looking around.

Time is indeed a tricky thing here in the Faerie Realm. When did it get so late? Have we walked so long and so far, that half a day has passed? She clasped her arms around herself, suddenly chilled with the fear that Samhain could come and go on earth without them, and her da would be gone forever.

MORE

The Faerie Realm
Outside of Time

Ka searched for Cali where he suspected, and feared, she would be-in the Unseelie Court, deep in the dense forest of the darkest part of the Faerie Realm, a fitting place for the Darker Faerie Court. He had told Mairi, Anne, and Jamie he needed to return to his body, which was actually true as his essence faded more and more, but he had really gone to find Cali and get another of her faerie hairs. Besides, he wanted to see what Cali was up to now.

Cali had been a liaison to the Seelie Court, something she'd detested, but was duty-bound to undertake. *Not that I saw any good come of it.* Ka wondered why such a tradition came to be, an Unseelie Faerie living in the Seelie Court and vice versa. *A form of Checks and Balances, I suppose, so that both courts will have an idea of what is going on in the other Court.* Ka had figured out that long ago, the two Courts had been at war with each other, fighting over control of their shrinking land as the Human World slowly but surely pushed the Faeirie Realm farther away, into this other dimension-a dimension that was much smaller in land mass. Now there was a grudging truce for peace, but Ka could feel the tension rising and it worried him.

Ka crept through the Dark Forest, as it had been dubbed, for the trunks of the trees had barely room for small creatures to pass between; the outspread branches overhead blocked out the light that should have been streaming in from above, for the sun had not yet set. An owl screeched from high above, and though Ka knew he couldn't be harmed by talon or beak, not in his current depleted state, any creature residing in the Faerie Realm was not normal and Ka could certainly be hurt by magic. If harm came to his spirit and he was unable to return to his body, his body would die.

But owls weren't too likely to attack a spirit form like Ka. Owls were predators and needed to eat. Ka wasn't dinner material. Ka was more concerned about Red-Capped Gnomes and Pixies who could throw spells at him, so he stepped with caution around every tree and searched for signs of Fey at every turn as he followed the one path that would lead him to the center of the Dark Forest where Queen Mab, as she was most often called, and her brother, King Oberon sat on their thrones of bones and moss. Ka pricked up his ears, a shiver ran down his back . . . it was oddly quiet, other than the one screech of an owl, and Ka wondered if he was racing into a trap.

Finally, the path opened into a clearing and Ka's fur stood up a little more. It was still dark in the clearing for the branches above did not separate. They made a thick canopy that covered a wide circular space where no tree trunks stood. Old trees that were wider in girth than five grown men, stretching fingertip-to-fingertip, could reach around surrounded the area. This part of the forest was ancient, older than the Egyptian civilization where Ka had borrowed his spirit name. That was how long ago the Faeries had been being pushed out of their Earthly domain. While the Throne Room of Queen Titania had been festive and uplifting, full of joy and hope, this Throne Room was full of despair and resentment. The Fae who lived here were angry and sought revenge on any they decided were to blame for their exile from their earthly home.

The clearing was filled with mobs of Red-Capped Gnomes and Pixies in their rainbow of skin colors, as well as stunningly gorgeous, gazelle-like tall Fae men and women in their flowing tunics and dresses dyed in shades of dark purples and dark forest greens. While the Seelie Faeries wore clothes to reflect all aspects of Light, so the Unseelie wore all the modes of Shadows and Darkness. Their wings, still made up of orbs of flowing light extending from their bodies to above their head, were more akin to the purple "black" lights of the 1980s. The older and more malicious the faeries were, then all the darker was the glow of his or her wings. The only fae Ka didn't see gathering there were the mermaids, for obvious reasons.

Searching through the sea of Fae Folk, Ka spotted Cali on the other side of the clearing, sitting at the foot of Queen Mab's throne. The throne was a high-backed seat made from the arm and leg bones of humans and faeries alike, cushioned with thick greyish-green moss. A holly tree covered in spiked green leaves and bunches of red berries hanging in clumps from the branches reached majestically above it. This was a tree that Ka recognized as having highly poisonous berries. His mother had shown it to him during his botany lessons, and she had explained that one seed could kill a person, but people loved using the branches covered in bright colored berries and evergreen leaves as décor for the holidays during the bleak and barren winter months.

How fitting that Queen Mab has a poisonous tree decorating her throne room, Ka thought.

Looking at Cali surrounded by several other faerie maidens with raven-black hair and milk-white skin, Ka made his way around the clearing, staying behind the large trees and out of sight from the Unseelie Fae Folk. He knew he shouldn't risk encountering these unruly faeries, but he needed what Cali could give. He had to have a strand of her hair that would give him a more tangible body to run around in, for the one he currently wore had lost its potency. Ka could feel his tenuous hold slipping from him, his body attempting to reel him back into the carbon prison of immobile flesh and bones.

And if I'm going to catch up to Mairi and make sure that my plan is followed through, so she has the powers I need to be healed, I'd better get through with Cali quickly. Though Ka did regret that he'd have to give up information as his bargaining piece to earn the strand of Cali's hair. He just hoped that with Mairi more powerful than ever, it wouldn't matter if Queen Mab and King Oberon knew they would be coming for James on Samhain.

SEEKING

The Faerie Realm
Outside of Time

Mairi sat on the edge of the Golden Meadow which was sandwiched between the Dark Forest and the ocean, watching the groups of exhausted humans in tattered clothes dancing wearily in circles and groups. This was indeed where humans lost in the Faerie Realm were kept, moving in eternity dancing through time, and the humans were from many different eras. Some wore the remnants of silken ball gowns, while others wore threadbare blue jeans and t-shirts, and still others appeared to be from years ahead of Mairi's own time for they wore fabrics and styles she had never seen on Earth. Their faces were gaunt, their eyes rimmed by deep, dark shadows, yet still they smiled, and laughed hysterically as they moved to a joyous music Mairi's ears could not hear. Whether she couldn't hear because she was part faerie and thus immune, or if there simply wasn't any music, she had no idea. With the hope in her heart starting to wane, she desperately kept an eye out for her dad, most likely dressed in a surfer shirt and swim trunks. Yet, if he wasn't here, where was he?

Mairi had already been there for the better part of the day, having arrived at midmorning after traveling all through the dawn along the edge of the Dark Forest. She'd had an uneventful trip, curiously alone, unmet by a single fae creature save for the deer she'd come close to mistaking for Elen before catching a glimpse of devil-red eyes and razor-sharp teeth. *Thank goodness I didn't follow her. I doubt that particular deer is a vegetarian.* She also thought she had seen a giant, and had spent several long minutes crouched behind a boulder wondering if she'd have to dive back into Anne's time as they had to before. But this giant figure, while taller than any grown man she'd ever met, wasn't as tall as the rock giant who had chased them. This one was also covered in fur, not unlike an ape, and had left really huge footprints in the soft mud along the riverbank. Gratefully, Mairi decided it seemed gentle as it stopped to smell the flowers growing near the river and it had moved into the woods without noticing Mairi, traveling slowly, barely disturbing a single tree leaf.

Standing and stretching out the aches she had acquired while crouching for so long in the tall grass growing on the edge of the Golden Meadow, she was rubbing her eyes that were threatening to tear up in her disappointment when Mairi noticed something new and completely out of place. A fluffy white cat was bounding through the grass, winding its way through the groups of dancing people, seeming to be chasing a butterfly. When the white cat came closer and noticed Mairi, the only person standing still, it stopped and stared, its green eyes growing large.

Letting out a plaintiff "Mairi!" that shocked Mairi almost to her knees, the white cat raced at her and would have knocked her on her back if it hadn't simply passed through her. Mairi turned in time to see the cat skid in the grass, flip around and mutter to itself, "Oh yeah. I'm not solid anymore, now am I?"

"Gran . . . ?"Mairi managed to gasp. "Gran! What are you doing here?"

Gran, once again in her fluffy white cat form named Star, though not at all solid but wispy . . . a spirit . . . walked over to Mairi's side and settled down on her hind legs. "I've been practicing transforming myself into a spirit cat like Anne showed me in September. I realized I could think about where I wanted to be then project my Self into my spirit cat form and I'd end up at that place."

"So you thought about being here?"

"Yes! Well, sort of. I thought of all the stories I'd ever heard about the Faerie Realm and so I've been to several places in this fairyland. I can't stay very long or my body becomes ill, so I have to keep returning. I'm going to have to go back in a minute, actually."

Mairi noticed Star was not as clear of an image as Ka's spirit form usually was. "But wait...why would you picture being here, at the Golden Meadow where Changeling humans are kept?"

Star shrugged her little cat shoulders. "I was hoping to find James. When you children went missing . . . your mother is very upset, by the way! But when you went missing, we all guessed you were trying to save James. I want to help so I've been doing my own searching."

Mairi frowned. *It's always about James! What about my dad?* she thought, saying instead, "Yeah, I haven't seen him either. I really hope we're right in guessing he'll be with the Wild Hunt and we can save him like Janet saved Tamlin."

"Right! I hope so, too." Star attempted to pat Mairi's hand, then sighed when her paw went right through. "Okay, I have to go. I'll tell your mother I saw you . . . " She looked around, as if just finally realizing Mairi was alone. "Where's Jamie? And Anne? Aren't they with you?"

Mairi crossed her arms over her chest. "They wanted to

talk to Queen Titania. I felt we needed to hurry here. We went our own ways, but I suppose they'll come here eventually." *I hope they're okay, but they should have listened to me! We wasted enough time with our side trip to Skye and Ewan's ridiculous Witch Hunt.* Mairi harrumphed.

Star looked at Mairi askance. "You know that family is the most important people we know. You should have stayed together. I'll help look for them when I can return. I must go, though. I'm sorry." And Star's form winked out of sight.

Ka came out of the shadows of the ancient Dark Forest in time to see Mairi talking to a white cat before it simply vanished from sight. Taking his time making his way to Mairi, so she wouldn't realize that he'd seen her gran, as he guessed the cat was. When he did finally stand by her side, Mairi was sitting with her body curled over her knees, head in her arms.

"Ahem," Ka cleared his throat.

Mairi turned her head towards him, shaking her wildly tangled red hair out of her eyes. "Oh, hi," she sighed. "I couldn't find him. I guess he's not a Changeling. I guess he really did die, and I just have to let him go."

Here was the moment Ka had been banking on. Now was his opportunity to get Mairi to the Isle of Avalon, to the apple tree that was an ancient ancestor to the gnarled old apple tree standing guard over Titania's throne. Finally, he'd be able to convince Mairi to eat the apple, which would enhance her powers that would enable her to heal his sickly body. *Then why do I feel bad?* Standing up and stretching, Ka made up his mind. It was all a long shot, anyway—trying to get his body healed, and get Mairi to see her dad.

"Look, Mairi, I can't make any promises that he'll still be there, but since your dad has been . . . " he fished for the kindest way to put it as Mairi narrowed her green eyes at him, making his breath catch, ". . . gone for less than a year, there is a good chance he's still in the 'in between' which is on Avalon. We could go to look for him there."

She stared for a moment before saying, "He's on Avalon . . . the mythical island? Is that place real?"

"It's as real as everything you've been learning the past few months. It's where the spirits of people who have passed away go to figure out what lessons they still need before moving on." *As well as where the Gods and Goddesses dwell, but I won't say that: it might scare her off.*

"Moving on where?" Mairi uncurled and crisscrossed her legs, facing Ka straight on. "And where exactly is Avalon?"

Ka looked out to the ocean. "Out there, through the mist. Avalon is a realm of its own, neither in the Faerie Realm nor on Earth. You can reach Avalon from either place; it has its own entrance on Earth, but it's easy to get lost in the mist no matter where you start."

Mairi stood up and brushed the bits of grass and dirt from her pants. "Let's go. Maybe that is all my dad meant in my dream, that I'd be able to see him again if I found him on Avalon . . . or something."

MALEVOLENT FAE

The Faerie Realm
Outside of Time

Anne and Jamie had followed the deer deep into the forest, realizing the path they followed was so tangled and windy they might not be able to find their way back to the river. In the distance, they could hear a steady drumbeat echoing off the trees, and as the sky darkened in an eerie sort of pre-dusk, the glowing orange light from a bonfire could be seen in the distance. Stepping carefully through the deep hollows between gnarled roots of ancient trees, madrone and oak, holly and pine trunks so big around that grown men would not be able to reach their own fingertips if they hugged them, Anne's heart was beginning to tighten with fear.

"Jamie," she whispered, tugging on his shirt as he stepped past her. When he failed to stop, she tugged harder, whispering more harshly, "Jamie, stop!" That got his attention.

"What?" he asked, his eyes glazing over, more from lack of sleep, Anne thought, than from any sort of magic. He stumbled to a stop next to her.

"I dinnae think we should be following this deer anymore. My skin is full of gooseflesh and my fingers are tingling. Something feels terribly wrong." Anne glanced at the deer that had stopped a few yards ahead of them, flank facing them with indifference. Then the head with rabbit-like ears, and a rack of antlers as pointed and gnarled as the tree branches mirrored overhead, slowly turned to face Anne and Jamie. Where big brown eyes should have been, there were blazing, red glaring orbs and the lipless muzzle snaked into a grin of malicious intent, exposing razor-sharp teeth no deer on earth was known to possess.

Anne gasped. Before she could tell Jamie what she'd seen, he was pulling her down and to the side, yelling, "Trap!"

It didn't matter. A net of barbed rope, as if spun from cacti skin, fell on the top of them, pinning them to the ground with the weight of the boulders tied to each corner. Yelling banshee cries, little men with long white beards and brownish-red pointed caps brandishing weapons in miniature jumped out from behind the nearest trees. Pricking Anne and Jamie in the back and arms, freeing ever more drops of blood from their already punctured skin, their cries of pain only loosened laughter from the little men's horrid, blood-caked lips.

"Anne...? What can we do?" Jamie cried out.

"I dinnae know! I am a healer, nae a warrior like your sister." *Even in the Witch Cage I could not bring myself to do anything to protect myself from the rocks being thrown at me. But they had only been children, brainwashed by their parents. These fae men are the size of children, but they are ancient, and their hats are soaked in the blood of their victims.* "I do nae want to be their victim!" She had spoken out loud without meaning to, fear making her lose control.

"Use your healing powers against them," Jamie suggested. "Numb their senses, or stop their hearts or . . . something . . . anything!"

That did it. Jamie was afraid, and to protect her younger cousin she would do something to help. Ignoring the pain of the prickles from the cacti-net as the blood-thirsty gnomes pulled them deeper into the forest, Anne searched inside herself for something that might work. As the dirt was stirred up from the ground, Anne began to cough, trying to keep the dirt from entering her lungs. Jamie was coughing, too and that gave her an idea.

"Jamie, can ye grab handfuls of dirt and throw them at the men's faces? I think I might be able to do something." *I hope so, anyway.*

Jamie began grabbing at the dirt beneath them, but he couldn't free his hands enough to throw the dirt anywhere, let alone at the gnomes' faces.

Anne sighed. *It is nae going to work.* She settled into herself again, feeling her clothes shredding under her, her skin becoming more exposed to the ground, feeling the earth beneath her. Using all her experience, she summoned as much energy as she could, trying to call on the Earth Energy as she'd seen Mairi do before with Water, Air, and Fire. But it didn't work. She couldn't make the dirt move into the mouths and noses of the little fae men. She opened her eyes in exasperation.

She turned to Jamie in apology, but saw him grinning. "I have a knife," he whispered with glee. He was brandishing the Sgian Dubh he'd pulled from outside the Realm entrance and was sawing a hole in the net as fast as he could.

He was busy with his knife while I was busy with my magic. Anne admired his tenacity.

With a final cut, they were slipping free. As suddenly as they were in the net, they were now out of it and the gnomes were falling over themselves as their heavy burden became decidedly lighter. Jumping to her feet, Anne grabbed Jamie's hand and pulled him back the direction they had come, following the wide trail of broken plants and disheveled soil. Behind her she could feel Jamie slashing at their pursuers with his knife. Chancing a glance back, she could see that he was really just waving it back and forth, keeping the gnomes at bay. Anne remembered it was iron, and faeries don't like iron. *How is Jamie able to hold it?* she wondered, as she assumed he was allergic to iron just as she was.

The red-cap gnomes finally gave up pursuit as their legs were shorter and they soon fell behind. Anne kept running though, fear filling her with adrenaline. Like a moth to a flame, she pulled Jamie toward the raucous drumming taking place deep in the Unseelie Forest. She yanked Jamie down beside her behind a gnarled tree, breathing hard.

They were too deep to go back and unsure of how to find their way to Mairi. Anne suggested they stay hidden until, hopefully, Mairi arrived, which she was bound to do as ultimately the Wild Hunt would be their next adversary.

ANTLERS

Isle of Avalon in Another Realm
Outside of Time

Mairi found the coracle on the beach where the river flowed into the sea. It was hidden from sight by cattails and thick reeds, but Ka had been confident there would be one if they searched hard enough, and he'd been right. The little rounded boat was difficult to get through the waves, which were blessedly small, as Mairi had to get used to paddling in a way that wouldn't send her into a spin. Ka was no help since he couldn't wield an oar; even if he hadn't been a spirit, his paws were useless for that purpose. She finally figured out to sit in the center and stay very still, like she did when she used to do the stand up paddle boards with her dad, mom, and Jamie in the San Diego Bay, only she realized right away that sitting rather than standing in the coracle was necessary.

Battling the current and the waves, Mairi pulled the paddle hard through the water and was just about to the outside where the waters were calmer when a milky white hand with webbed fingers grabbed ahold of the side of the vessel. Stunned, Mairi just stared until another hand grabbed onto the side and a face surrounded by a halo of blue-green hair appeared. The mermaid looked at Mairi with unblinking over-large eyes before smiling, showing her rows of pointed teeth. The extra weight of the mermaid caused the coracle to start tipping precariously close to the water, and Mairi shook herself as it dawned on her that the mermaid was slowly pulling the ship and occupants into the ocean depths.

"No!" shouted Mairi, and she whacked the mermaid's hands with the paddle. "We will not be visiting you in your watery kingdom."

The mermaid's eyes narrowed viciously, and she opened her mouth to release an ear-shattering scream. The waters all around the coracle began to churn with the hundreds of fishtailed women that appeared.

"Now would be a good idea to call on your magic, Mairi." Ka spoke the words as calmly as was possible, considering the circumstances, though the realization that he could easily leave her and save himself also crossed Mairi's mind.

Nodding her head, she called on the stars overhead and the water beneath her, gathering as much energy from the ethers as she could muster. Holding her paddle out like a Martial Arts staff, she felt the energy flow from her body into the wooden paddle and then blinding white light shot out in opposite directions from the ends of the paddle, blasting the mermaids on both sides. Rising to her knees, stabilizing her core muscles to keep from toppling over, she slowly spun her body. Trusting Ka would stay low and out of the way, she sent the arc of energy out in 360 degrees until the mermaids tired of the difficult prey and dove deep into the ocean depths.

Mairi sank to the floor of the craft and took several deep

breaths. "Eat," Ka reminded her, so she took out a handful of nuts and dried fruit and ate them. There were only two handfuls remaining in her backpack and those were soon gone, too. Taking up the paddle again with shaky hands, she began paddling forward, only to see that a wall of mist had formed before her, just as Ka had said there would be.

"What now?" she asked, daring to hope Ka had a map or something with which to guide them through the mist.

"Row straight through. If our intentions are true, and unselfish, we will be allowed to find the shores of Avalon."

"And if they're not true or unselfish . . . ?"

Ka shrugged, "We become hopelessly lost in the mist. And since I suspect I am not the one who will be tested since I'm a spirit," *at least I hope not*, he thought, "you best concentrate on your intentions of finding your dad's spirit."

"I just want to say one last good-bye," Mairi choked back a sob, still refusing to start crying. "I just want to know that he is really gone, and then I promise to stop looking for him."

Ka nodded his head. "I think that's as good as any reason anyone ever gives."

As if Ka were in charge and he'd commanded it, the mists parted like curtains on a stage, and the coracle ran ashore on the Isle of Avalon. Mairi climbed out, her sneakers getting wet in the salt water, and she pulled the small boat high onto the beach, not wanting to risk it being dragged out to sea leaving her stranded. "Where do we go now?"

Ka responded from the dry sand on the shore, "I've never been here before; I've only heard stories, so let's make our way inland and see if your dad shows up."

As an answer, Mairi swung her backpack onto her back and started the trek up the green hillside where the sand ended.

Mairi looked all around at the rolling, grass-covered,

very empty hillsides. The only thing breaking the horizon was a single tree in the distance. Wiping a bead of sweat rolling down her temple, she headed towards that tree, the only shade on the entire island.

"This looks like any other boring island. Where are the faeries? Where are the ghosts?" She stopped and frowned at Ka, hands balled up on her hips. "Why are we here?"

Ka sat down under the tree, curled up in the overlarge exposed roots of the primordial twisted and knotted apple tree. "I've heard tales of people who have been here. This is supposed to be where King Arthur is buried and where Guinevere met Lancelot. It's supposedly where the dead come before moving onto the afterlife, a sort of Elysium. I'm just as surprised as you that there is nothing here but this old apple tree." Ka put out a black paw and gently nudged an apple on the ground, startled when his paw was able to touch the apple and not simply go through it. The strand of hair Cali had given him was more powerful on this island.

Mairi was eyeing him. She might have noticed the same thing. Throwing down her backpack, she plopped down beside him. "Nothing is ever easy." She sounded defeated. "I thought if I just made it to the Faerie Realm I'd find my dad as a changeling and I could speak with him. Then you got my hopes up that I'd find him here. Now, there's nothing . . . nothing at all. And I'm hungry."

Without the prodding Ka had been expecting to have to give her, Mairi picked up the bright red apple from the ground, perfect in every way. "I might as well throw caution to the wind and eat faerie food, if we are even in the Faerie Realm anymore," and she bit into it, chewing and swallowing.

Ka's eyes widened in shock at seeing her eating the apple. It had been too easy. *Will it work?* He wondered as he searched for any signs of her changing.

Mairi took another bite and chewed some more. "This is

the best apple I've ever eaten," she announced, her eyes turning glassy, her smile growing. She ate the rest of the apple, core and all, before laying her head on her backpack and falling asleep.

Ka sighed. *Not what I expected, but we don't exactly have time to lay around taking naps.* He walked over to Mairi and pushed on her shoulder, but just as quickly jumped backwards when he saw something moving in her hair above her forehead and temples. Staring, caught in mid-step, he watched as two small points of bone or something just as hard, pushed through Mairi's mop of unruly red hair. The points grew and grew, branching out once . . . twice, until a set of eight-inch antlers stuck out from her head, seeming to have reached their full length in less than ten minutes.

HIGH PRIESTESS

Isle of Avalon
Outside of Time

Mairi awoke from her deep sleep and sat up, rubbing her forehead.

"Oooh . . . I have the worst headache." Rummaging through her backpack, she pulled out her water bottle and finished off the last few sips along with a couple of white willow bark aspirin.

"How long was I asleep?" Mairi asked Ka, finally looking up from her bag, only to gasp at what she saw all around them. "Ka!" she whispered harshly, "do you see?"

Ka shook his head, "what . . . ?" but Mairi didn't let him finish, just scooping him up and turning him to face out from the tree. He too gasped.

"You see it now, don't you?" she asked him, gawking at the change the island had gone through while she napped. For all around them, the island was now covered in little grass huts and gardens with winding pathways leading from each hut to a central building, still made of mud and grass, but much larger. Every hut had a garden filled with colorful flowers and one or two fruit trees, all in season with bright full fruit, oranges and apples and pears, and even more that Mairi couldn't quite make out. And most fascinating of all were the people, most of whom seemed to be women, dressed in robes of varying shades of purples and blues.

Staring as they were, Ka and Mairi were startled when a shadow fell across them and a gentle voice spoke. "Ah, I see we have visitors."

Mairi looked up into the gentle brown eyes of a girl about her own age, her skin a chestnut brown color the same as her hair, and a purple moon painted between her brows. She held a clay pot in her hands.

"Who might you be?" The girl asked, setting down her pot and sitting cross-legged in the apple tree's shade.

"I . . . " Mairi coughed to clear her throat, unsure of what to say. She looked at Ka who shrugged, as if to say he didn't know what they should do. Mairi decided to go with honesty, as she had the distinct feeling this place was magic and they would know all her deepest secrets anyway. "I'm Mairi, and this is my friend Ka, a spirit animal. We rowed a coracle over from the Faerie Realm, in search of my dad who di . . . uh . . . died a few months ago. I'm hoping to find him, to speak to him . . . to . . ." her voice caught, and she whispered that last bit, " . . . to say good-bye, I suppose."

The girl nodded, "Yes, that is often why we get visitors. People in search of their departed loved ones. Your dad is probably around here somewhere, but the spirits don't show themselves unless they want to be seen. I can't promise you will find him." She stood and, picking up her pot in one hand, gestured with her other hand for Mairi to follow her. "My name is Alyssum. I'm a Maiden of Avalon, studying to become a priestess. I can show you around our island."

Mairi set Ka down and put on her backpack as she stood. Ka shook his head. "Wait! It all disappeared when you let go of me." Mairi frowned at him, but she could see the maiden was smiling at him.

"You'll have to pick him up again. This journey is yours, not his, so he is unable to see what you are seeing unless he is touching you. Besides, he cannot eat the apple of our Mother Tree as you have." Her eyes drifted up to the top of Mairi's head.

Mairi put her hand up to pat her head and pulled away as if zapped by lightening. *Did I just feel antlers on my head?* She reached up again, and yelped. "No wonder I have a headache. How . . . ?"

The maiden patted Mairi on the upper arm. "It's okay, you will get used to them. As to how . . . well, you must have eaten an apple from our Mother Tree," she indicated the tree they stood under, "and I'm guessing you ate the seeds, too. Her apples are endowed with the power to bring out your true self. You must have old magic in you to have been blessed with the antlers of Elen Herself."

Ka rubbed against Mairi's leg and she automatically picked him up, the same way she would have if she were home with Peaches. "I'm able to hold you, without my hands going through you . . . is it because of the antlers?" She'd asked Ka, but the maiden answered.

"I'm not sure. He has faerie magic about him. Perhaps it is a combination of both. But come now, we'll stop to fill my pot, and make our way to the central building. Perhaps our High Priestess can help you."

Trailing behind Alyssum, Mairi walked along the cobblestone paths of Avalon, admiring the abalone shell designs intricately worked in with the small round stones. The gardens were immaculately cared for; the scent of rosemary and lavender, chamomile and rose filled the air. A gentle breeze blew past them, carrying the sweet smell of ripe apples and golden honey. On distant hills,, the "maaa" of goats could be heard and little girls could be seen skipping around them.

The path they followed led them to a fountain made of blue and white tiles with clear water bubbling up from the center with a gentle splashing sound. Several other maidens, all dressed in the same light blue robes as Alyssum were stooping to fill their own clay pots, joyfully chattering with their friends. They appeared to represent people from all over the world, some with light skin and blonde hair, others with ebony skin, or alabaster white. When Mairi stepped up to the fountain, the chattering stopped, and Alyssum told the other maidens about her companions.

Once her pot was filled with the fresh spring water, and Mairi had filled her own water bottle, they took a path that circuitously led them to the central building Mairi had noticed earlier. As they walked, Alyssum explained how this island was the entryway to the realm of the Celtic Gods and Goddesses. The Priestesses lived here studying and worshipping them, keeping the Old Ways alive for eternity. Often the Goddesses would join them, but the Gods had their own places for entertainment. The spirits of the dead too came here on their way to their next life, sometimes interacting with the Priestesses, but primarily keeping to themselves as they meditated on their previous life.

Mairi had been so enthralled by all that Alyssum was explaining, that she was almost disappointed when they arrived at their destination. Stopping at the entryway, they set down their loads and removed their shoes; Ka leaning against Mairi's leg when she couldn't hold him, then they entered through the archway on silent feet, moving the thick gray wool curtains aside so they could pass through.

The room was surprisingly bright, and Mairi saw that there were several large window openings with their own curtains pulled aside and tied, letting in the morning sun.

The air was thick with incense, a mixture of sage and rosemary, and several women of varying ages and coloring sat crisscross in a semi-circle around a large copper bowl of water in the center of the room; each was dressed in a varying shade of purple and indigo, and had a crescent moon tattooed in the center of her brow. Alyssum stood before them and bowed her head, with the palms of her hands pressed together at her heart. Mairi stood beside her and bowed her head, too, the weight of the antlers growing heavier. She tried to press her palms together, but Ka was still nestled in her arms.

Alyssum indicated the eldest woman sitting in the center of the semi-circle, dressed in the deepest indigo-dyed cloak and gown. Her long white hair was braided elaborately and pinned to her head, while a circle of herbs rested atop the crown of her head. "This is our High Priestess. She will guide you in your search for your father."

With a wave of her hand, the Priestess indicated Mairi should come towards her. She gestured to the ground between herself and the copper bowl of water, so Mairi kneeled, setting Ka beside her and he nestled against her leg.

The Priestess took Mairi's smooth hands in her wrinkled ones, closing her eyes for a long moment. Nodding to herself, she spoke, "You seek your father who has passed away from your plane of existence. You have a need to see for yourself that he has truly died, and that his death was not in vain. Though you have learned much since his dying," and the Priestess looked pointedly at the antlers and then at Ka resting beside Mairi, "and have come into your magical abilities with surprising force, you do not yet value the balance of Life and Death, of Light and Darkness. You wish to take your father back to the living with you, though death comes to all in many forms over our lifetimes. This is a lesson you must learn at your own pace, and I can feel the presence of Elen of the Ways guiding you in this."

The Priestess smiled at Mairi, staring into her eyes. "You are very lucky. Elen has taken an interest in you, nudging you along a path both enlightening and dangerous, a path that teeters precariously between the Balance of Light and Dark. You have many choices to face ahead of you." With a squeeze of her hands, the Priestess let them fall.

"Let's look into the Scrying Bowl, and see if your father is indeed here." Mairi stood and moved to sit on the other side of the bowl, noticing the waters within had begun to swirl in a rainbow eddy of Light and Dark. Ka jumped into her lap while all the Priestesses began to hum a low vibration and the waters swirled faster and faster in unison with the song. Mairi felt a longing to touch the water, and with embarrassment realized she had stretched her hand out and was indeed about to put fingertips to the swirling mass of water and light. She looked up into the High Priestess's ocean blue eyes and saw she was smiling.

"Yes, follow your instincts. They are correct. Don't let your mind get in the way."

So Mairi touched the water's surface and everything came to a sudden stop. The surface became smooth and an image not unlike the reflective image of a mirror began to take shape. It was Mairi's face looking back at her and beside her reflection was her father's face. He smiled, put up a hand to caress her cheek, then turned away.

"Wait! Where is he going?" Mairi looked around herself, panicking that he had been so close that she could feel him, almost smell his after-shave, but then there was nothing. He was gone.

The High Priestess smiled at her. "He is on a Journey in the Afterlife and cannot stray from his own path, but there are many opportunities for you to speak with him from your Earthly plane. One of which is about to dawn, the Eve of Samhain is nearing. Set up an Ancestor Altar, put out a bit of the food your father used to like to eat and his Spirit will be drawn to you. He will visit you at each of the days that the veils between worlds are thinnest if you only invite him, and if he is not busy in his Afterlife. For that is what you must come to understand. There is Life after Death, though it is not such a Life as you are accustomed to from your Point of View."

Then she turned to Ka, who sat quietly in Mairi's lap, taking it all in. "Ah, little kitty, though that is not who you truly are. You understand the Spirit Life much better than your friend, but it is the Physical Life you seek to enjoy more." The Priestess nodded her head, "Yes, you are on a Quest of your own. It will be time to share the specifics of your Quest with your friends, very soon, or you will lose them."

Clapping her hands, she announced, "Let us give you water and food and send you on your way. Your friends need you and you must not delay this journey you are on together."

Young women, Maidens like Alyssum, Mairi assumed, arrived with a bag of bread and cheese and golden pears, as well as clay carafes of water. Alyssum bowed to the High Priestess and left the room, so Mairi followed her lead, bowing and exiting the room, disappointed to not have achieved at least speaking with her dad and uncertain what the future would bring.

HURRY!
The Faerie Realm
Outside of Time

Mairi stepped from the coracle as Ka leaped onto the sandy shore. The trip back to the Faerie Realm had been uneventful, not a single mermaid had surfaced, and the sky had remained clear the whole way. *Are the mermaids doing mischief somewhere else, or did I frighten them away for good?* Mairi wondered as she pulled the little round boat into the reeds where she'd originally borrowed it, doing her best to camouflage it the same way as when she'd first found it.

"What now?" she asked Ka. "Do you have any idea where Jamie and Anne are? Or where we can find the Wild Hunt?"

Ka started walking up the embankment, calling over his shoulder, "This way. I know the Wild Hunt is lining up at the Unseelie Court, and hopefully we'll find Jamie and Anne on the way."

"Hopefully? What if we don't find them?" Mairi felt the worry creeping into her gut and up her into her chest. *What if we leave them here? Who will fight for Uncle James if we can't find Anne? I'm not sure I love my Uncle enough to save him and it's obvious from the story of Tamlin that someone must love the person very much or they won't be able to hold on through all the beastly changes. Ugh! I should not have run off without them!*

As if reading her thoughts, Ka said, "You should have waited for them. This is a very unsafe place for humans."

Mairi growled, "Yeah! I get that! But Anne has powers and Jamie is smart and has a little power. They'll be okay." *I hope!*

They made their way through the Golden Meadow where the humans were dancing for eternity. Mairi looked wistfully at them, wishing it had been so easy with her dad, that he had simply been a Changeling after all. *He's really dead. That's all there is to it.* She briefly thought about what the High Priestess of Avalon had said, about there being more to life than living and dying. *Is there really a sort of Life after we die? I felt my dad's spirit in the Central Hut on Avalon, and I felt him when I dreamed of him at home.*

She stared at Ka walking ahead of her, his black fur shining in the morning sun, his long tail twitching like a flag in the wind being carried in a parade. *He's a spirit. What would happen if his body died? Would his spirit disappear, or would it still exist without his body? Would Ka still exist?*

Mairi stopped then, struck with the sudden question she realized she should have asked a long time ago. "Where is your body, Ka? Who are you, really?"

Ka also stopped and sat on his haunches, looking at Mairi with a steady gaze. "I've been wondering when you'd ask me that. I promise I will tell you, even show you, but here...?" Ka looked towards the Dark Forest they were drawing closer to. "Not here. It's dangerous to let the Unseelie Folk know who we really are."

Mairi nodded, agreeing for now, *but I will ask him again.*

"Meeow?"

Mairi whipped her head to the right, staring off into the meadow running along the edge of the Dark Forest. A fluffy white cat was bounding through the grass, making her way towards them.

"Star! Gran! You're here! You came back!" Mairi grinned, struck with a sudden inspiration. "You can help!" Star came closer to Mairi and nuzzled her ankle, though she really just passed through, sending a chill up Mairi's spine. Ka stared, which reminded Mairi to introduce the two.

"Ka, this is my Gran. You may call her Star. Gran, this is Ka...my friend, I guess."

Ka looked at Mairi with a withering glance, then back to Star, "Yes, I am her friend."

"Oh, you're a Spirit Shape Changer, too!" Star grinned. "I'm just getting the hang of this. Isn't it so much fun?"

Ka nodded, "Yes, but let's get going. We've wasted valuable time."

Mairi brought Gran up to speed on their situation as they walked, and Gran told them that it was indeed Samhain morning, at last, and that was what she'd come to tell them. "Look, Gran, can you send yourself to Anne and Jamie, find out where they are and come back to us? We need to find them. Anne is the only one who can save her dad!"

Star nodded and disappeared. Mairi and Ka kept their steady walk toward the Unseelie Court. The walk felt like a death march, like they were making their way to their doom. There were no living creatures around them, and the silence was ominous.

Star reappeared as they entered the trees in the Dark Woods. "They're hiding on the edge of the Unseelie Court.

They said something about accidentally following an evil red-eyed deer because they thought it was Elen, and battling a band of Red-Capped Gnomes, but they were able to hide before being recaptured, so they've only just been panicked about where you are. They're relieved that you're on your way."

Mairi shook her head at the thought of them fighting Unseelie Fae. Sighing with relief that they were okay now, she decided to only focus on getting through the woods, so everyone could be reunited. It was dark as an almost-moonless night in the shadows of the Dark Forest, and there wasn't much of a path to follow even in the brightest daylight. Ka led them over fallen logs as often as he took them under them.

Ancient giant oak trees reached to the sky with bent and twisting branches splaying out in all directions; Old Man's Beard hung down in heavy clumps. Holly trees, their sharp leaves blanketing the floor in a dense carpet, mingling with the oak leaves, stood tall and watchful like sentinels as their red berries brightened the murky darkness. Other trees stood close by, but Mairi was too busy pushing branches and brush out of her way, wiping the occasional spider web from her face, to note what kind they were.

If something wants to attack us, now would be a good time. We're too busy defending ourselves from the forest to fight properly. She held her breath for a minute, her eyes wide. Looking around, she breathed out as she realized, *we* are *fighting the forest. It doesn't want us to reach the Unseelie Court. The Dark Woods* are *Unseelie,* as she thought this, she pulled loose from the grasp of a prickly-leafed branch, *especially the holly trees.*

"Ka!" She whispered loudly. "Ka!"

Ka stopped and looked at her, biting at a vine that had wrapped around his paw. "What?" he asked, after spitting out the greenery.

"The forest is defending the Dark Faeries. It's working with them to keep us from entering the Unseelie Court."

"Yes, I imagine that's true. I've never had this much trouble before. Perhaps try your Druidic skills to blast our way in?"

Mairi looked at him for a long moment. Then she looked around the forest. There was no sunlight filtering in, just a shadowy sort of light like when the sun is beyond sight in the evening, but it's not actually night time yet, but just that gloomy hour of dusk. *There's plenty of greenery and brown decay, so I can draw from the Earth, and if I listen I can find Water, maybe, and though it's stale, there is Air, but I wish there was sunlight for Fire. I'll just have to do what I did before in the underground.*

Planting her feet firmly, she felt the Earth Magic entering through her feet, she heard in the thick silence of the empty woods the trickle of water, and she pulled what she could from its Water Magic. She sensed the air begin to swirl around her and the Air Magic entered through her Heart Chakra.

Then she reached out to hold the trunk of a particularly huge oak tree, and she experienced a rush of both Fire Magic from the photosynthesis in the leaves and the Earth Magic flowing in stronger through her bare hand. She thought she could feel a faint surge of joy. *Weird! It's as if the oak is cheering me on . . . maybe the Oak is really Seelie?* Yet, it all had a dark taste to it, like a seasoning she couldn't name. It felt tainted by the Dark. *No, not tainted exactly. Controlled . . .*

Mairi opened her eyes and took a step forward. The plants curled back as if bowing to a queen. Moss-covered boulders rolled aside, and trees leaned away to clear the trail. Mairi walked unhindered with the two spirit cats close on her heels.

"Mairi!" Ka called out. "Stop! We can't make this huge of an entrance! Tone it down a little, and I'll let you know when we've gotten close enough for you to stop altogether."

Mairi nodded and reigned in some of the power, or at least she hoped she did. It was not so easy to hold all her power in check after filling up like she had. It was bursting to come out and she'd never asked it to stay within her before. Her skin began to crackle with little bursts of lightning, her hair stood out like hundreds of copper wires on top of her head, not unlike a dry static day when humans and animals get a little spark when they touch, and their hair stands up on ends. But Mairi knew this was so much more and she didn't know how long she could contain it.

UNSEELIE COURT
The Faerie Realm
Outside of Time

Anne and Jamie still huddled together behind the gnarled tree, watching the Dark Faeries gathering there. Anne had used their time there to heal them of their many puncture wounds and to pull the cactus needles from their skin. She'd even healed the burn-like rash on Jamie's hand from his holding the Sgian Dubh longer than his faerie blood could take. Other than their torn and bloody clothing, they appeared to have had nothing go wrong on their journey in the Faerie Realm. And now that they had spoken with their gran, they felt better about their situation. They continued keeping an eye out for her dad, but so far there hadn't been any sign of him.

Where are they keeping him? Anne wondered. *Is he with the Dark Faerie Queen? I have nae seen her either.*

She and Jamie hadn't spoken almost the entire time they had huddled together, which had been what felt like an entire day and night. There was only one time they had uttered a sound, and it was when Jamie had recognized one of the dark faeries, a tall willowy lady with black hair and a long lavender dress, her gossamer wings of pure energy arching high above her head. Jamie had whispered in her ear, "That's Cali. I met her in the Seelie Queen's court and she acted really sinister, like Snape always acted in Harry Potter." Anne hadn't understood who Snape was, or Harry Potter, but she did understand sinister. Cali gave off a feeling of frustration and malice. Anne hoped to never cross paths with such a faerie..

There really wasn't a need to be too quiet because the tree-lined clearing was becoming louder and louder as more and more fae folk arrived, and many of them were carrying instruments of one sort or another. The deep thumping rhythm of the drums had become more emphasized as several giants joined the crowd. Blending in like gargantuan trees, they even had skin that appeared like bark, though she'd seen a couple that looked a bit like rocks. The giants tapped their toes to the beat, and Anne felt her body move in a steady bounce as the earth vibrated beneath her.

Along with the drumming there was a woeful crooning coming from wooden pipes played by gnomes and fauns alike. The music was beautiful and alluring, but mostly made her want to cry. She had a strong suspicion that if the fae knew humans were nearby, the music would change to a magical quality that would capture them in some way.

By the time Star had appeared and disappeared, Anne had seen more of the Fae Folk than she cared to ever see again. There were tiny pixies with green skin and sharp fangs, splatters of red on their tiny spider-silk tunics. The red was blood, she knew, because she had watched a band of pixies attack a blue bird who had flown too low into the trees and they'd eaten it in a matter of minutes, plucking the feathers and spitting out the bones. Anne shook her head trying to get the image out of her mind. She'd also seen red-capped gnomes with evil grins, demon-eyed forest animals, and all manner of creatures she could not name. She couldn't wait to leave this realm.

Mairi and the two spirit cats hid behind a very large fallen log and gazed in horror at the freaky party taking place in front of and all around the Dark Faerie's throne.

"Where are the Queen and King?" she asked Ka.

"They're probably with their faerie soldiers getting ready to mount their horses for the Wild Hunt. We need to get past all of these folk and go through that tree behind the Queen's throne before the Wild Hunt goes through, that way we can be waiting for them on the other side, like Janet in the story of Tamlin."

Mairi nodded, turning to Star. "Can you go to Jamie and Anne? I'll try to sense where they are and if they are closer to the tree entrance than we are, then we'll come to you."

Star smiled, her fangs gleaming behind her white fur covered muzzle. "I'll go to them. If you aren't with us in several minutes, I'll find you."

Star blipped out and Mairi closed her eyes, testing if she could sense her gran somewhere else in the clearing. Mairi still felt like a cooking pot full of electricity with a lid that barely contained all of the energy within her. With the antlers that Elen had bestowed upon her when she ate the apple, Mairi felt like she might explode at any moment. Focusing on Star was a relief, it was some place to put her energy. Her head began to tingle where the antlers attached to her, and they acted like antennae, tugging at all the different auras in the clearing until she felt the two she was most familiar with, and they were with Star. They were just on the other side of the milieu of faeries gyrating to their wild music, not too far from the faerie door. Unfortunately, she also sensed Cali and the druid Ewan near the faerie door. That was a problem she might be dealing with sooner rather than later.

Mairi and Ka made their way slowly towards Jamie and Anne, careful to hide if they were too close to any of the fae. The way was longer than she expected, and she was utterly exhausted once she joined her brother and cousin.

When Star had shown up again, Anne was relieved to hear Mairi and Ka weren't far behind her. Mairi gestured to them to follow her and they crawled on hands and knees past everyone until they finally reached the faerie door. Knowing they would be in full view when they went through the door, they had to be quick. Anne followed behind Jamie with Ka and Star behind her. The last five feet stretched long in front of them. Glancing around at the Unseelie Court, Anne realized they wouldn't be noticed in all the bedlam taking place. They just had to be quick. On a cue from Mairi, they ran past the empty thrones made of bones and holly tree, and leaped through the faerie door, tumbling into the dark tunnels beyond.

"Where to now?" Mairi asked Ka, glowing more like a faerie than ever before. Anne could see there was something decidedly different about her cousin since they were last together as they had arrived at Queen Titania's court, but she could only see a stronger energy, and something going on above Mairi's head. There just simply wasn't time to focus to figure out what was different.

Ka ran down the tunnel, "This way! Hurry!" There was shouting behind them, and Anne didn't have to be told twice to run. Risking one glance over her shoulder, she saw the Arch Druid Ewan MacDonald enter the tunnel, blinking in the dark. She couldn't be sure if he was following them, or if he just happened to be entering the tunnel at the same time. Turning back the way she was running, she saw Star disappear. *She must need to return to her body. I wonder if she'll be able to bring help? Granda, maybe? Or Aunt Shaylee?*

The tunnel was a short one, though, and they soon exited through another door, entering a cool, bright green forest of the tallest, reddest trees she had ever seen. After the noise of the Unseelie Court and the fear in the tunnels, this forest felt like a sanctuary with the gentle silence and sunlight filtering through the wide-spread canopy overhead. She didn't have too long to admire it, though, before Mairi was grabbing her hand and they were squeezing behind a huge fallen tree. Muttering a spell under her breath, Mairi began to bind the smaller plants surrounding them. The plants grew and wove a wall around them, coming together as a canopy of ferns and wood sorrel that covered their heads, a green tent with one wall made by the red bark of the fallen tree. Everyone breathed a sigh of relief as they watched Ewan pass them by, unable to see them, though they questioned his intentions when he too tucked into a clump of ferns and hid.

"Is he waiting for us to come back from whence he thinks we have gone?" Anne whispered to Mairi and Jamie. Mairi shrugged, her eyes never leaving the spot where Ewan had hid. Anne smiled at Jamie, who grinned back, but Mairi did not look at her, wearing only a grimace. *I wonder if we will ever be okay?* Anne wondered. She noticed that Ka was gone, probably he had returned to his body like Gran, and hopefully bringing help, too. *Maybe Danny will come.* Her cheeks reddened at the thought, then she shook herself to refocus on the upcoming battle she must face to save her da.

WILD HUNT
Ancient Redwood Grove
Samhain, Pre-Dawn

Mairi stood on the soft carpet made of dropped Redwood needles and damp ferns, sweat glistening on her forehead despite the gloomy wet weather of thick fog enveloping them in the forest. They waited. What might have only been mere minutes felt like long excruciating hours as they anticipated the Wild Hunt's emergence from the Faerie Realm. She and Anne and Jamie had managed to crawl out the back of their makeshift shelter and move away from where Ewan hid without being seen. They wanted a view of the Faerie Door and a space Anne could easily maneuver from when her dad rode by.

Mairi shivered as the first sound of bells and a horse neighing reached through the gray day. Gripping the grandmother redwood tree Mairi and her companions had stopped behind, Mairi peeked out to see if the Wild Hunt was near. She could feel Anne's heartbeat echoing through the tree as she leaned in beside Mairi.

"Did you hear that?" Mairi whispered to her cousin.

"No! What did ye hear?" Anne asked.

Mairi frowned. "Maybe I imagined it . . . " then a horse neighed near them again. Mairi peeked out and announced, "They're here!"

Anne stuck her head under Mairi's arm to see. "Where? I only see a glimmer of light in trees and fog and . . . "

Mairi hissed, "Right there!" She pointed where the first of the Unseelie Queen's mounts could be seen crowning the burned-out hole in the eons-old trunk of a redwood, new growth giving the illusion of several young trees growing in a crowd, in fact creating life from the bones of their mother.

Mairi watched the first horse pass through, black as night with silver bells and sat upon by the black-haired Queen of the Unseelie Court. She had skin as white as milk, glowing in the murky light, and gossamer wings arching up several feet above her head and shoulders, wide purple-hued eyes searching.

Next came her king consort on an equally black horse with demon red eyes, snorting and stamping his hooves . . . his was a warhorse of some evil intent. "Be calm, you'll eat soon," Oberon soothed his stallion.

"We cannae see anything, Mairi. Can you?" Anne nudged her again.

Mairi frowned. "Why can't you see? They're right in front of us?" She leaned down to look at Jamie behind Anne and bumped her antlers on the trunk. "Oh!" She reached up and felt her velvet soft antlers. "You really can't see . . . like I can . . . " It dawned on Mairi that the antlers allowed her to see through whatever glamour hid the Unseelie Court. Stepping back from her viewpoint, she took Anne's hand, saying, "Now look."

Anne gasped. "Och! For the love of Elen! They are terrifying tae see in this serene forest!" Jamie came forward to see and Mairi held his hand with her other, and he too gasped.

"Shshsh!" Mairi hissed at them. "Don't let them hear you!"

"Oh!" Anne cried, putting her hand to her mouth, trying to stop the noise escaping. "Do ye see the little ones bound by the delicate chains? They are human children, forced to march beside the fae. They dinnae look so happy."

Jamie nodded, "I think they must be the changeling children stolen from human homes."

"Do ye think that is what would have become of my wee little sister if we had nae managed to help her to escape?"

"Yes!" Mairi hissed again, "now please be quiet. I'm sure they could hear us if they knew to listen, and we have more important things to discuss. Jamie, what was it the story of Tamlin told us we had to do to rescue James?"

"I think he will be on the last horse in the back, a white one, after the Queen and King pass on the black horses, and the faerie soldiers pass on the brown. Anne will have to pull him off the horse and hold on to him as he changes into many terrifying beastly shapes," Jamie explained.

"Right," Mairi agreed. "And now I understand what Ewan is doing."

Anne and Jamie looked at her from either side, but Anne was the one who asked her, "What is it he is doing?"

"He's watching for one of us to make a grab for James. Remember, Ewan only ever wanted revenge on the family who killed his father." Mairi took in a deep shuddering breath before letting out a ragged whisper, "and I'm the one who killed Ian. Ironic, isn't it? I am dealing with my dad dying, then I go and kill someone else's dad." Her head dropped for a second.

"Mairi..." Jamie started, "you did it to save us. It was self-defense."

Mairi's head snapped up, all signs of sorrow gone. "I know. I had to do it, though I would probably have not killed him if I actually knew what I was doing, the way Anne always seems to know." Shrugging off Anne and Jamie's looks of sympathy, she stood straighter. "It's fine. I would do it again, if necessary. So, here's what is going to happen. The second Uncle James shows up, Anne and I will lunge for him. Once Anne has a hold of him, I will let go of her and go after Ewan, who will surely be about to attack us. Jamie, you have to stay here and get that plaid ready to drape around our Uncle, because isn't he naked in the end?"

"Yes...yeah, okay!" Jamie stuttered, stoked to have something important to do, even if it wasn't actually battling with anyone.

By this time, Mairi could see the train of brown horses emerging from the Faerie Door, long obsidian colored tails swishing behind them. Several of the horses neighed and pranced, bells hanging from their gold brocade halters jingling in the earth-scented air. Creatures of all shapes and sizes, in varying degrees of hideousness, were riding on and dancing alongside the horses, laughing with wicked glee. Cali sat perched upon the last brown horse, a haughty look of satisfaction on her face as she held tight to the reins of the horse behind her about to emerge into the forest. Then the last horse in the Wild Hunt parade stepped into the forest, its white muzzle in stark contrast to the darkness within the tree, followed by a blue-eyed head and a yellow tone mane. Sitting atop the docile horse was Uncle James.

Mairi could see that James had a glamour of some sort over him, his blonde hair sometimes appeared brown, his tattered clothes sometimes appeared to be the elegant finery of the fae. *What has Cali done to you, Uncle?* Mairi worried, but could see he didn't seem aware of his situation. *At least, his horse isn't a demon horse. It would probably eat Uncle James if it were. Good! Makes our job easier.* Anne squeezed Mairi's hand indicating she was ready, and Mairi squeezed back attempting to indicate she wasn't a bad person or anything.

"Ready?" Anne asked.

Mairi whispered back, "On three—1-2-3!" They ran out from their cover and Anne reached for her da with her free hand, pulling him from his horse. Mairi saw that as her Uncle James fell his shape shifted into an angry grizzly bear with five-inch claws. The look of pure hatred on Cali's face nearly shriveled Mairi, but not quite.

BATTLE
Ancient Redwood Grove
Samhain, Dawn

Anne let go of Mairi's hand and everyone except her da and Mairi disappeared from her view. Pulling her da from the horse, his full weight crushed her as they landed on the ground. A heart-beat and he morphed into a humongous creature covered in matted fur. His claws, as long as her hands, slashed the air above him, and she held on with all her strength. *Magic must be helping me because I could not possibly hold onto something this big. Nae! Not something . . . .he is my da! I must succeed; it is the only way he will survive all this.*

Anne's eyes opened wide in her shock at how much harder this was than she'd expected. She was not finding it so easy to keep a hold on him when his ferocious snout, filled with razor sharp teeth, kept getting close to her face, hot spittle landing on her cheek. *This feels so real!*

Just as she managed to find a way to work with this

shape, her da shifted again, snapping at her with the long gargantuan jaws of a hideous creature wearing scaly skin and a long thick tail. He took advantage of her surprise to twist in her arms, his jaw opening to envelop her head. "Da! Nae!" Anne cried out. "Do not eat me! I am your wee lassie, Anne." Tears streamed down her cheeks, but the creature pulled back, the hideous teeth closing with a snap! She got a view of its eyes. She gasped. *They are blue, they are my da's eyes. This IS my da!* Resisting the temptation to close her eyes again, worried the action might ruin the magical antidote somehow, so she kept them open and stared into her da's eyes. He looked afraid. She felt her heart beat steadily, a rhythmic *th-thump*, *th-thump*, and focused on that rather than the fear coursing through her blood. Then her da shifted yet again.

She tightened her grip and vowed to never let go, just as the first tiny teeth punctured her skin, teeth not belonging to her da's grotesque shape. *What now?* She cried inside, not daring to let go to fight this other danger.

Mairi heard the steady drumbeat, the forlorn pipes, the wild laughter as she felt the teeth biting her shoulder, the sting of tiny vicious claws in her hair and on her arms. Instinctively, she swatted at them as if they were mosquitos, or rats, but it was ineffective. The second she pushed one pixie away, three more took its place. Glancing at Anne, she saw she was under attack, too. It reminded her of a swarm of bees and the idea of jumping into a pool of water popped up in her mind.

That's it! She stopped fighting, though now she spotted a red-capped gnome coming at her to join the pixies, and took a deep breath, calling the energy seething within her. She focused on feeling the energy covering her like a waterfall, flowing from the filtered sunlight and down her head, over her shoulders, down her arms and legs and pooling at her feet, over and over and over. She envisioned the flow of energy becoming a shield around Anne and her da. When Mairi felt she was free, the creatures washed away by her energy, she looked into the surprisingly calm eyes of Cali.

"I do not like my games interrupted," Cali stated, cold intent seeping through each word. Then she looked up and shouted, "Ewan! Now!"

Mairi, pumped up with adrenaline and energy crackling under her skin, grinned at this sinister faerie who seemed to thrill at messing with people's lives. "Another time, another battle, you and me . . . " Not knowing why she had said such emboldened words and needing to draw the battle away from Anne's own struggle, Mairi ran, hoping the feisty little pixies would follow her . . . hoping Cali would not follow, simply because to do so would draw her Queen's attention to her games.

After ten long strides, Mairi turned and saw that Anne was safe from the Dark Fae who now stood beside their Queen, their frenzied music stopping as they realized Mairi was under a strange protection. She glanced at her cousin and uncle, noting James was in the shape of a muscular writhing python, thick body swirling around Anne, long sharp fangs poised to strike. *Oh Lugh! Please protect Anne and her da!* Mairi hoped calling on the Celtic God would be helpful. She figured he was the one that might take a sporting chance to help her cousin. *Don't let that creature bite Anne!*

Aware that the Unseelie Fae might be after her again, she looked around to see what her next move should be. She spotted Ewan, creeping out of his hiding spot, arms raised to attack her with the fireballs burning in his hands, aimed right for her. A glance behind her told her the entrance to the Faerie Realm was finally empty, and the carnival of crazy creatures had started playing their wild music again, bumping away and cheering for Anne's certain death. Mairi didn't matter to them anymore. As they were preoccupied with that battle, Mairi bolted for the entrance, luring Ewan away.

Ewan ran after the red-haired witch, the young lass with more power than he saw fair for her to have. *She is too young to be controlling the weather as she did when she helped the black-haired witch escape my cage. She is too young to have the power to have killed my da. Most of all, she runs around the Faerie Realm as if she belongs there as much as she is human and belongs on earth. No matter! I am powerful, too, and nae so old as my da was. I WILL have my vengeance.*

He rounded a corner in the pitch-dark tunnel and saw her ahead. *She glows like a faerie! So that must be her secret. She is faerie-human offspring, after all. It is known to happen. The old stories, the fairy tales, tell us so. There is even rumor we MacDonald druids have faerie in our ancestry, and that is the source of our druidic powers, just as Cali hinted at.* He shuddered at the thought of faerie and human consorting together. *I have nae desire to claim such connections.*

Mairi raced along the tunnels. *Maybe I should try to lead him back into the Faerie Realm or into some other place and time, except I don't actually know how to exit these tunnels unless an opening happens to appear. I should have asked Ka more questions.* She berated herself for being so obsessed with her dad and changelings. *Ka knows how these tunnels work. What can I do?* Running was possibly getting her absolutely nowhere, so she skidded to a stop. *It's now or never, I suppose.* She turned and faced Ewan.

"Good, Witch! Face me!" Ewan called out. "Prove that you are deserving of a title. Are ye pretending to be a druid, as your robes indicate? Well, ye are merely a witch, dabbling in herbs and the stars and magic, as is fitting a woman." Ewan nearly caught up to her, stopping a mere several feet away, taunting. He would not fuel her power by admitting to her how powerful he knew her to be.

Mairi held her ground. "You say 'witch' like it's a bad thing to call me that. Maybe I am a Witch. Maybe I am a Druid. What difference does it make?"

Ewan laughed. "Witches *are* less than Druids. Witches have nae the power, nor the training that Druids have. Witches are women, not men, and only men ought to be Druids. So ye are a Witch."

"Ha! You are definitely from the 17th century! Only in your archaic time do the men get away with trouncing the women. In my time, women stand up to men, and men are being held accountable for treating us as less. So, call me Witch. I do not care. I can be a Witch or a Druid, because I am ME either way, and I am more powerful than you can imagine." She let a few tiny blue bolts of light flash about her fingertips to make her point.

"Enough babbling, girl! I will have vengeance for my father's death. That is all that truly matters to me at this moment." Ewan raised his hands and blue orbs of fire surrounded his hands.

Mairi enveloped herself in a green shield of Heart Chakra energy.

"I am also a MacDonald, you know," Mairi stated, assuming it was information that would anger Ewan further, buying more time for her Uncle's transformation to be complete. *Though it might not be wise to make him too angry.*

Ewan drew in a sudden breath, lowering his hands, glowering at Mairi. *What is this she says? A MacDonald like me?* "That is nae possible! I am aware of all the MacDonalds in Scotland who have shown signs of power. I have records. I have watchers. They bring me all the children in our clans who might possibly become druids and they receive the training they are most suited for."

"So, as a girl I would have received no training at all? Just a label of 'witch' and clansmen watching me to be sure I behaved like a proper girl? Good thing for me I am not from your time," and the girl laughed.

"Enough! I am nae here to learn about you. I am here tae eliminate you." Ewan sent forth a streak of the blue light, the hottest fire he could summon, to melt the girl like she'd apparently done to his father.

Mairi was ready. She understood what fueled his anger. He was broken-hearted over his father's death, so she added layer upon layer to her bubble shield: red from her Root Chakra, orange and yellow, all the chakras until she was surrounded by a rainbow-orb in a matter of seconds. Ewan's blue fire ricocheted off, picking up the layers of Chakra Energy filled with positive energy, cooling off the blue fire and slamming back into him. Ewan was thrown to the ground, still as stone.

Mairi lightened her defense, reducing her bubble to something requiring less from her Energy reserves as she walked over to Ewan. She cautiously checked Ewan for a pulse. His heart beat steadily. Mairi sighed with relief. She was determined to never kill anyone again, so she hoped her plan of only sending energy coming from Light, but magnified in strength from Ewan's own powers, would fundamentally change him and, at the very least, knock him out, so she could return to Anne. She stood and ran back to her cousin's side.

Anne gasped as her da became liquid metal, a vibrant beautiful gleaming gold. Her mind screamed that she could not possibly hold him, even though she'd held him through bear, giant lizard, humongous snake, overlarge raptor bird, and so on. *But this is nae a creature! This had not been in Gran's story. Da should be back to his own shape now. Has it nae been long enough? Brigid help me!* She called to the goddess her Irish gran had taught her about. And she called her again, by her Scottish name, *Bride! Dinnae let me be burned by this hideous stuff.* She felt the hot metal oozing between her fingertips, flowing around her arms, her skin feeling as if it were burning off of her very bones. *How much longer can I do this? How can I hold onto something that nae longer even has my da's eyes?*

But she knew she would hold him as long as she had to. The healer in her couldn't let harm come to her father as she held him. The daughter that she was couldn't stand the thought of losing her father again, perhaps permanently. Her heart pitied the pain Mairi was going through, and she did not want to go through it, too. She squeezed tighter, feeling the muscle and bones that was her father, though her eyes told her she held hot liquid metal.

Then it was over. Her eyes saw what her hands felt. Her father lay in her arms, and Jamie was throwing the dark blue MacLeod plaid over his naked form. He blinked up at her, his eyes clearer than the last time she'd seen him, when he'd been sick with an incurable flu.

"Anne?" he croaked.

"Aye, Da, it is I. We have saved you." Anne choked back a sob.

Mairi ran forward, then, placing her hand on Anne's shoulder. Anne gasped, for only then could she see the Dark Faerie Queen and her entire raucous Court, swaying and gyrating to the bizarre orchestra, surrounding them.

Queen Mab flicked her fingers at her Court and the music stopped. "I see there are those who still listen to the old stories and learn from them. I will not be so careless in my choice of tithe next time. Perhaps Cali has much to explain." Cali stared straight ahead, shoulders rigid, under the scrutiny of her Queen.

The Queen spoke again, her voice cold, sharp and

smooth like an icicle in winter. "The world is once again remembering the Faeries. This could prove to be helpful in our battle to win back what was once ours." She looked at Mairi, settling her gaze on her antlers and nodding once. "I see someone has been training you. We'll see about ensuring your education is not all biased to the Light. Without Dark, there is no Light." Looking directly into Mairi's eyes, she said, "Best to remember that."

With a flick of her ivory white fingers tipped like daggers with berry-red nails, the Queen and her consort were away, rhythmic drumming fading into the distance.

What havoc will they wreak on the world? Mairi wondered, as she and Jamie sank to their knees beside their uncle and cousin.

"What now?" Anne whispered.

REBIRTH

The Tunnels of the Faerie Realm
Time Unknown

Rubbing his head, he sat up, uncertain where he was. There was only darkness surrounding him. Patting the ground, he felt hard-packed dirt. Reaching out to the sides, there were walls of crumbling earth and long tubular roots. As if by instinct, the man flicked his hands, expecting light but got nothing, not even a tiny spark. He was too weak to make a light of any type. He dragged himself to his feet, wondering what had happened to make him feel so useless, so incapable. *Where am I?* He wondered. *How is it I came to be encased in a room of dirt?*

Shock rocked his body and he grabbed at his chest for breath. A most horrific realization had hit him. *Who am I?* Not one memory could he conjure in his mind, not one image, save a sound, a word. *A name! My name, but not only mine . . . MacDonald.* There was a feeling of belonging to that name, but he knew another name should be part of it. It flitted about his mind like a caged bird, teasing him. *No matter. It will come to me in time.* Accepting that and not fighting to capture that word, his name, brought peace and he wondered if he was dead.

Turning in a slow circle, contemplating if this was what death looked like, he saw a small beam of light reaching for him, coming through a hole where the wall swept down to become the floor. Lying flat on his stomach, he peered through with one eye and saw a festival on the other side. Scrabbling at the soil, pulling out stones and small boulders, music reached his ears and the golden light grew brighter. Using a dried root, he found on the ground, he worked continuously to enlarge the hole. When the opening was big enough for him to squeeze his body through, he did so, wriggling and inching his way into the world the same way as a newborn baby.

He stumbled out of the hole in a hillside and into a green meadow filled with the smells of food, and the sounds of joyous laughter and friendly music. Thus, he realized he was still alive. As soft as a butterfly leaving a flower, his name whispered through his lips, "Ewan."

Yet he knew no more than his name as he was swept into a stream of costumed people dancing in a ring.

ALL HALLOW'S EVE

Ancient Redwood Grove
Samhain, Present
Noon

Mairi watched as a hulking shadow peered out of the hollow leading into the Faerie Realm. Thick furry fingers held the burnt bark of the redwood tree, narrow eyes darted side to side, scanning. The creature stepped with an overlarge foot into the light of day, its leg covered in matted fur, followed by its hulking form. It wasn't an ape, exactly, nor was it a human. *It's the creature I saw in the Faerie Realm on my way to the Golden Meadow! What is it?* She nudged Jamie, shushing him at the same moment as she pointed. Jamie followed her finger to see the creature sniff the air then pad away on surprisingly silent feet into the wilderness.

Jamie gasped, "It's Bigfoot! Bigfoot is real!" He continued in a whisper, "I read about them in my books about Native American stories, essentially their fairy tales.

I think all the myths of the world hold more truths than modern civilization acknowledges. Just like Queen Mab said, all of the fae creatures are returning to our Earthly Realm as humans show renewed interest in the old stories and a love for nature." He grinned at his sister.

Mairi nodded, both admiring her younger brother's wealth of knowledge and wondering what it meant for the realms to be intermingling again. Humans were reconnecting with nature, thus taking care of the wilderness, while simultaneously becoming greedier than ever, destroying the natural world for resources just to acquire more money. *What will this mean for the Faeries and the Humans?* She lay her head back down to rest as she pondered this larger picture of what was happening in the world.

Mairi, Anne, Jamie, and James lay on the naturally carpeted floor of the Redwood Grove. Mairi sprawled with her arms and legs reaching out like a star, her palms spread out to touch as much of the earth as possible, her shoes kicked off, so she felt the breeze on the bottoms of her feet. Jamie had offered Mairi a bite of chocolate to help her regain her energy after she'd told of her battle with Ewan, but she'd declined. Being surrounded by the dense grove with the sunlight filtering through the branches was rejuvenating her without a need for food. She could feel the Light Energy of Earth, Fire, Air and even Water from the lush greenery as it flowed into her every pore. The tension of the past several weeks drained away, replaced with a positive feeling of connection to the world, both seen and unseen.

Jamie had wondered what had become of Ewan after Mairi had knocked him out, and Mairi had said she hoped that he'd woken and returned to his home. When Anne had asked, "What now?" they had all agreed to take a break for several minutes to rest and come up with ideas, so they lay on the forest floor and thought about it.

When Anne's question had finally knocked on Mairi's consciousness loud enough to come up with an answer, Mairi dragged herself back from the bliss of doing absolutely nothing. Sitting up, she looked at her family lying in their own patches, exhaustion seeping away where they'd fallen asleep after telling James all that had happened since he'd become gravely ill. For his part, James could remember nothing beyond when he first became sick in his own home.

"We need the Silver Faerie Chanter, or Ka, or both," Mairi stated, breaking the silence.

Anne stretched where she lay and smiled up at the sky peeking through the canopy. "It will be so nice to go home."

James sat up, "Aye! Now we've rested I need to return to my wife and wee babe. They must be sick with worry! Wills, too. And I need a good long walk through the moor to sort out what just happened."

Jamie rolled over and rubbed his eyes, sitting up and nodding his agreement. "And a really big hamburger for lunch would be nice, too!"

As if on cue, or perhaps some of their conscious thought had reached through the ethers and called to him, Ka arrived. "Sorry to have missed out on all of the excitement," Ka sat back on his haunches. "I wasn't idle, though. Danny's ready with the bagpipes, so let's get back to your Granny Kate's house and see if we can get Jamie his hamburger."

Arriving back at Granny Kate's house, Kate had pulled out some of her deceased husband's old clothes for James. He'd luckily been a man with a large frame, so his kilt and billowy shirt fit James perfectly. "Oi! If I weren't so desperate for better coverage than this overlarge scarf, I would nae take too kindly to wearing the plaid of a

MacDonald." Being surrounded by a handful of MacDonald family members did not deter James from speaking his mind. Shaylee, having dashed over when Kate had called to tell her, was busy alternating between hugging everyone, so relieved they were all alive, and berating them for leaving without telling her what they were up to.

Sitting down to an indulgent lunch of fast food burgers delivered by Danny, Jamie wasted no time in tucking in. "I have missed real food so much!" to which his uncle grunted his agreement, savoring the flavorful burgers from his teen years that he'd nearly forgotten about. Through huge bites of burger crammed in with fries and gulps of soda, Jamie, Mairi, and Anne filled in Granny Kate, Danny, and Tobias' mother on all they'd been through.

"You know," Granny Kate said, "your grandfather's name was also Ewan MacDonald. I suspect it's a very common Celtic name."

"I never thought about his name," Mairi admitted. "He was always just 'Papa' when we talked about him." Danny and Jamie nodded their heads in agreement.

"It is too bad you three never met him, nor did your father," she said to Mairi and Jamie. "It's a shame your Papa died when he did, though he was a workaholic so he might not have been around much, anyway." Her voice trailed off.

Jamie turned to Danny and asked, "Did you get a chance to look at the Silver Faerie Chanter while you kept the bagpipes?"

"I did. I'm not sure I found much. The chanter is carved with what looks like several different Celtic Knots, but when I looked more closely, there are only four knots depicted in slightly different styles."

"Which knots are they?" Mairi asked.

"The Trinity Knot, the Protection Knot which is also known as the Witch's Knot, the Faerie Knot or maybe the

Lover's Knot. That one was a little harder to pinpoint. And finally, the Eternity Knot, which I've found in both the Celtic and Sanskrit. I'm just not sure why they are carved on the chanter."

"Maybe the knots are the source of the magic?" Anne suggested. Danny shrugged.

Mairi fingered her pendants. *I'm wearing two of the four. Does that mean anything?*

As her cousins seemed lost in thought, Anne turned to Sonja and asked how Tobias was. "Why is he nae out here with us?"

Sonja's eyes filled with tears. "He's been so weak lately. For the past few weeks he's been in and out of consciousness. There have only been a few rare moments when he woke and attempted communication through blinking eyes. I've sat by his bedside almost constantly, hoping to figure out what is wrong with him, but there is no way for him to tell me." She ran her hands over her exhausted face then took a long drink of her black tea. "In fact, I better return to his side right now."

Anne put her hand on Sonja's shoulder. "I am a healer, ye ken. I would be happy to take a look at him."

At Sonja's look of hope that lit up her eyes, Anne quickly clarified. "I am nae a miracle worker. I will do my best, but I cannae make any promises."

Ka jumped up on the table then, to everyone's surprise, and cleared his throat. *Now or never, I suppose.* Danny nodded to him as encouragement. "Uh . . . I have a confession to make," he said once he saw that everyone was looking at him.

Addressing Mairi and Jamie, he said, "You have been wondering who I am really. I have only, so far, let Danny in on my secret," Danny smiled at him and Ka took courage. "I am now going to tell all of you, and implore that you help me."

He sat down and looked at each person until he stopped at Sonja. "I am Tobias."

Sonja dropped her water glass and Anne's hand flew to her mouth to cover her astonishment. Mairi and Jamie jumped out of their chairs.

"What did you say?" Mairi gasped.

"I am Tobias, and I'm hoping that today, while their powers are at their strongest, since it's Samhain, Anne and Mairi can use their magic to heal my body from that which has caused me to be a quadriplegic."

TOBIAS

San Diego, California
October 31ˢᵗ, Present
Samhain, Afternoon

Once everyone had regained their composure, Ka led them out of the kitchen and into Tobias' bedroom. Tobias appeared to be sleeping in his bed, tucked in neatly under a sheet and a thin blanket. His eyes were closed, and he breathed in shallow breaths, a slight gurgle to each out breath. His pale skin was now a shade of gray, the shape of his skeleton showing where the blanket did not cover him.

"He's been like this for weeks," his mother said softly. She leaned over Tobias' still form and held his hand. "Unresponsive, perhaps asleep. I've never seen him out for so many weeks on end."

Ka leapt onto the bed, placed his forepaws onto Tobias' chest and looked directly into Sonja's eyes. She gasped when she looked into the vibrant blue, almost lavender eyes. "You are truly my Tobias?" she whispered.

He nodded, "Yes, mother."

"Oh Tobias!" she gasped, looking from Tobias' body in the bed to Tobias' spirit in front of her. "How?"

"Do you really have to ask? I was raised by witches, after all." Mairi could almost hear the smile in his voice. "If Mairi and Anne are willing to try to heal my body, I will finally be whole. Anne is a powerful healer, and Mairi is just simply powerful. Together . . . well, together there is hope."

Taking that as her cue, Mairi crossed the small room to Tobias' bed, standing on the side across from his mother. Anne stood beside Sonja, who appeared stunned.

"Mother, please let Anne stand there. Trust me," he added, when she seemed unwilling to let go. She looked into first Anne's eyes, then into Mairi's across the bed, and finally she let go of Tobias' hand. She stood at the foot of his bed, instead.

Ka looked around at everyone in the room. Danny and Jamie stood by the door while Kate and Shaylee hustled about lighting candles and murmuring various spells. They'd understood right away what would be needed. Satisfied that all was ready, Ka gave a nod, and padded over to Mairi. "Please remove the charm from around my neck."

Mairi reached over and felt for the thin strand of faerie hair blending with the soft cat fur. Having located it, she gave a gentle tug and the strand snapped. Ka's form wavered and lost solidity. Mairi smiled at him gently, "See you soon." The black cat smiled a feline smile, turned and leapt into the body of Tobias, which gave a visible shutter as spirit rejoined physical form.

Mairi reached over for Anne's right hand with her left, each girl taking one of Tobias' hands, then they looked into each other's eyes before closing their own in unison. Mairi focused on imagining all her healing energy flowing from her hands into Tobias and adding to Anne's. Mairi's red hair began to glow like it was made of copper strands of wire wildly waving about, Anne's black hair shone like a pearlescent oil slick on a silvery sea, and Tobias' body began to glow an eerie, sickly green.

Anne gasped. Everything stopped then, as if a light switch had been turned off. "How did this happen? I sense bones were broken and nerves were severed in an accident of some sort." Her throat caught, and she whispered hoarsely, "but overlying that I can sense he was harmed further. Someone deliberately cut into his spine, tried to reattach the broken parts . . . and that made everything worse."

A sob broke the near silence, and Sonja hung her head. "It was me, I allowed the surgeons to try something experimental. I never should have, but Tobias' father was so angry after the accident . . . after Tobias," she stroked her son's foot through the blanket, "our beautiful perfect boy . . . he was jumping on the trampoline when he was 12. He was always so agile, so capable. I never considered something so terrible could go wrong."

Sonja stopped talking, breathing heavily and gulping down her tears. Finally, she continued. "It was his birthday party. He did a flip, I was told by his friends. He landed on his neck, and they heard a crack . . . I heard them screaming. When I ran outside, Tobias was silent, eerily so, and still . . . so very still."

Sonja paused again, and Shaylee put her arm around the frail woman. "His father called the ambulance, and we went to the hospital. Tobias was paralyzed from the neck down, permanently. My husband was so angry, with me, with the world, with himself. It was his idea to buy the trampoline. I had been afraid of something like this happening." Sonja looked up to all of their eyes watching her, "but I'm always afraid of terrible things happening. My husband felt so much guilt he disappeared before Tobias' thirteenth birthday came around and I've never seen him since. I kept hoping Tobias' body would pull through, or I'd find a spell, or medical science would find a cure. Something . . . anything . . . but nothing ever worked."

Tears streamed down her face, dripping onto the blanket covering Tobias' feet. "Tobias became depressed, suicidal. His caseworker became more and more worried as he discovered Tobias was using any technology we gave him, and his new group of friends with varying paralysis, to search for ways to commit suicide. It haunted me, day and night, so when a new experimental surgery was offered, I decided we should try it. Tobias wanted to, and for the first time I saw hope in his eyes, so I consented . . . "

Sonja heaved a huge sigh, ". . . and it went wrong, terribly wrong. He lost the last control he had over his body, his face. He could no longer talk or blink. My only consolation was he couldn't commit suicide now. But that felt wrong of me. He'd lost all freedom of choice, so I adopted optimism, and searched in the alchemical realm through my Witch Sisters. I didn't really think it would come to fruition. Inside I'm not nearly as optimistic as I try to be for my son." She hung her head, limp hair hanging like a shield over her face as she whispered, "I'd actually given up hope . . . "

She looked up again, eyes shining bright, "Until now," she whispered, her voice husky from sorrow. "Can you help him? Is it truly possible?"

Anne smiled gently. "Aye, I do see a way. His energy, his nervous system I saw in an anatomy book on Shaylee's shelf, is blocked by heavy scar tissue at the base of his skull, not allowing the flow of connection between his brain and his body. It would be too much for me on my own. I would tire before the blockage were to budge and heal smooth enough tae work again, but with Mairi's strength I can do it. I am certain of it. I just . . . knowing that this is how modern medicine attempts to heal shocks me. I did nae expect a battle wound, only a birth defect. To take up knife and cut open the human body in such a way, seems cruel and unnecessary. Modern medicine is archaic for it has foregone all that Nature has offered to humans."

"But we aren't human," Jamie said. "We are part faerie, so our way of healing isn't actually the human way."

"Then we must learn to unite the Fae and Humans, to help each other. I do nae like bloodshed and death . . . we need to try harder to be the bridge between the two."

Mairi nodded. "I agree. Fae and Humans need each other. I don't like bloodshed and death, either, but I've learned there is a time and a place for both. It just shouldn't be deliberately inflicted. So often the motive is greed or anger. But we need to finish this, Anne. At least healing Tobias is something we *can* do."

The witches and druids filling the room nodded, this time understanding the battle needed all powers present to participate in order to win. As Mairi and Anne drifted back into their trance, Mairi heard Shaylee whisper to Jamie that he ought to go out to the garden and play a tune on the bagpipes. The music was full of its own power. Danny held hands with Kate and Shaylee, and Sonja held Kate's other hand while Shaylee and Sonja each placed a hand on Tobias' feet, exposed from under the covers, completing the circle. As the clock struck 2:00 in the hallway, golden sun rays filtered into the room from the green gauze covered French doors behind Mairi that Jamie had just left through, letting everyone know night would soon be descending. A soft breeze blew in carrying with it the scent of lavender and chamomile, calming their nerves, as well as newly decaying leaves as Autumn grabbed hold of the world.

The power in the room was palpable and the antlers on Mairi's head, only faintly visible to those who had set foot in the Faerie Realm, tingled like antennae on a bee. For hours they stood there, eddies of energy pulsating through Tobias' healing, unclogging his energetic flow, until the clock struck 4:00 and Tobias sat up with a gasp of pain. His distinctive eyes stared directly into his mother's duller version, and her mother's love could be felt by all.

It was done.

Tobias was whole once more.

CALLEACH BHER

Isle of Skye, Scotland
October 31ˢᵗ, 1700s
Samhain, Late Afternoon

James and Jamie were several yards ahead of Mairi and Anne on the moor near Anne's home, discussing the best methods of sneaking up on deer and enemies. Mairi could hear Jamie laugh at his uncle's impressions of surprising an enemy clansman one early morning several summers past. It was good to see Jamie looking bright-eyed at a grown man. An uncle could never replace a father, but Uncle James felt like a man they could turn to if needed.

"Are we good, Mairi?" Anne's soft voice broke through her reverie.

"What do you mean?" Mairi asked.

"Are ye still upset with me, or are ye okay with me?" Anne asked, rephrasing her question.

"I was never upset with you," Mairi denied.

"Ye seemed mad at me for most of our journey," Anne

whispered.

Mairi let out a breath she'd not realized she was holding, tension draining from her shoulders. "I . . . I didn't know you could tell I was upset." Mairi shrugged her shoulders, trying to shake off the seriousness of the conversation. "But obviously you could."

Mairi walked a few more steps before she took Anne's hand and squeezed it. "I'm sorry. I didn't mean to take out my frustrations on you. It's just that you had powers and knew how to use them. You *know* how to use them," Mairi amended. "I have powers and I'm only just beginning to know what I can do with them, but we're the same age and I was just mad that you grew up knowing all about our family heritage and I didn't. It took losing my dad to finally be told what I am."

Anne squeezed Mairi's hand back. "I am sorry ye were not told. But knowing ye have powers would nae have helped save your da. First off, your powers dinnae show up until yer da died. It was most likely the shock of his death that opened the door to let yer powers free. Second, I would nae have been able to help your da, had I been there, even though I knew how to wield my powers when he died."

Mairi stopped and stared at Anne. "How do you know that? How do you know that if I'd been allowed to hone my powers, assuming I would have had them if I'd been told of the possibility, I wouldn't have been able to save my dad from cancer?"

Anne took Mairi's hands in hers again, "because we have cancer now, in my time, and I cannae heal those who have it. I can only ease their suffering. Magic must still work with what knowledge we *witches* have, and I have nae the knowledge to stop cancer."

"Well, maybe we will have to study it. Now that we've healed Tobias, I feel like we can learn how to heal anything."

Anne smiled at Mairi, "Perhaps. That is a very nice

thought, and I ken that I would like that vera much."

Anne threw her arms around Mairi and gave her a tight hug. "We'll change the world, together."

Mairi grinned and pulled on her cousin, so they could catch up to the guys.

Anne's mother cried in alarm when they entered her house. "Are ye demons? Or dae I dream?"

"Ma, it is me, yer own dear Anne. And Da is with me." Anne ran to her mother's bed and fell to her knees, hugging her mother and baby sister Caroline both at once. James strode across the room and hugged them all.

Mairi and Jamie stood to one side just inside the door, shuffling with embarrassment to be witnessing such a tender moment.

Wills walked in at that moment, arms full of wood for the fire. He stood dumbfounded in the doorway, waiting for his mind to catch up with what his eyes took in. "They are back . . . " he whispered, more to himself than to anyone else. Dropping the wood on the floor, he ran across the room and flung himself into the bunch. "Ye are back!" he hollered with total abandon, like an exuberant six-year-old.

After they untangled and wiped their tears, Jamie and Mairi helped Anne retell the story so that Anne's mother and brother knew what all had taken place since last, they'd been together at the Fall Equinox. Begging off any dinner, insisting they had promised to return to their time right away, they made plans to visit again with news at the Winter Solstice, and finally they parted ways.

Mairi and Jamie trudged part of the way back to the other side of the moor, wishing to have some privacy from the village when they time traveled. They stood beside the rock with a fissure in it that Danny had once hid in over the summer. They were poised to time travel with Mairi's hand on Jamie's shoulder when they heard a loud cracking sound. Before their eyes, the rock split further along the fissure and out stepped a woman so old and bent over, covered in wrinkles to resemble a shriveled apple, her skin as blue as the sky on a clear day. She cackled when she saw them, a twinkle lighting up her one eye set in the center of her forehead, and she smiled at them with her almost toothless grin. Waggling a gnarled finger at them, she took off walking at an unnatural speed, her white and gray plaid cloak pulling behind her, a frigid wind lifting the edges. Before they could blink, the woman was gone with the world becoming a frozen winter land in her wake.

"The Calleach," Jamie gasped. He looked at Mairi, "we've just witnessed the coming of Calleach Bher, bringer of Winter . . . a goddess!"

Mairi watched as the mountains in the distance turned white, as if painted by an artist, snowflakes swirling about their faces.

"Let's go home," Mairi held her necklace and her brother's shoulder as he struck up a tune. "I just wish to be home."

ANCESTOR ALTAR
San Diego, California
October 31ˢᵗ, Present
Samhain, Early Evening

Mairi couldn't believe she had finally returned to her own house. Sitting on one of the two couches in her family room, feeling comforted by the eclectic array of vibrant colored throw pillows and Mexican blankets covering the couches, she fell into a deep sleep. Jamie had already fallen asleep on the floor, bagpipes resting in their case beside him. They would have stayed that way all night, except they were startled awake by the doorbell ringing. Mairi stumbled to the entry way, wondering where her mom was, and opened the door to Granny Kate standing on the front porch looking refreshed in a black dress embroidered with richly decorated multi-colored skulls. She carried a bouquet of marigolds in one hand and a tray of artistically decorated sugar skulls in her other.

"It's past time to set up your Ancestor's Altar and

properly honor our departed loved ones. Go to my car and get the box in the backseat full of decorations for the altar," she commanded. "We need to prepare the altar before we can celebrate our Dumb Supper at midnight." Granny Kate went on to explain that the Dumb Supper would be celebrated at Mairi's house rather than at her's, as it had been for the whole of Mairi's life, because this was the home of the most recently departed relative.

Jamie's bloodshot, tired eyes alighted on the sugar skulls and Granny indulged him with one to suck on as he attempted to appear cheery, stumbling out the front door. Mairi was slower to act, staggering a little as she led her granny to the dining room.

"It's okay, my dear. Sit down and rest. You've depleted yourself." Granny Kate handed her a tiny sugar skull decorated with a pink rose on its forehead. "A bit of sugar will help you, too. Now go get dressed properly."

Plucking at the filthy druids robes she hadn't yet managed to take off, she was relieved to escape to her bedroom where Peaches lay curled up on her pillow. Sitting down beside her kitty, she petted her calico fur. "Please don't tell me you're not a real cat. I like you just like this. Soft, snuggly, and simple." In response, Peaches purred loudly, rolling over onto her back, exposing her even softer underside. Mairi grinned and obediently rubbed her tummy. *I think it's safe to accept she is simply a cat, nothing more.*

Having carefully dragged a black sweater over her antlered head, and changed into black jeans, she pulled her red hair into a manageable yet messy bun, carefully arranging it around the supposedly invisible antlers. Mairi exited her bedroom sanctuary with a weary sigh. *Ain't no rest for the wicked,* she thought, remembering the lyrics to a popular song. *Not that I am wicked, but hopefully all the wicked ARE resting by now,* Mairi thought of the dark faeries on their Wild Hunt parade through the Realms and even the MacDonald druids, though she felt deep inside they weren't really wicked.

"Ah Mairi, there you are and looking quite lovely in black. Perfect for the occasion." Granny Kate sat at the dining table and smiled at her. Looking at the antique sewing table, Mairi could see that her granny had been setting up an altar to the dead. Levels were added to the table by stacking boxes of various sizes in the center, then covering the whole tower with black satin fabric. In the heart of the top level there was set a large ceramic skull decorated with vibrant swirls and floral designs in front of the bouquet of orange marigold flowers. Photos of deceased loved ones would also be placed on the altar and little plates of their favorite foods set before them, similar to the Dumb Supper they would hold later that night. Candles of differing heights were arranged on the table and Jamie was adding a few of the tiny sugar skulls.

At least he didn't eat them all, Mairi thought with a laugh.

Setting up an Ancestor Altar with a strong Dia de los Muertos influence was something they'd done every year at their Granny's house. Living on the border of Mexico, Granny Kate had acquired a love of the Mexican culture and a holiday meaning Day of the Dead that was celebrated the day after Halloween had charmed her Celtic senses, easily wrapped into the Celtic traditions she'd learned from her long line of female ancestors, and more recently, her late husband. So Mairi had grown up celebrating Dia de los Muertos. It was a way to honor Mairi's grandfather who had passed away at the end of the Vietnam War, right before her dad had been born.

Papa MacDonald, as they'd always referred to him, had been working his way up in the army when he'd died. Reaching for the photos sure to be in the box of decorations, she pulled out the pile of framed photographs. Mairi looked with admiration at a familiar picture of him in his uniform, hair cropped short. *I'm not one for the military, but he wanted to protect our country. He did what he thought was right.* Running a finger over the lines of his face, noticing for the first time that his hair must have been red when he was younger, she realized he looked oddly familiar.

Didn't Granny Kate say earlier today that his name was Ewan MacDonald? A sinking feeling slowly crept its way out of her stomach and into her heart, her mind racing.

No! He can't be! It's not possible!

Or is it?

Shuffling through the photos of him, she had to be sure, so she asked, "What did you say Papa MacDonald's first name was, Granny?" but she didn't hear her granny's answer. She didn't need to.

"Ewan!" she gasped, dropping the pile of frames with a crash and sitting down hard on the dining room chair. Jamie's head whipped around from the altar at the loud crash and he ran over to his sister's side.

"What is it?" he asked.

Mairi showed him the yellowed photograph she held in her trembling hand. Written in Granny Kate's neat handwriting were the words "San Francisco, Summer of Love, 1969" on an old-fashioned color photograph of a much younger Kate with long, straight, blonde hair down to her waist, dressed in a flower crown and a bohemian style ankle-length dress. Beside her, looking more than a bit bewildered, was the druid Ewan MacDonald, long red hair and beard flowing to his waist, white druid robes draped over his broad shoulders and distinctive barrel chest. He looked the way he had when Mairi had last seen him . . . *wasn't that only hours ago? . . .* right before she'd blasted him with his own spell plus every bit of Chakra Energy she could muster, determined not to kill, but only to disable until they were away from him for good.

For good . . . but then, what happened?

Unaware, caught up in her memories, Granny Kate

fondly touched the photograph. "That's the day I first met your grandfather. He seemed to be tripping on some drug or other at that time, mumbling stuff about seeing faeries and a Wild Witch girl coming after him. It made me giggle a little, my being a witch, after all." Finally catching a whiff of her grandchildren's rigid bodies, hearing her own words, she whispered her question, "You were the Wild Witch girl . . . weren't you?" finally putting two and two together.

Mairi slowly nodded her head.

Shaylee came out of the kitchen where she'd been preparing dinner, carrying a pot of hot peppermint tea. Seeing the photo and catching Kate's last words, she set the pot down with shaking hands. "Just when we thought our world couldn't possibly throw any more surprises our way."

Mairi felt like she might throw up.

DUMB SUPPER
San Diego, California
October 31ˢᵗ, Present
Samhain, Sunset

The Ancestor Altar was finished, a photo of her dad at the beach in the place of honor at the highest point as the most recent person to have passed away. His favorite treat of ginger chew candies filled a small clay bowl sat beside his photo. The next level down held pictures of Granny Kate's parents, her mom in a bright mu-mu dress she'd worn on a trip to Hawaii right before she had died, her dad's death following a year later, and Granny's younger sister who had been killed in a car crash ten years ago. The final level held their Papa MacDonald in his uniform, since he'd been gone the longest, just over 40 years.

Mairi shook her head, *I can't believe this man, Papa MacDonald, and Ewan the Druid are the same. After my spell hit him, he must have lost his memory and wandered out of the tunnels into another time . . . the 1960s . . .*

running into my Granny Kate. The Fates must be having a laugh as they weave our lives together.

Mairi set down the last plate on the dining table that they had covered in a black tablecloth. At the two ends of the table, the chairs were shrouded in black cloth, intended to be for her dad and her Papa. Her mom was busy making her dad's favorite dinner, salmon on rice, and Granny Kate was making Papa's favorite dinner of venison barbecued with beer. *I can't believe I know Ewan's favorite meal. I know this setting is for my Papa, but I knew Ewan better than I knew my Papa . . . he was just a story told to us since we never actually got to meet him.*

A new thought crept into her thinking as she carefully placed the silverware in mirror image order at each place setting. *What if Ewan visits us? I want my dad to visit, I want to finally see him in spirit, but I don't want to see Ewan, not even if his hair is short and white and he doesn't remember me as 'the Wild Witch' or whatever names he's called me.* Mairi sighed and walked back into the kitchen where Jamie was helping put the finishing touches on the fish for their dad.

When the door into the kitchen closed behind her, she spoke. "What if Papa . . . what if Ewan visits us? I know we've never had spirits visit before, but we might manage to open the veil this time, and he'll come. Will he remember the feud? What do I say?"

Granny Kate set her very soft and wrinkled hand on Mairi's. "Let's let it play out. I've never done more than stated the invitation for your grandfather to visit, and he's only answered the call once, before you were even born. This year, we may open the veil and perhaps he will come this time. Perhaps he won't. With the spirit world, we do not worry ourselves trying to predict what might or might not happen." She put her finger to her lips, reminding Mairi they were to now be quiet, as was the custom for the Dumb Supper.

Mairi nodded, and went to her post at the front door to wait for Danny while everyone else carried platters with steaming food to the dining room. He would be eating supper with them and then spending the night on their couch. He had been just as shocked as she had when she'd called to tell him about Ewan. When Danny arrived, Mairi greeted him in silence as was the custom and they walked together to join the others at the table.

The clink of silverware on plates was the only sound they could hear. Mairi glanced up at her dad's place setting from time to time hoping to see something, though it was hard to see much of anything since they had turned off all electricity and the room was lit only by the orange glow of flickering candle light. She had already finished eating the chocolate cake her mother had baked earlier, and Mairi had taken her first bite of the venison. She still disliked any fish because it reminded her of throwing up tuna over a year ago, but now the venison reminded her of the encounter with the deer hunter. She chewed on the venison and was just deciding she wouldn't eat anymore because how could she when she wore antlers herself and her favorite goddess was a deer woman. *I still can't get the image of Granda's neighbor shooting that deer out of my mind.* She grimaced, despite the delicious flavor of the deer meat.

Mairi shivered as a cold breeze blew through the room and the candles sputtered. She looked up and nearly dropped her fork when she saw her dad sitting in his chair as if it were the most normal, everyday thing for him to be doing. He wore his customary surf brand t-shirt and smiled at her as he ate his fish. Mairi was about to call out to him when she remembered that speaking was a sure way to break the connection, so she contented herself with just staring at him and smiling back, hoping she wouldn't start blubbering like a baby, her arms aching to hug him.

Another breeze blew through and the candles flickered

again. Mairi looked down the length of the table and saw Papa MacDonald sitting primly in his uniform. He nodded to her when she looked at him. She was considering if she should nod back or smile or what, when he frowned, and his image shimmered. Now Ewan MacDonald, the red-haired Arch Druid sat before her. She looked around and saw that everyone else had noticed the change. *Had her dad?* She looked back at him and he was paused in his eating, seeming to be puzzling over the change in his father.

Looking over at Ewan, Mairi saw that his hands had curled into a fist. Mairi's breath caught in her chest and her instinct was to start *feeling* around for sources of Energy. *There's Air and Fire Energy from the candles, and I can feel Earth and Water Energy from the houseplants. It's not a lot, but better than nothing. Will I really need it to defend myself?*

Then it happened.

Ewan lunged at Mairi, a wave of hatred preceding his spirit form. Just as Mairi was putting up an energy shield, her dad's spirit was in front of her body, blocking Ewan from reaching her. Everything froze for a moment, as the two spirits faced off, looking the way two magnets with like poles do when put together. Ewan and her dad didn't seem able to touch each other. Finally, they bounced back to their own seats. The air in the room felt like just before a thunder storm. Across from Mairi, Shaylee wore a look of fear and Jamie was on his feet, fingers sputtering sparks. Danny, too, was on his feet, shock registering on his face, while Granny sat up rigid in her chair, eyes wide.

Ewan's spirit was shimmering again, flickering between the druid Ewan and Papa Ewan. He looked at Granny Kate, then down the length of the table at his son, then back to his wife, and finally his military self seemed to be taking hold.

His spirit is waffling. Didn't he remember who he was once he died? Or is it that with Granny Kate he is Papa and with me he is Ewan?

As Ewan looked at Granny Kate and his form became only Papa again, Mairi felt Granny reach over and take her hand. Mairi looked at her Granny and saw that she was keeping eye contact with Ewan . . . Papa. *She's showing him that I am her granddaughter.* Mairi was in awe of the simplicity of Granny's approach. Ewan shimmered back into the Druid form for a moment, so Mairi concentrated on sending a wave of love in his direction, through Granny Kate's connection, focusing on how she might love him as a grandfather.

Mairi hesitated a moment, then set her hand near her dad's spirit form. He smiled at her and set his translucent hand on hers. Love radiated into her being. Her dad did the same to Jamie beside him, and Shaylee took Jamie's hand beside her and Danny's across from her. Ewan, still in his Papa MacDonald form, offered his spirit hand to Danny and Danny accepted it.

Through this figure-eight of hand holding, a ripple of green Chakra Energy, heart energy, rippled through all of them, and this time when Ewan looked at Mairi, he smiled. Forgiveness washed over her like a wave crashing on the beach. Mairi had to fight not to gasp out loud. On a whim, she sent the forgiveness back at Ewan. The decision seemed like the right one to make.

Then she felt the warmth of love, like the hot sun on a summer day, radiating from her dad, and she looked back at him. He was gazing at her and smiling, and she felt his love wrapping around her. She tingled like she did with the Energy she garnered from Earth, Fire, Air, and Water, but it felt different, stronger. *Love Energy is more powerful than all the others!*

The clock struck Midnight in the hallway and the spell broke. Her dad and Ewan . . . her Papa . . . were gone. The connection was broken, yet the feelings remained. *Maybe the story of Cinderella is full of truths, too,* Mairi realized, looking around at the living people still sitting at the table, smiling. *Midnight does break spells.*

Yet, the spell of love lingered as the table was cleared and they all tumbled into a deep sleep.

CYCLE OF LIFE
San Diego, California
November 1ˢᵗ, Present
Dia de los Muertos

Mairi sat on the bottom step of the stairs leading into the canyon. She shivered as a cold wind swirled all around, signaling that the Santa Ana winds had moved on and winter would inevitably arrive, even in Southern California. The wind whipped the leaves off the Anna Apple Tree her dad had planted for her when she was a baby, when they'd first moved into their house. She stared as the leaves drifted to the ground.

Ironic, Mairi thought. *Apples* . . . She reached up to feel the antlers that no one could really see except for her, the antlers that weighed heavily upon her head. She knew they meant she would be returning to the Faerie Realm, to the Isle of Avalon. There was no other way to remove them.

She watched a leaf get caught in the eddy of a wind draft, swirl up high in the sky and settle down on the ground before another blast of wind could catch it. The leaf landed near the hooves of a deer.

Deer don't live around here. Looking up into the golden-brown eyes of a doe, Mairi said "Oh! Hello, Elen."

The doe walked over to Mairi and laid its head on Mairi's leg, enjoying Mairi scratching behind her ears and at the base of her antlers.

Taking a step back, the doe shook herself and transformed into a woman with long brown hair sprinkled with orange and yellow leaves, clothed in a suede tunic and bare feet, velvet soft antlers protruding from the crown of her head.

"Hello, Mairi." Elen sat down beside her on the steps, smelling of the forest floor after a rain, the rich scent of soil ready for sleeping plants to grow, come spring. "You've been through quite a bit since the last time we spoke. I trust last night brought some healing."

"Yes," Mairi smiled at this woman, this goddess, who had chosen to be her guide. Mairi decided it was time to ask her some questions. "You take an awful lot of interest in me. Why is that?"

"Because you are a vessel, empty and ready. Few humans, even those with faerie blood like you, are as open to filling up with power. And even fewer humans are capable of holding such power as this universe offers without becoming something terrible. I am pretty sure you are able to do great things, a greatness that will lead the Realms of this world onto a path of Goodness and Light."

"You said 'pretty sure.' I suppose that means I might not be able to do good, to make the right choices. Besides, that's a lot to expect of me," Mairi stated, sounding braver than she felt.

"I've seen you in a possible future, so I know you are capable. But yes, no future is for certain, and you are also just as capable of failing me, failing everyone, especially yourself. We will just have to see what choices you make as time unfolds." The deer woman leaned in and touched her forehead to Mairi's, their antlers clinking a bit like champagne glasses. Mairi felt as if they might be toasting to her future. Then Elen was gone, and Mairi was alone, the weight of the world settling on her shoulders, uncertain herself of what choices she would make.

I'm still just a kid. I want it to be okay that I just want the world to be simple again.

As night fell, Mairi stood beside Danny and Jamie looking at the photo of their dad in a wetsuit jacket and bright Tommy Bahama shorts, carrying a longboard. Below his photo was the one of their Papa MacDonald in uniform.

"We're his grandchildren?" Danny whispered. "We're Ewan MacDonald's grandchildren? And Ian's great-grandchildren?" He shook his head. "I finally understand how come my dad is so naturally cruel. He got all of Ian and Ewan's cruelty, and your dad got all of Granny Kate's sweet kindness. I just wish it was his photo on this altar, not Uncle Aiden's."

Jamie nodded his agreement, then said, "Ewan showed us he wasn't only filled with cruelty. He was also good. Maybe your dad will have a similar change." Danny smiled at the hope in his younger cousin's voice.

"I think the cruelness left Ewan once and for all last night," Mairi agreed. "I was filled with a feeling of forgiveness from him, and love. Didn't you feel it?"

"I think I did," Jamie said, "I know I saw his and dad's forms at the table, though they were sometimes difficult to make out, like a poorly developed photograph."

"I must have been able to see them more clearly than you guys because of my antlers. I guess?" Mairi said.

"Me, too, I saw their faint spirit forms, and yeah . . . " Danny jumped in, "I felt those feelings, too."

"I think what it really comes down to, though, is whether we can truly forgive him," Mairi pointed out. "We're the ones who have to live with these feelings, after all." Jamie and Danny nodded their agreement.

"Let's go, kiddos," Shaylee called to them to join her and Granny Kate at the door. "Let's get to Old Town for the Dia de los Muertos festivities." Her voice was more cheerful than Mairi had heard it in a long time.

She definitely saw or felt something last night, Mairi concluded.

"I can't wait to see everyone with their faces painted like skulls and the mariachi bands playing traditional Mexican music," Danny said. "I haven't been to this event since I was a little kid."

"I just love seeing people celebrating death," Granny Kate declared.

Everyone stopped and frowned at her.

She shrugged, "The motto for Dia de los Muertos is 'If we don't forget them, they aren't truly gone.' So a celebration of our dearly departed is a celebration of death, and death is a part of the cycle of life. It's better than being afraid of it."

"Well, all I want to do is to eat a *carne asada* burrito." Jamie, as usual, had his mind on the food.

RELEASE
San Diego, California
November 2nd, Present

Mairi sat on her bed, petting Peaches' silky fur, letting the tears stream down her cheeks. As drops of salt water slowly fell on her cat's fur, Mairi stroked her back in a deep, repetitive motion, the tears disappearing in the warmth beneath her hands. It had finally sunk in. Her dad was gone. Really gone. Physically, his body would never appear before her again.

Sure, there was some relief in knowing his spirit was still around, that he visited her in her dreams, that she could, if she wished, make the journey to the Isle of Avalon and request audience with him, that he might come to the Dumb Supper with her. But she knew his spirit would be moving on soon, becoming a new body and having a new adventure without her. She knew that they would never, ever go surfing together again.

The crying, the release, felt good, though. The ache in

her chest was seeping out with each tear, and finally Mairi collapsed onto her bed in a deep, dreamless sleep. At some point, Peaches silently snuck out to eat her evening meal and search for crickets to play with.

As the sun sank lower in the sky, the shadows stretched across her bed, covering it in a shroud of mourning. Mairi heard a gentle knocking. Looking up, she saw Jamie peeking into her room.

"Dinner's ready. You okay?"

Wiping at her puffy eyes, Mairi sat up. "Yeah, I guess so."

Jamie sat down on the bed next to her. "It's okay to cry, you know. I did it a lot, right after Dad died."

"I know it is," Mairi replied, in a tone more curt than she meant to be. "But you're also so much happier than I am most of the time. I just don't know how to be happy anymore. Not really."

"I focus on being happy because Dad would want us to be, you know."

Mairi looked at her little brother. *When did he get so much wiser than I am?* "You're just like him. Dad was always so optimistic, so positive. Just like you. You're lucky. I'm grumpier, even though I don't mean to be. I *want* to be a happy person."

Jamie put his arm around her shoulder, "You're not so bad, not really. Don't be so hard on yourself."

The last golden ray of sunlight disappeared behind the houses across the street, leaving Mairi and Jamie sitting in the dark.

Mairi rested her head against Jamie's, "Let's go surfing sometime. We'll take Dad's truck. Just you and me." Jamie nodded his agreement and somehow, that felt like the perfect antidote to their sorrow.

ACKNOWLEDGEMENTS

Thank you to my mom for her endless patience as I prattle on and on about all my ideas and inspirations. Thank goodness she likes the same topics I do! Also thank you to my close friends Darcy, Isis, Kelly, Marina, and Raina, who offer sage advice in my efforts to penetrate the world of becoming a recognizable author. I am especially grateful to all my readers who take the time to meticulously read as well as critique my storyline and characters. Emilia, Lily, Daphne, Jazmyne, Jane, Ann, Wayne, Neda and Aden. Without your insights I wouldn't know how to dig deeper and try harder. Finally, a special thanks to our family friend, Marni, who edited my final draft, dealing with weird formatting issues and ridiculous mistakes. I appreciate everyone who is willing to take a little time (and quite often, a lot of time) to help me create as perfect a novel as I am humanly capable of. I also appreciate that my human abilities appear to be improving with practice.

COMING WINTER 2019

Celtic Magic Book 3

The Faerie Knot

Celtic Magic

Be wary the gifts the faeries may give;
We know not how they influence the life we live.

The Faerie Knot

Winter is the time for solitude
When living creatures disappear.
Silence echoes, dividing families,
And dark nights embrace our fear.

Thank you for reading **The Witch's Knot**. I hope you have enjoyed the story as much as I do. Please leave a review on Amazon and Goodreads. Visit me on Facebook at Wild Rose Stories and on Instagram at Wild Rose Stories and Tales.

mòran taing

Gaelic for "many thanks"

Made in the USA
Columbia, SC
23 November 2019